MW00904119

Life Raft

Life Raft

Paula Ashcraft

Library of Congress Control Number:		2019911765
ISBN:	Hardcover	978-1-7960-5211-4
	Softcover	978-1-7960-5210-7
	eBook	978-1-7960-5209-1

Print information available on the last page.

Rev. date: 08/19/2019

To order additional copies of this book, contact:
Xlibris
1-888-795-4274
www.Xlibris.com
Orders@Xlibris.com
798209

CONTENTS

PROLOGUE

Chicago

His phone rang once then stopped. Looking down, he studied the small piece of electronics lying in his hand. It was original issue—slim and sleek, about half the size of his palm. Easily hidden and quietly nesting, he'd carried it for the last five years. Until today. It was around noon that he'd felt the buzz, signaling an incoming text message. A simple cipher, reacquainting him with a life that he'd all but forgotten. Now here he was, listening, counting, waiting for his two worlds to collide.

The second call came the standard five minutes later. The phone rang once then twice before silence fell. There was nothing significant about the digits; in fact, he knew that it was a different number from the first, and it belonged to someone who had nothing to do with the operation at hand. If it hadn't been preceded by the text code in the same day, it could have easily been explained away as a wrong number.

He walked to the window and peered down at the lake, watching as the boats bobbed up and down in the reflection of the sunset. He turned, taking in his surroundings — his private elevator, his special ordered Italian leather furniture, and his gourmet kitchen. Life was good. For the first few years, he had focused on the end of his assignment, but as time passed, his perspective had changed. He had found his niche, and his new life had welcomed him. Could he really go back?

By the time the third call came, five minutes after the second, he still hadn't decided where his loyalty lay. He was pacing back and forth across his oak floors when the ringing halted his steps.

"One." He focused on the count.

"Two." He took a deep breath, choking, as his throat tightened.

"Three." The sound of his voice was barely audible.

Three calls. Three unknown numbers. One ring from the first, two rings for the second, and three rings for the third. The message had been sent. The code had been received. Two calls projected the hour; three the half hour. He had received three. It would take place on the half hour. He looked at the clock to verify—1-2-3-0. It was going down at 12:30 a.m. He had been warned.

He knew his duty. He had to protect his identity. But was he ready to walk away? Then what? A new town? A new persona? Days turning into months. Months turning into years. Could he really start over on a new assignment?

It was eleven thirty as he pulled his car out of the parking garage. The night was filled with distant sirens and people scurrying across the street entwined in pairs. It was raining. The streets were blanketed with teardrops falling from the sky. Was it crying for him? He pondered a different life—one filled with a loving wife, children, and a nine to five job. A beep behind him halted his musings. He moved forward and rolled down his window to scan his magnetic card. The air was heavy—the kind that weighs on the lungs and restricts ones breathing. Hesitating as the parking arm raised to allow him to exit, he felt a sense of foreboding. He pushed it away. Rolling up his window, he turned right into traffic. He had chosen this life. Regrets were just interruptions.

He could be at the warehouse in thirty minutes if he hurried, leaving plenty of time. But time for what? Was he to be a siren of warning or a purveyor of justice? Either way, he would need to be careful. Being seen could get him killed or expose his undercover status, which would blow his credibility. His credibility? What did that really mean? Was he trying to take down a crime boss or solidify a place in his organization? If only he could just call and warn him. But that would be a fool's errand. He knew how his boss's mind worked. Bastos had his protocols that had to be followed. He just had to get there in time. Figuring out what to say without exposing his own secret identity in the process, would take some serious thought. He didn't have much time. If only he knew who brought in the FBI. He needed a fall guy. His life depended on it.

Police cruisers blocked his approach as he pulled up to the scene at the warehouse. He had arrived at midnight with a half hour to spare, yet he was too late. It was all over. The FBI had moved up the operation. They had stormed the place early and left behind a sea of carnage. He had been played. Someone didn't trust him, but who? Who could have known? He had been very discreet. No one would dare take down Bastos without help. There had to be another inside man. Yet something wasn't right. Why was he given the wrong time? This screamed of deception. Was it a test of loyalty? Would they have killed him if he was in the warehouse when they arrived? Was he to have been sacrificed in the take-down?

He parked the car by an abandoned building a couple of blocks away and joined the fray of reporters and onlookers as they made their way to the edge of the cordoned-off area. It was unusual to see this much activity in this corner of the warehouse district, where each building had seen the neglect of decades. Nevertheless, buildings, like people, were deceptive. This structure of disrepair had been completely renovated on the inside, ready to withstand any force that came against it. So how could they be rolling out gurneys of dead bodies, including Nicholas Bastos himself?

He thought back to the last meeting in Bastos's office. All the top players were there. He examined each of their faces in his memory—nothing seemed out of the ordinary. Had he missed something? How could this go down without a peep right under his nose? It certainly wasn't from the information he had left for his handler, which was just enough to appease his bosses on both sides.

Who could have done this? He knew everyone who worked for Nicholas Bastos, yet someone whom he trusted had obtained enough information to take him down. He had to be in Bastos's inner circle in order to pull this off. There had to be another undercover agent. He had been replaced.

He took in his surroundings watching for any interest that might be steered in his direction. Yes, he had been warned but with false information. Did his FBI status protect him, or did his rescuer expect him to protect Bastos and be there for the take-down? As he took in the faces focused on the scene, he felt alienated. They were all strangers to him.

Movement at the entrance of the building hushed the crowd as the final gurney was rolled to the waiting ambulance. There was no tubes or wires protruding from the still body. He was dead. Nicholas Bastos was dead, and they had rolled him out, exposing their prize for all to see. The cameras around him began to flash, lighting up the black night.

He felt sick. He needed air. His chest was being squeezed from the inside. Panic had taken over. Tears were forming in his eyes, blurring his vision. He had to leave. He couldn't watch. Slowly, he slipped away from the chaos of the crowd. Why was his body acting this way? What was wrong with him? He was an FBI agent undercover, watching his target being taken down. So why did he feel like he just watched his own father dying in front of him. Should he have made that call? Maybe Bastos would've believed him.

His world had been changed in an instant. He had to get away. His only hope was a transfer out of Chicago. It was time to call the only person who could help him right now—his handler, Supervisory Special Agent Smith.

Victor Ramos took several deep breaths, pulled out his phone, and turned and walked away.

01

The Snitch – DC

The parking garage stunk of exhaust and urine, causing Jason to roll up his window to release the breath he was holding. How long would he have to wait? It was late. The bustling activity of the day had ceased, leaving the night deathly still, though an uncomfortable silence hung in the air. His training nagged at him to take security rounds, but as soon as the thought entered his mind, he pushed it away. This meeting was not his idea, and it was dangerous. However, Julio called, and it was his job to calm his snitch.

Morning had come early with a call from Sierra, saying she had a recruit for him. Finding a reason to be in her company was a pleasure he enjoyed. So, picking up her recruit would allow them to work closely together. Of course, if she would have accepted his offer for dinner . . . Perhaps it was for the best. He was too tired tonight. All he wanted to do was finish this last meeting and succumb to his tired bones. He leaned his head back against the seat, closing his eyes.

"Finally." A bright light penetrated through his stupor. He leaned forward across the steering wheel as he studied the man getting out of the car in front of him. Why did Sierra feel this man was the one to take down Perrone? Okay, he might be a likeable-enough guy, but he seemed too loyal, too dedicated to turn on his boss. Yet she was so sure.

Still, he wasn't her snitch. Time would tell, but this meeting wasn't a good start. It was too dangerous. Yet here we were . . .

Jason turned on his lights and stepped out of the car. "What's going on, Julio? I thought we had an understanding."

Julio was nervous, pacing through the beam of his headlamps, struggling to find the words he felt he needed to say. He had agreed to be an informant for the FBI to stay out of jail. They had set him up on charges of drug possession and had promised to drop the charges if he would snitch for them. His connection with Juan Perrone had tagged him for recruitment. He was the inside man, a warehouse security guard, a low-level behind-the-scenes lackey whom Sierra had been working with for months. They had him now, but was he capable of the task? His assignment was simple: switch out the bills in Perrone's next shipment and report. Yet here he was, pacing, nervous as an alley cat.

Julio had tried to convince himself it wasn't a big deal, but he knew that going through with it meant signing his own death warrant. His only choice was to convince Jason he had the wrong man, and with that look on his face, it wouldn't be easy. He still couldn't believe he was doing this, but he had to try. He had to stand up to Jason and make him understand. There was no way of sneaking anything under Juan's nose—nothing got past him. Between Juan and his new protégé Vic, no one was spared.

Perrone had his ways. For Julio, it was that extra pat on the back that turned his insides to stone. He had been too clingy today. He had to know. It was time to fix this and protect himself. He needed Jason to understand. He was skating on thin ice, and the cracks were already forming.

Jason squinted through the strobe effect his snitch was causing, waiting for some big revelation as to why he was jeopardizing their safety. He had waited long enough.

"I said, what's going on, Julio?"

Jason had no patience for this sniveling idiot. It was not a good idea to have two meetings with a snitch in the same week, let alone the same day. Informants were always a crap shoot. It was usually the stupid ones who got arrested and ended up the eyes and ears for the police. Half the time, their information was made up to appease their handlers, claiming innocence when they were caught lying. If it wasn't for Sierra's insistence, this one would have been thrown back.

Sierra, he thought for a moment, *what a beautiful woman. If only . . .* His thoughts faded into the sound of Julio's voice.

"Jason, you have to let me out of this deal. I-I tried, but he's on to me. There was a look in his eyes. He hardly let me out of his sight all day, and when he did, he sent me on this stupid errand with Vic. He doesn't trust me anymore. If I do this, he'll kill me." Julio's eyes were wide and darting back and forth.

Jason nervously looked around. "Did anyone follow you?"

"Not that I noticed. I did just what you said. I drove around for a while, crisscrossed through town, went into a store and bought something, drove around some more, then made my way here." He was pacing again.

Jason tried to blink through the strobe lights. "Stop pacing—you're blinding me." He took a deep breath.

"Julio, if Juan was on to you, he would've followed you here. If he suspected any deception, you would already be dead, yet here you are. Stop being paranoid and just do the job you agreed to do, or I can arrest you right now. What do you think your life will be like tucked away in jail? Do you think Juan's reach is only on the street? Your chances are much better working for me than locked up with his crew, especially when I tell them you were my snitch."

Julio stopped pacing and looked at Jason with a new sense of fear.

"Julio, look around you. Did anyone follow you? No. It's just us here. Fear can make us nervous. You'll be just fine. So, get rid of your paranoia, and just get the job done. You will feel much better when it's over, and you can go back to kissing up to your boss and getting back in his good graces."

Julio looked around and seemed to relax a bit. "Okay. Okay. You're right. I'm probably just being paranoid. You're right. I would be dead if he knew. You're right . . . You're right . . .," Julio continued muttering, trying desperately to convince himself.

"Where is Juan?" Jason asked, a prickling sensation creeping up his spine, knowing it was time to end this conversation and leave.

"He's at the docks, preparing the boat for Saint Maartens." Julio's mind turned to his boss's smuggling operation.

"So did you switch the money?"

Julio couldn't believe that Jason just came right out and said it. He scanned the garage one more time, only partially concerned that the headlights only illuminated a small section of the mass expanse. He didn't see anyone, but he was getting a funny feeling. It was time to leave and leave now.

"No," Julio said timidly, "but I'm working on a plan."

"WORKING ON A PLAN?!" Jason was furious.

"I-I mean . . . I-I have a plan. It will be d-done tomorrow, I-I promise," Julio stuttered. "I'll let you know—our n-normal signal, right?"

"You should remember what that is," Jason quipped. "I'll be waiting. The next time I hear from you, the deed better be done. Or I'll haul your butt in, and we'll see what Juan does to snitches."

"Okay, I'll . . ." Julio slammed his car door and jammed his car into gear. Jason just shook his head as he watched Julio peel out of the parking garage, laying a line of rubber on the pavement.

The spine prickling was back. Jason knew he had stayed too long. He hurried toward his open car door as a stinging sensation took his breath away. With one hand on his chest and the other reaching for his gun, he turned and peered through the blackness. His muddled mind was racing for a solution. He didn't see the color of the warm liquid running between his fingers, but he knew. His legs collapsed, slamming his body to the pavement. "Julio, you idiot . . ." was all he could muster as the cold darkness enveloped his conscious mind.

02

The Warehouse – DC

Julio was glad he left the parking garage when he did. He couldn't put his finger on it, but something wasn't right. He hadn't worked for Perrone for this long without knowing when to leave. He also knew that if he had any hope of making this work, the money had to be switched tonight. The boat would be loaded first thing in the morning and on its way around sunup. Juan didn't mess around when it came to his shipments. It was now or never.

The warehouse was dark as he swung his car into the corner of the parking lot, choosing his space carefully to avoid the cameras.

Perfect, he thought, *no one is here. I can slip in, swap the money, and get out. I should have thought of this sooner—in and out with no one around.*

In the three years Julio had worked for Juan Perrone, keeping the warehouse secure had been his job. There was a time when a simple cot in the corner was home, but things had changed. His life was pretty good now. He and his mom had their own apartments. He had his ranking in Perrone's organization, and to top it off, he owned a black customized Dodge Challenger with ground-effect spoiler, high-intensity running lights, and a 6.1 HEMI engine. It was perfect for blowing off steam—racing his fellow street racers.

Julio stood looking at the warehouse. He had worked hard to build this life, and now the FBI was threatening to take it away. His chest tightened as he crept alone the boundaries of the camera angles and made his way to the side door. He pulled out his key. He would thank his mom again for the lighted key ring she gave him for Christmas. This made each key easy to see in the dark. He tried his warehouse key.

"What the . . .?" He stifled his voice just in time. "Shh." He brought his finger to his lips and glanced up at the cameras.

Perhaps the keys got mixed up. He tried each key on his key ring, even the car key, but none fit the lock. Anxiety moved through his extremities as his mind went into overdrive.

My key worked just fine yesterday. That's it. Forget about the FBI. I'm outta here. They can threaten me all they want, but if I double-cross Perrone, I'm dead.

His trip back to the car was faster, but his legs felt like jelly. Easing into his car seat, his nerves were on fire signaling his pulse to quicken. He was in trouble.

"Think, Julio, think." He slapped himself on the cheek. "According to Jason, if Juan was suspicious, he would've had me followed."

He looked around, relieved to find only blackness.

"Maybe I should just leave town and go into hiding." His hidden thoughts were voiced. "Would fifteen thousand really get me anywhere, except jail?"

He laid back against his head rest and tried to weigh his options. His path had been paved by the forces around him. The only way out was to play along. Sitting forward, he smacked the steering wheel in frustration. He had to switch out the bills tomorrow morning before the boat left. It was his only way out. But he would have to be watchful. Perrone wasn't stupid.

Shaking, he started his car and slowly left his parking space, not turning on his lights until he was a quarter mile down the road. He kept a vigil through the rearview mirror, his eyes darting—left, right, front, rear, over and over. His head was pounding in frustration, but he didn't see anyone following him.

"Stop acting crazy!" he yelled at his eyes in the mirror as he pulled up to a stop light. "No one is following you. Juan probably changed the warehouse lock to protect the shipment, and you will get your key in the morning. See, there is an explanation for everything." He lowered his eyes as the light turned green. "I need sleep, that's all. Things will look better in the morning. The shipment doesn't leave until sunup, and perhaps I can still switch the money and get Jason off my back. However, working in Perrone's periphery will be difficult. I'll have to be careful."

The alarm sounded, and it nearly sent Julio for his gun before he realized it was three o'clock and time for him to get up. Thoughts of betrayal had filled his restless night with terror. He had to make this switch just right, or he would be in jail or, worse, dead. This was his only chance to clear his record with the FBI. Once that was done, he would figure out how to schmooze Perrone and let him know he was loyal. Perhaps Jason was right; he was just being paranoid.

Julio was on the road by three thirty, heading toward the warehouse. If he got there in time, he could volunteer his services and watch for an opening to switch the bills. If Juan was true to character, the shipment would be loaded that morning and transported to the dock.

It was nearly four o'clock by the time he pulled up to the warehouse. His nerves were already fried. Who knew there were aggressive drivers so early in the morning? The DC commuters were many. What a life to spend hours just driving to and from work each day. Julio was grateful for his nine-to-seven shift and his usual thirty-minute drive. Once again, the warehouse was dark, and there was no activity around. He parked his car and waited until five, still not a soul in sight. Had he been too late? He started his car and drove to the dock, hoping to arrive before anyone else to scope out his options.

The dock was bustling with activity. There was Juan Perrone talking to a man on the bow of a boat with the engine running. This had to be the captain. Julio had never met Captain Max, but he had heard the others talk about him. He was an old friend of Perrone's or something and the only one Juan would trust with a boat going to the Caribbean. He looked around. There had to be half a dozen men lining the dock watching the two men converse. He parked his car and headed for the boat.

"There he is!" Juan yelled over the engine noise. "Julio, where have you been? We have been waiting for you. Come aboard and meet Captain Max."

Julio's back stiffened. What was Perrone talking about? "We have been waiting for you?" No one told him to meet at the docks this morning. He walked between the six minions lined up along the gang plank. He only recognized two—this was odd. He thought he knew all Perrone's men. If more bodyguards were hired, why wasn't he informed? Julio didn't have time to mull this over. He was being watched and scrutinized with each step.

"I was over at the warehouse, waiting to help with the shipment, sir," Julio said apologetically as he approached the two men. "Sorry I got here late."

"I'm sure it was just a miscommunication." Perrone put his arm around him and, in a hushed voice, said, "I have a different job for you, one that is much more important." His Cheshire grin put Julio on edge. "I have arranged for you to ride the boat to Saint Maartens. Meet Max, he is your captain on this voyage, and you are his official first mate. Your job is to make sure my shipment arrives safely into the right hands. I am relying on you. You are responsible for this boat and its contents. Do you understand?"

"Yes, sir." Julio's head was swimming. He had been put in charge of Perrone's money, and he didn't even know how to drive a boat. This seemed so out of character for his boss, taking a simple warehouse worker and putting him in charge of a money shipment.

Juan walked him toward the railing. "Here, take this phone. You are to contact me every six hours—every six hours! I want to know where you are each step of the way. Do you understand?" Juan was eyeing him carefully.

Julio relaxed a bit. He had thought for sure that Juan Perrone knew of his betrayal with the FBI, but if he did, he wasn't letting on. In fact, he trusted him. Perhaps Perrone was none the wiser. He wouldn't put him in charge of such an important shipment if there was no trust. His mind was struggling to work this out; this assignment could give him access to switch the money and take him out of the country away from Perrone and Jason—it could be a win-win.

"When do we leave?" Julio was making a mental note of all he needed to do.

Juan's eyes were like daggers as he took a step closer. "Max is ready, and you are leaving right now."

Julio couldn't help but flinch. "I-I need to ga-garage my c-car, get someone to wa-water my plants, and get my pa-passport. Then there's my ma-mom, I need to tell her I'm going to be out of town for a few days, an-and I need to p-pack my bag . . ." His voice faltered.

Juan's big grin returned. "I sent Victor to find you last night. He checked all your normal hangouts, even talked to your girl—Sierra, right? He said you were nowhere to be found, so I went to your place and packed your bag. Don't worry, I grabbed your passport and will handle the rest. The shipment is ready, so off I go, and off you go. Don't let me down, Julio. I can always find you if I need to . . ." He trailed off. Juan was on the dock, heading for Julio's car. He turned back. "Get his keys before you throw the lines, boys."

Victor Ramos looked at Julio who was all but frozen in place. "Throw me your keys, Oo-lio." He mechanically followed the request, but his mind was pondering what his boss just said. "I can always find you if I need to . . ." Anything after that was a blur.

What did he mean? Did he know about my meeting with Jason last night? Was he there? Why was he sending me with Max? Was he to be my executioner and the sea my grave?

"Hey! Pull your head out and pay attention." Max was at the helm, screaming out the window. "Wake up. Quick—grab the lines! They're throwing them at us. If you're with me, you have to pull your own weight. This is not a pleasure cruise."

Julio's mind jumped into gear. He turned and caught the mooring lines that were coming toward him as Max maneuvered the boat from the dock. Just like that, his sturdy foundation was no more. He was floating out to sea on a boat headed for the Caribbean. As the shore disappeared, he saw Juan's minions tearing apart his car. They were looking for something. The money? There was no doubt now—Juan Peronne knew. Julio may have just boarded a cruise to his final destination.

Julio's eyes watched the sunrise peeking over the horizon illuminating the shadows of the trees dotting the shoreline. Perhaps it was his sense of foreboding, of never seeing these sights again, that heightened their splendor—his home. His DC, with all its colors and majesty; the fall with its reds and oranges, the spring with the frosting of cherry blossoms in shades of pink and white. He knew he would miss the beauty, but it was the thought of leaving his mother without saying goodbye that darkened his heart.

03

First Mate – Macon it Easy

Julio lost sight of his car as the boat trolled through the channel. They were on their way. It had all happened so fast. He had been outmaneuvered, and just like that, lost his footing on solid ground. He didn't know what to think or how to feel. It was all too new. Focusing on the sights around him only heightened his fears. On one side, he could see Haines Point Park where his boss had invited him to play a round from time to time during his golfing phase. There had been backslapping and laughter. It was at these times he had felt like family. That was then, before his fall from grace and before his respect had been changed to trepidation. He turned away. Across the channel, he could see the warehouse roof, his second home. That part of his life was over. He lowered his eyes, and there was the sign for the Titanic Memorial. A chill ran up his spine. What was going to happen to him? If he died, who was going to take care of his mom? His mistake had sealed his fate and most likely hers. He loved his home, and now it was slipping away. He couldn't watch anymore.

Julio turned from the rail, leaving his tortured memories behind. He needed to clear his mind. Making his way inside, he looked around the living room area-called a salon. He was impressed. It was a beautifully decorated entertainment space about the size of his apartment. There was a plush sofa, decorated with two throw pillows, centered in the

open space. Two armchairs cradled the sides of the sofa facing toward
a built-in entertainment center. Against the back wall stood a cabinet
containing books of different genres. Connecting on one end of the
room was the kitchen – called a galley; and on the other end steps going
up to the helm - where Max was driving the boat. Neither end appealed
to him at the moment. Julio made his way to the sofa. Stretching out
the full length of the surface, he hugged one throw pillow and cradled
his head with the other. The humming sound of the engines lulled him
into unconsciousness. Sleep washed over him. Peaceful, peaceful sleep.

He was rocking, rocking. He awoke with a jolt. Where was he? He
looked around as his heart darkened. The boat—it was real. No amount
of sleep or dreaming could remove this living nightmare. He looked at
his watch. What time was it? What time had they left the dock? Five
thirty or six? The phone—where was the phone? The sun was just
coming up when they left, and now it was overhead. He couldn't believe
it was one o'clock already. Had it really been six hours?

He dialed the number. "Hello, Juan?"

"No.

"Vic?"

Who's this? Oolio, is that you? What do you want?"

"Put Juan on the phone!"

Julio never liked Victor Ramos. The first time they met was six
months ago, when he'd walked into Perrone's office only to find a
strange man sitting behind his boss's desk. He immediately drew on
him. It had been a standoff since Victor had also been quick on the
draw. He didn't know what would have happened if Perrone hadn't
walked in at that moment and explained how he had hired Victor
Ramos to be his second-in-command. Julio had been confused. First of
all, he hadn't been told, and second, Perrone had never trusted anyone
enough to relinquish authority. But comply he would because Perrone
was the boss.

Vic never forgave Julio for almost killing him. He would often leave
the employment section of the paper with circled janitorial ads on Julio's
desk. He knew they were from Vic, trying to get rid of him. He would
just crumple up the paper and throw it away. Then things began to

change. Peronne became more distant as Victor Ramos became more prominent in the organization. Faces changed, replacing the old team. It seemed subtle at first then became more progressive. Juan Perrone was his boss, but some days he questioned who was really in charge.

"You're late, Julio." The impatience in Perrone's voice brought him back to the present. "Where are you?"

Julio hurried up to the helm. "Where are we?" He asked Max. "Perrone wants to know."

"Three-eight-point-one-five north and seven-six-point-six-four west, twenty miles southeast of the Highway 301 Bridge." Max pointed to the chart plotter on the helm.

Julio relayed the message to Juan. "Sir, did you call my mo—m?" The phone went dead. Would Juan call his mom? What was going to happen to her? To him?

He sat down at the table in the corner. Max turned toward him, and with a voice that was soft but insistent, he said, "Julio, It's time for your first driving lesson. For us to make our schedule, we'll have to take driving shifts." He didn't wait for a response. "Come over here." Julio stood up and walked to the captain's chair.

"First of all, what do you know about driving a boat?" This was a simple question, and it didn't take him long to answer.

"Absolutely nothing."

Max gave him a concerned smile. "Okay, the first thing you need to know is a boat steers like a car." Max stood to the side of the captain's chair and pointed for him to take a seat.

Once Julio was seated, he began. "What's important right now is this—this is called a chart plotter." Julio's gaze followed Max's finger to a colorful monitor attached to the helm. "This dotted line is our planned route. As you're steering the boat, you need to keep us on this dotted line. Now this over here is a depth finder. It shows us how much water is under the boat. There should always be more than ten feet. If the depth finder is beeping, pull this lever—the throttle, vertical, to stop the boat—and call me. If we run aground, a distress call will have to be made. The coast guard coming to our aid would be better than being boarded by pirates, but for us, if the coast guard boards us, we'll be arrested, and they will take possession of the boat. If by a strange twist of fate, we were to survive that, then we'll be in Juan Perrone's hands, and neither one of us wants that. To put it simply, pay attention at all times."

He continued, "Now it is very important that you watch for other boats on the right and left. If someone is approaching from the right, they have the right-of-way, and we need to slow down and steer clear to avoid them. If anyone comes within a hundred yards of our boat, you need to take measures to avoid any collision."

Max gestured toward the console on the right. "This is the vessel's management system. It watches all our systems. If it starts making any noise, call me immediately. Your job is to keep us afloat and be aware of all our surroundings. It's important to always make wise decisions and never—ever—fall asleep at the helm. If you are tired, you let me know. Understand?"

Julio nodded and turned as another monitor began beeping. "What does this do?"

"That's a multifunction monitor. We can talk about that later. But for right now, just keep your hands off." Max yawned and stretched. "You've got the helm." Max stepped back and watched. "Just follow the dotted line on the chart plotter."

Julio caught on quickly to steering. It took a little more effort to get used to watching the boats coming straight at him and coming up behind him, plus keeping an eye on the depth finder and the chart plotter all at the same time.

Max watched him until he could see his shoulders start to relax. "Have you got the hang of it enough for me to get something to eat and relieve myself?"

Max wasn't comfortable leaving Julio alone for too long, so he hurried below without waiting for a response from him, listening intently for any unusual sounds.

All Max wanted was a nap. He was up most of the night, receiving instructions, and then Julio was thrown at him that morning. He'd known Juan for most of his life, but it always surprised him the depths he would go to control another person. He didn't know the whole story behind Julio's banishment, but handing him over like this was wrong. His own relationship with Perrone had always been well defined, but now he was changing the rules. It's not that an extra set of hands on the boat wasn't welcome, but there were other expectations. Max wanted out, and Perrone had agreed to let him go after this run. It was time. But the price was high. He had his orders. Taking care of Julio was one thing but convincing his contact in Saint Maartens that he could trust his old friend was risky. The news of Bastos being taken out in Chicago put everyone on edge. New partners were harder to find. Trust required proof. No matter how this trip turned out, his freedom was worth the risk. Things had changed, and it was time for him to disappear.

"Well, it looks like we're still in one piece," Max jabbed as he returned. "I'm going to sit right over here and eat my lunch." Julio nodded at his words. He didn't dare turn his eyes to look where Max pointed. He made him nervous, and he would do his best to look competent in front of him.

"Listen," Max said between bites, "we need to come to an understanding. You were a last-minute addition to this trip, and I told Juan I didn't want you. I would much rather work alone than with someone I don't trust."

"Why wouldn't you trust me?" Julio only caught a glimpse of Max's eyes, but they were dark and troubled. Was that guilt? Regret? Anger?

"Keep your eyes on the helm. You're off course. I don't trust anyone I don't know, and I don't know you. Are we back on course?" He looked at the chart plotter to answer his own question.

"I am not sure you understand the gravity of our situation. If either of us screws up, we could both end up dead. This trip will take us over a week to get to Saint Maartens. We'll have to take shifts and sleep when we can. We don't have the luxury of anchoring at night, and we need to limit our exposure to the shore. If you are not someone I can use or trust, I need to know now. If I can't depend on you, I'll throw you overboard and save me the aggravation of dealing with you later. I don't need deadweight." The seriousness in his tone only left Julio room for one answer.

"I'm in." Julio wanted to ask what he meant by "the aggravation of dealing with you later," but he knew this was not the right time. He filed his curiosity for later.

"Since you already had your nap, it's my turn. You've got the helm—just follow the dotted line. We'll see if you're someone who will be an asset or a liability." Max opened a cupboard under the bench seat and pulled out a pillow. Obviously, this was not the first time Captain Max had slept on the helm.

Julio was left alone with his thoughts. Max's words felt like another threat. How was he going to survive the testosterone thrown at him in the last twenty-four hours? It all started with an abrupt awakening in his jail cell. He still couldn't remember being arrested or appearing before a judge for a bail hearing. He only remembers Jason's blurry face, telling him he had been picked up on possession with the intent to sell. Sell? Drugs? They weren't his thing. He was a part of Peronne's security team, and he had a no-tolerance policy when it came to drugs. They were strictly forbidden. Julio had respected that about his boss. How had he been arrested for possession? It had to be a setup. Perhaps it was another gift from Vic, hoping to get rid of him? It didn't matter who turned him in, only that he now had to deal with threats from Jason, implied threats from Perrone, and now Max.

Julio had always been careful when it came to the law, not doing anything to draw attention. He stayed away from fancy clubs, sticking to his local bar as his preferred hangout, living a quiet, unassuming life. He didn't have close friends, except Sierra. She was the bright spot in his nightly bar visits, always making special time to sit and chat. She had been his last real memory until Jason woke him up in jail. Then of course, there was the so-called offer he couldn't refuse—work for the FBI or they would tell Perrone that he was working for them anyway, which would guarantee his death. So he'd agreed. Now here he was, floating away from everything he knew and loved.

Then there was the money. When Perrone didn't find it in his car, he would search his apartment. Then what? His mom's house. His eyes started to tear up, but he blinked, refusing to cry. Had he signed his mother's death warrant? Perrone would not spare her life if it meant leaving a loose end. Julio had to know she was all right. He pulled the phone out of his pocket and dialed.

With Max snoring away in the corner, Julio held the phone to his ear and listened. After the fourth ring, the answering machine picked up. His mother's voice filled the void between them. He listened but decided against leaving his voice on the machine. He ended the call. Something nagged at his senses—sadness, anger, pain? Was his mom already dead and he was here on this boat to nowhere listening to Max tell him he was going to die? "The aggravation of dealing with you later" sure sounded that way. He needed a to come up with his own plan and be ready when the opportunity presented itself. It was time to focus—focus on the boat. He needed to learn all he could about her, and perhaps, when the time came, he could change his destiny.

04

Julio's Bag – Driving the Ocean

Julio was actually enjoying his time as captain. Who would have thought this inner-city boy would enjoy driving a boat? Max was stirring in the corner, and true to his word, it had been exactly an hour since he dozed off. He seemed to have his sleeping down to a science—his body knowing just how long to nap. How he managed on other trips without anyone else to drive was baffling. Max was definitely a curious character.

Julio couldn't remember Perrone ever using anyone else to transport his shipments. He had heard that the two had a history together—they were related or old school friends or something. It seemed that Max was only present when there was a shipment. Of course, Perrone did most of his business with people who knew how to be invisible.

"How far are we from Smith Point?" Max wasn't really asking him; his eyes went straight to the chart plotter to answer his own question. "You did good. I'll be right back to take over." He disappeared down the steps and returned fifteen minutes later with crackers and coffee. "I'll take the helm. We are coming up on a section of tricky currents where the river narrows." Julio gladly surrendered the captain's chair.

"Where did Perrone put my bag?" he asked as he stepped back.

Max lowered his eyes, refusing to make eye contact. "I don't know. I never saw him go into the cabin. You'll have to look." He was checking some gauges on the monitor. Julio didn't figure it was a good time to ask what he was doing, so he just watched.

"You may want to find something to hang on to or brace yourself. We have a choppy ride up ahead."

The river narrowed quickly, and he was glad Max was driving. It was interesting watching him maneuver the yacht through the swirling currents and flawlessly squeezing past an ocean cargo liner.

"That was too close for comfort." Julio sighed as he took a deep breath and headed straight for the staterooms to search for his bag. This was his first time in the belly of the boat. The first stateroom he came to was very small with only a pathway between two twin beds. The storage compartments hung from the ceiling, making this a cramped space for anyone over five feet tall. He squeezed into the space and did a thorough search through each cubby, leaving empty-handed, no bag.

He moved on down the hall to the next cabin. This room, like the first, seemed undisturbed, new, fresh from the factory. It bolstered a full-size bed, high ceilings, and room to walk around. This would be his room. He quickly vetted each storage area and once again exited without his bag.

Down the hall was a head or a small bathroom and a master stateroom. Ruling out the head, he entered the large master suite. He was impressed. The workmanship presented before him was exquisite.

"I could live here." He paused for a moment to take it all in: the king-sized bed, the double closet with built-in storage, and the private head with marble tile sink and a full-size shower. "Nice."

He moved on. A quick sweep of the room only produced Max's travel bag lying open on the bed. Glancing inside only revealed a couple of sets of clothes he hadn't taken the time to hang up, a shaving kit, and some personal papers along with his passport.

Stress was setting in. Hot blood was flowing through Julio's veins. His bag was his only connection to reality. He took the steps two at a time, sprinting toward the salon, searching every nook and cranny, behind pillows and under cushions, then on to the galley. The galley wasn't logical, but nothing escaped his search, opening and closing all the cupboards and even looking under the sink. He slid down the wall and sat across the stove. He needed to calm himself. He looked from the salon to the galley and lowered his head into his hands. He had to relax, to breathe.

"So, Mr. Galley and Ms. Salon, where is my bag? Salon? Galley?" He understood why they would name a kitchen a galley, but why label a living room a salon? He would have to ask someone that someday.

He stood up and looked around at the mess he had made and walked on by. He was in no mood to fix anything. He needed his bag. He needed some normalcy in this situation. If his bag wasn't on the inside of the boat, perhaps it was outside. He remembered seeing some handles on the deck as he was boarding. He hurried down one side, across the back, and up the other. He searched each compartment that he could find, but they were filled with boating and fishing supplies. He slowly walked back to the bow, watching the water glance off the side as the boat cut through the current.

"What are you doing?" Max yelled through the window of the helm.

"Searching for my bag!" he yelled, hoping Max could hear him over the wind.

Max just shook his head. "Did you check below in the engine room? The stairs are aft, off the salon."

Julio couldn't imagine why his bag would be left down there, but he didn't want to leave any stone unturned. He found the door and climbed down. The engine room was so noisy with only a narrow path between two huge diesel engines. He opened each cabinet door, but all he could find was a tool bag. He looked inside only to find a flashlight, a basic hammer, a screwdriver, a socket wrench, and a set of pliers. He climbed back up to the salon, double-checking each space. Nothing. Refusing to give up, he headed back to the helm to once again question Max.

"You still looking for that bag?" He felt his energy deflate as he looked into Max's eyes. His legs began to tremble, and his stomach felt sick. He lowered his body to a sitting position on the floor, leaning against the wall.

"My bag's not here, is it?" Max averted his eyes but said nothing. "When did he tell you I was going on this trip?"

Max remained silent. Julio looked around the helm and saw a locked cooler in the corner. "What's in there?"

Max turned his eyes to the corner where Julio was pointing. "That's just my personal survival kit. I carry one on every trip for emergencies. It's my own private business, and *you* need to stay out of it!"

His answer seemed odd, cold. Why would you lock a survival kit? Max didn't seem to want to say more, and Julio wasn't in the mood to grill him further. Without his bag, he would have to stay in the same clothes for the rest of the trip. He could wash out his shorts and do fine, but what about when he got to the Caribbean? He would be arrested without his passport.

"I'm going to lie down." He stood up and headed for his stateroom.

Julio sat on the bed, phone in hand. All he wanted to do is throw it against the wall. He had to think. He had to plan. What was he going to do? The tears were coming—he had no time for tears. He turned the phone over and over in his hands. He had to call Juan in about an hour. What was he going to say? He studied the phone. What was he going to do? Where was his bag? Was that Juan's plan to have him show up in Saint Maartens without a passport?

"Get a grip, Julio." His voice in his own ears sounded strange. He didn't mean those words to be spoken aloud, but he was falling apart, and he had to get his mind to focus. There had to be a reason why Juan didn't put his bag on the boat.

I'll ask him where my bag is in the next phone call. I'm sure it was just a misunderstanding, or I missed it somewhere.

He felt part of his mind relax. In an hour, he would know for sure. He looked at the phone—his only connection to the real world—for answers. He found the alarm feature and set up reminders for each of his calls to Juan—every six hours.

He stared at the phone. Could he take a chance to call his mom again? Juan would have given him an untraceable phone. He wouldn't take a chance of it leading back to him. He dialed his mom's number. He had to know if she was okay. The phone rang once, twice . . .

"Hello." He didn't recognize the husky voice on the other end. "Hello, is anyone there?"

"Is Mary Torres there?" He altered his voice to copy one of his mom's friends.

"Mary is unable to come to the phone right now. Can I take a message?" Julio didn't recognize the voice as one of Juan's men, but then again, he had hired some new cronies.

"This is Dorothy. I need to tell Mary I am running late. I will be there in twenty minutes to pick her up for bingo. Could you tell her, please?" Julio knew his mom played bingo every Wednesday. She would know it was a lie, but she would have to be alive to relay that information to the man on the phone.

"This is Detective Danny Cross of the Maryland Police Department. I am sorry to have to tell you this, but your friend will not be playing bingo today." Detective Cross was using a gentle tone.

Julio pressed end. Realization sat in his mom was dead. Juan had sent him to a watery grave and had killed his mom to tidy up loose ends. Julio took off his shoes and lay down on his bed, hugging his pillow as the tears flowed. How long had it been since he really cried? It had to be years. It was his dad's funeral, the last time he really felt like a boy. He was eleven years old when he became the man of the house. He had promised his dad that he would take care of his mom, and now he had failed. Tears blanketed his pillow and flowed until he drifted into a fitful sleep.

The alarm on the phone sent him to his feet. The ache in his head was similar to a hangover. "How do women do this crying stuff? Wow, it really drains you." He blinked his eyes to try and clear the fog from his brain as he turned off the alarm. It was time to call Perrone. With phone in hand, he headed for the head to wash his face then climbed up to the helm.

"I'm going to need the coordinates—it's time to call Perrone." He sat down at the table in the corner and picked up a pad of paper and a pencil.

"Three-seven-point-four-nine and seven-six-point-one-seven. We're in the Chesapeake Bay." Max hardly even looked at the plotter.

"Thanks." Julio picked up the phone to dial.

"Wait a minute." The strength of Max's voice brought Julio to attention. "When I give you specific information or directions, I want you to repeat it back to me. This is called closing the loop. It is too important when dealing with coordinates and ship controls to casually receive information. You have just as much responsibility for our safety on this trip as I do. What you tell Juan affects me. When given information, I expect you to repeat it back to me and double-check it on the equipment. Got it?"

Julio couldn't believe the sudden mood change in this man. "So you want me to repeat three-seven-point-four-nine and seven-six-point-one-seven, we're in the Chesapeake Bay, back to you?"

"Yes." The answer was so quiet and casual Julio wasn't sure if he was serious or just messing with him. Another guy with power issues. Whatever.

He found Juan's number and pushed send on the phone. The phone was ringing before his thoughts were turned back to his task.

"Who's this?" It was Vic again. "This is Julio. Please put Perrone on the phone!" He was not going to give Vic the satisfaction of giving him grief.

Perrone must have been standing right next him. "Have you reached the Chesapeake Bay yet?"

"We're in the Chesapeake Bay—coordinates three-seven-point-four-nine and seven-six-point-one-seven." Julio relayed the coordinates like a pro.

"Did you say six-seven-point-one-seven?" Juan was writing it down.

"No, that was seven-six-point-one-seven. Yes, everything is going fine, but I can't find my bag or my passport. Where did you say you put them?"

"Victor left them in the car. We mailed them to Saint Maartens. My associate will meet you at the boat with the bag and your passport. That's what happens when you can't trust those that work for you . . ." Juan's voice cut out, and the line went dead.

05

Into the Dark – The Ocean

Julio put the phone back in his pocket and got up to leave. "Wait a minute," Max summoned. "We need to talk about nighttime driving. I have devised a driving schedule so we can both sleep. Your first shift will be in three hours, and it will be dark."

Julio stayed silent, doing his best to hide his nervousness.

Max continued, "A boat drives differently at night, so you will need to know a few things. First of all, I'm in charge. You follow my lead. This boat can't be docked without me. So there are emergency protocols you must follow. If any message comes across this radio and I'm asleep, you must wake me up immediately. If, by some chance, I fall overboard while the boat is moving, you need to press this red button on the chart plotter to store a waypoint."

Julio stepped closer to the chart plotter for a better look.

"Then throw this float over the side." He pointed to a life ring with a beacon on the top hanging on the wall. "You will need to slow the boat down, turn it around, and come back and pick me up—just don't run me over. Now let's talk about driving this boat when you're blinded by the night sky. The darkness can distort your views, especially if you are in foreign waters. This makes your equipment your best resource." Max reached up and turned a few knobs on the multifunction monitor, displaying a round picture with lights.

"This center spot," Max pointed to one of the lights, "is us, our boat. The other points of light on this screen are other solid objects around us. See that ridge over there to the starboard? That's this group of lights on the monitor. See these faint rings that circle out from the center of the monitor? Those are range rings. They tell you how far away objects are. Right now, each ring represents a quarter of a mile. These buttons change the magnification of the monitor. The distance between each ring is shown by this number in the corner. The scale of your radar is very important. Any questions?"

"I think I got it?" Julio reached up, pushed the button, and watched the display change.

"There are two different kinds of solid objects on the screen. See this one that is moving quickly? It is that boat right over there. If there is a light above your point on the monitor, that means there is an object in front of us." Julio followed the movement of the boat and the point on the screen. "Your job is to keep your distance. These other displays are used to help us see the hidden angles. The infrared camera is turned on with this button on the multifunction monitor. It will switch the screen to display what the camera sees. You can zoom into an object or zoom out to discern an image's distance." Max demonstrated how to switch the monitor back and forth between displays.

Max only paused briefly, then moved on. "This display is a depth finder. It monitors what is below us. There should always be more than ten feet of water between us and the ocean floor." He turned and caught Julio's eyes. "I can't emphasize this enough each display has a purpose. They are very important to our survival on this trip. It only takes one wrong decision and the water easily becomes our grave. Once we get to the ocean, the real challenge begins. We'll be working around the clock getting as far as fast as possible. Driving a boat requires you to be alert and aware of all your surroundings. I'll be monitoring the weather patterns, so hopefully, we can avoid any storms coming across our path. All these systems are our lifeline. We are blind out here without them. They are serious pieces of equipment and are not toys! If you don't understand anything, or if you have any questions, ask me—don't guess. This box over here is the weather radio. I want you to understand that it is HANDS-OFF!" Max looked at Julio for a minute, wondering if he was making a mistake trusting him.

"By the time you relieve me after midnight, we'll be on the open ocean, heading south. You will be required to stay awake when you are driving. Now go get some sleep. You need to be back up here for your twelve-thirty phone call to Juan, and then you will take over the helm. Good night."

In the sudden silence, Julio turned and headed for his stateroom. He wasn't sure he understood everything, but he would figure it out when it was his turn to drive without Max's prying eyes scrutinizing his every move. Right now, he needed sleep. Too much was happening too fast. Focusing on staying alive was his main concern, though he knew his mom's death would haunt his dark times.

Once in his stateroom, he undressed for bed. He hadn't thought about the money from Jason since he left DC. Now here he sat with a pouch strapped to his leg. Keeping it on his person allowed him to take it with him, but what good was FBI marked money? Customs would be sure to confiscate it when he reached Saint Maartens, but he couldn't think about that now. His current dilemma was whether to continue to wear the money or hide it in his stateroom. Max was an unknown, and he wasn't sure what he knew about his situation. His only option was to watch his own back. If Juan was telling the truth, and he was shipping his bag to Saint Maartens, then all would be well, unless he was pulling a fast one and waiting for him to be arrested or, worse, killed—this thought sent a chill down his spine. He would definitely need an escape plan. Perhaps this FBI money may be useful after all. It could get him started in a new area, and if that place was big enough, perhaps the marked bills wouldn't lead back to him. For now, he reasoned, he would keep the money strapped to his leg while he slept.

Julio crawled into bed. The pace Max was promising to put him through was going to be grueling. It didn't take long to fall asleep, but it only seemed like seconds before the alarm was sounding in his ears.

He reached for the phone to shut it up, but there was a moaning of metal that was still resonating. What was that noise? His stomach growled, but the noise from the boat all but silenced his body's internal complaints. He stood up and had to reach for the wall. "Wow, the boat is really rocking." He got dressed and headed for the galley for drinks and food, then up the steps to get the coordinates to make his scheduled call.

"Where are we now?" Julio had to raise his voice to be heard over the noise.

"You tell me." Max motioned toward the instrument panel. "I'll let you know if you're right before you call."

He laid his food on the table and turned toward the chart plotter as the boat dipped. He reached back toward the table just in time to catch his plate before it hit the floor. With food in hand, he walked to the display. "Let's see, thirty-six-point-fifty-three and seventy-five—"

"That is three-six-point-five-three . . .," Max cut in.

"Okay, three-six-point-five-three and seven-five-point-seven-three, and where are we on the water?

"We are about five miles south of the Virginia/North Carolina state line. You don't have to have this perfect, but Juan wants to know some landmark to give him a reference point along the way. I need to talk to him when you get done." He turned back and adjusted something labeled "stabilizer," which evened out the boat's rocking. Julio wrote down the coordinates to make sure he got them right.

"What'd you say? Why do you need to talk to him?" Max's statement had taken him off guard.

"It's none of your business! If you weren't here, that phone would be in my hand, and I would be the one checking in every six hours. You just do your thing, and I'll do mine."

Julio dialed the phone, and Juan answered. "Hello? Perrone? Yes. It's twelve thirty. We are three-six-point-five-three and seven-five-point-seven-three, about five miles south of the Virginia/North Carolina state line."

"Julio, if I don't answer this phone, you need to leave the coordinates on my voice mail every six hours. Do you understand?"

"Yes . . ."

"Hey, give me the phone." Max stood up and took the phone out of his hand.

"Juan, this is Max. I've got a weather pattern coming across my path. I'm going to pick up the pace to stay ahead of the storm." He looked tired and worried. "That will put us there Friday evening instead of Sunday morning . . . Yes, I will take care of it . . . Soon." He hung up the phone.

"What's this about a storm? Tonight? While I'm driving?" Julio's expression changed to one of concern.

"Does that scare you?" A grin came across Max's face. He was enjoying watching him squirm. He turned his eyes back to the instruments.

"This storm is a few days away, and if we pick up the pace, we'll miss it entirely. I just needed Juan to know so he can inform his buyer of our change of arrival." His words calmed Julio's fears at first, and then he thought about his bag. Would it be there in time?

"It's your shift. I need to know if you can handle driving this thing on the ocean." He moved aside.

"How did you get the boat to quit rocking?" Julio waited, but Max seemed to ignore his question, so he tried again. "What makes ocean travel so much noisier and rougher?"

Max sighed. "It isn't that it's rougher, the waves are bigger, and we're traveling faster, which creates more noise. Are you okay so I can get some shut-eye?" Max watched Julio intently as he settled into his chair and surveyed the monitors.

"Where are we on the radar screen?" Max asked, testing him.

"Right here." Julio pointed at the light in the middle of the screen.

"What's this?" Max pointed to another light. Julio noticed that the object on the display was moving at the same speed as almost everything else on the screen, which means it wasn't moving at all. "I don't know?"

"Take the infrared camera and take a closer look." Max moved over behind him to see if he remembered how to work the camera.

Moving the camera, Julio zoomed in on the object. "It looks like something floating with a flashing light."

"That's called a buoy. It's like a road sign on the ocean. They are color-coated to direct traffic on the waters. See this object on the chart plotter? It's that buoy. So, for now, all you need to know is to follow the chart plotter course and don't run over the buoys." He stepped back and watched Julio, wondering if he should just use the autopilot, but he had already committed to this course of action, and right now, he just wanted sleep. He stepped below and was back up on the helm in no time. He did a once-over on the monitors and equipment and headed for the corner nook, pulling out his pillow. It wasn't long until Max was snoring away.

Julio could finally relax, but with that came his exhaustion. The stillness of the black night taunted him to sleep, and it took every trick he had to keep his eyes opened. The snacks he brought worked at first, busying his senses for stimulation. Once they were gone, his battle began. It started with thoughts of home, but he soon pushed them away. He couldn't handle that pain right now. Staring off in the distance darkened his mind, and he found himself doing the head bob, followed by slow course corrections. It was only a three-hour shift, but he was glad when Max stirred.

"I'm heading down to the head and the galley and will be up shortly to relieve you."

Anxiety kicking in, Julio did a quick observation of all the monitors to be ready to answer Max's questions.

"How did it go?" Max's voice was there before he was.

"Fine." He yawned and stretched as he climbed off the captain's chair.

"Did you pass any boats or ships or see any coast guard cruisers?" Max walked past him and sat down.

"Was I supposed to watch out for coast guard cruisers?" Fear crept up his spine. Max seemed to enjoy winding him up.

Max shrugged. "You probably should observe any unusual things going on around us, and that includes boats that can arrest us!"

"Right. I'll be more vigilant next time. If anything, tonight was boring. The hardest thing was staying awake."

Max turned and gave him a penetrating stare. "You fall asleep and something happens, I'll kill you!"

Another threat from Max, Julio knew it was time to leave. He had to call Perrone again in just under three hours, and he needed some sleep. "Oh well, as long as I'm an asset, my life has value to him, right?"

06

The Plan – Ocean Travel

Julio found the next few days filled with three-hour driving shifts. His sleeping patterns gave him just enough energy to function but not enough to ever feel rested. He was comfortable in the captain's chair, and driving had become routine, which released part of his mind to wander. He had plenty of time to review his life and deride himself for all his bad choices.

It all seemed to come back to the decision he made when he was sixteen. His best friend had hooked him up with Soni, a girl unlike any other girl he had ever dated. She hung out with gangs, throwing caution to the wind. Her excitement was intoxicating, adding just enough danger to keep him on his toes. The world she introduced him to was untamed—liberating to an adolescent seeking to find his own place. Soni was smart, insightful. She had power in this world, and she used it. Julio had been an innocent bystander, like a patron in a movie theater, watching the action playing out before him. Looking back now, he could see that his relationship with Soni was the mistake that had set his fate in motion.

It was around his seventeenth birthday when Soni introduced him to Juan Perrone at a party for his daughter Natalia. Soni marched him right up to this well-dressed, stocky man who'd fit right in to any Olympic wrestling competition. He was definitely the man in charge.

"Sir, I want you to meet my friend Julio." He couldn't believe she was interrupting this man to introduce someone like him. That was the beginning of the end.

Things changed quickly after that, and Soni disappeared from his life. He told himself that she had tired of him and moved on. Now he wondered who she really was—a girlfriend or a recruiter for Perrone.

Juan Perrone turned out to be a likeable-enough guy, and he offered Julio a job right there at the party. He couldn't believe it. His mom, on the other hand, was not impressed and encouraged him to say no, but the dollar signs won out. For the most part, Perrone turned out to be a good boss. However, the job took the place of college, which nearly broke his mother's heart. She told him that to waste a good mind like his was a travesty. But Perrone convinced him that he just wasn't college material. "Universities are for rich guys who want to run businesses, and why would you want to do that with all their headaches and problems?" he would say. Juan promised he would take care of him; that if he was a good worker, he would always have a job and a place to live. If only he'd been smart enough to look past the money and the empty promises.

"I should've listened to Mom, and now she's dead." He looked out at the vastness of the ocean. "And it looks like I'll be joining her soon." He squeezed his eyes to stop the tears from forming.

The lull of the boat was soothing. He struggled to keep his eyes opened. After catching himself drifting off for the third time, he decided he needed something to help him focus. He centered his mind on his situation. What had he gotten himself into? There was Juan who wanted him dead, and then there was Max spitting vile comments at him every time he spoke. His warning played through Julio's mind. *"If you aren't someone I can use or trust, I need to know right now. If I can't depend on you, I'll throw you overboard and save me the aggravation of dealing with you later."* Was he just Max's problem to solve when he got tired of him? He needed to limit his contact and avoid him as much as possible. These short shifts were good for that.

His brooding, once again, had him looking for stimulation. He started playing with the infrared camera, zooming in and out, trying to make sense of shadows around him, but nothing was discernable in the blackness. The other buttons on the helm caught his eye. He couldn't help but touch each one to see what they controlled. Everything seemed to have an acronym: Wypt, Mob, Map, Fish. Dep Stab and Auto. Touching one would expose another list of buttons. He recognized some, but others were unknown abbreviations.

The weather radio made a noise, grabbing his attention. What was it Max said about a storm? He reached over and turned one of the knobs a few clicks, trying to find a weather report; all he heard was static. He turned it again to quiet the noise. Max seemed to shift uneasily then settle back down. That was close. The last thing he needed was more of Max's ire.

Focusing on the black night ahead, his eyes began to droop followed by head nods. He was so tired. He had to stay awake. There were two guarantees for death: wrecking the boat or Max finding him asleep at the helm. Of course, death might be a welcome change. The thought strangled him like a strait jacket. Death. Death was a cold enemy that took those you loved. Death stripped you have hope and peace. No. Death needed to stay far away—far, far away! He took a deep breath to calm his anxiety.

Did he have a choice in the matter? Was his story already written, just waiting for the final chapter to play itself out, or could he change its ending? Could he turn things around? Was there a possible escape, a possible way to challenge his fate—to rewrite his story? He felt the adrenaline wake up his mind. He had to find a way to keep death at bay. There had to be a way. There had to be an answer. He would figure it out. He would live.

There was movement behind him. Julio was ready and quickly turned the helm over to Max. He headed below to his stateroom. His shift was over, and his mind was ready for solace—for sleep. Yet there was a new light in his eyes, a new hope. The choice was made—he was choosing to live. No matter what Perrone and Max had in store for him, he would fight it.

Day and night were indiscernible in the windowless staterooms, making sleep come easier between shifts. The next few days were filled with the monotonous schedule of sleeping, eating, and driving. Julio made time every few shifts to take a shower, mainly because he was getting too ripe for his own nose. On his shower days, he was more alert, but sleep deprivation was taking its toll. There were times he would wake up and realize he was sitting in the captain's chair, checking the log to make sure he made the phone calls to Perrone, calls he didn't remember making. Those times scared him the most, causing him to question what else he may have done or said while he was functioning in his sleep.

When his mind was alert, he tried to focus on his escape, but his thoughts were jumbled. His distance from land and lack of navigation on the water quickly eliminated each idea as it formed. Even though he had taken swimming lessons as a child, he knew his skills were not good enough to survive in the ocean. Anger and depression became his constant companion as his mind turned to despair. He was angry with Perrone, he was angry with Jason, he was angry with Max, he was angry at the boat, but most of all, he was angry with himself for allowing his life to end up like this. Why hadn't he listened to his mom? Why had he turned a blind eye to Juan's dealings? And why, oh why, had he agreed to do this job?

A slap across the face would usually right his mind, but he soon turned to eating to help him stay alert. His diet consisted of canned beans and peanut butter sandwiches, which at first was a favorite of his but soon became his enemy as the waves tossed the boat about on the open ocean. His stomach would recoil during feedings, developing all kinds of dances. He then had to deal with a roaming boat as it veered off course while he was bent over the port side seeking relief. It was at these times he was glad Max was no longer sleeping on the helm. He tried fasting for a while instead of subjecting his stomach to the pain but soon found himself back to head bobbing. One thing was for certain, his pants were getting looser and his belt tighter. If he could see a silver lining in all this, it would be the pounds he was shedding.

Sleep deprivation was messing with his brain, causing his thoughts to wildly go from one extreme to another. He was excited when a new escape idea would surface and then immediately felt depressed as his plan would fill with holes. Thoughts of his past would make him sad.

Thoughts of his future would end in a dark stupor. He found himself checking his phone every few hours as a reminder of the date and time, keeping an ongoing count of the hours ticking by. This repetition seemed monotonous but served as a distraction. Challenging his brain with mind exercises calmed his stress and helped him stay alert. After running through math equations or poems he had memorized, he could calmly tackle his dilemma and turn his focus to his escape plans.

His contact with Max was a routine of passing shifts. The one leaving the helm would tell the other of any unusual activity or concern as they were heading for their staterooms. Most of it was mumble talk. "Nothing to report," one would say. The other would follow with, "Okay," and off they'd each go, whether sleeping or driving.

His phone calls to Perrone were nothing more than coordinates, most of the time leaving them on an answering machine. The lack of human contact was driving him crazy. He wished he had someone to bounce off ideas or thoughts. He didn't realize how hard it was to be left alone with his own thoughts for so long. He missed Sierra. She was his solace. She was his sounding board. His dreams were filled with her face. Why hadn't he seen how much she meant to him? He should have married that girl and taken her far away. Now his fate was sealed, his story ending, the last chapter playing itself out hour by hour, minute by minute, with each rock of the boat on the perpetual waves.

His escape plans were haunting him, coming and going, as his brain tore each one apart. His first plan was simple. He would knock out Max, throw him overboard, and steal the boat, but even though he had worked for Juan for many years, he wasn't one to end a life. This plan also scared him because he didn't know enough about the boat and where he was going to want Max gone. After that, each plan was a deviation of the first. Perhaps he would tie him up instead of kill him, then what? He knew his mind was not focused; not being creative, not forming a reasonable plan. It would have been easy to just give up, but his only other option was death. He had to keep trying. He may not have a mother or even a girl to return to, but he wanted much more from his life. He wasn't done yet.

He was trying to stay hopeful. When he would see land on the chart plotter, it was always too far away to be considered a viable escape plan. As he stared out the front window into the vast ocean, he would often see a dark patch that would resemble a land mass, but as they neared, it proved to be nothing more than a shadow. His mind was playing tricks on him. He often wondered how people he knew lived year after year on small amounts of sleep.

He was on the phone when Max appeared behind him. "I need to talk to Juan." Julio handed off the phone.

"Juan, the increased speed has burned more fuel than planned. At the scheduled fuel stop, we'll need to increase our fuel estimate. We should be there in just a few hours . . . Yes, this is the only stop, I think, we need to make unless the storm changes course. My calculation is around a thousand . . . No, nothing was said . . . I'll take a look . . . Yes, I know . . . Yes, before arrival . . . I'll take care of it south of Cay Sal in deep water." Max hung up the phone.

"We're stopping for fuel?" Julio felt a surge of energy. Maybe there was hope of an escape.

"We're taking on fuel in Miami, a quick stop at the fuel dock, then on toward Saint Maartens." Max was making notations in his logbook.

"What's K-Cell? Are we making another stop?" Julio's question was casual, but his mind was racing for possible escape options. He had to be careful not to sound too excited.

"My business with Juan is none of yours! I'll let you know what concerns you! I'm going to bed!" He stepped down to his stateroom and slammed the door.

Julio was stunned. "What was that about?"

Max's conversation with Juan was all Julio could think about during his driving shift. What was K-Cell? Did it concern him? Did it concern the money shipment? Julio looked around at the monitors, but nothing was labeled K-Cell. Why deep water—to bury something? The money and the boat were going to Saint Maartens, so that just left him. Was Max to do away with him? Was K-Cell to be his burial plot? He didn't want to think about Max killing him, but why deep water? The money had a destination and a path, but he was the added variable on this trip.

He looked out over the open expanse in front of him. In one phone call, just one-half of a conversation, it was all made clear. Max had a plan, and he needed one too.

Julio's eyes looked at the locked chest cooler in the corner. Was the money locked in there? Was that chest big enough for a million dollars in cash? He thought back to his search for his bag. All the compartments he went through, and there was no sign of any money. Perhaps the money was a ruse. Had he been duped all along? This was too much to think about right now. Besides, a dead man doesn't need money. He had to figure out how to get off this boat.

His mind was alive and vibrant. His need for sleep was pacified. He was ready. He could almost smell his freedom—just a few hours away. It all came to him. It was all too simple. He would make his escape in Miami. Max would pull the boat in for fuel, and all he had to do was push him into the water and make a run for it. The plan was set, and he would soon be free.

07

Murder at the Dock – Miami

Julio was so preoccupied with his planning that he didn't hear Max step up behind him. He jumped as Max's voice filled the stillness. "I'll take it from here. It's time to pull into the port of Miami. See over there, those buildings and large ships, we are going through that channel." Julio stood up and headed for his stateroom.

"Julio, I need you to stay up here and help me navigate through the channel and dock the boat. Your job is to sit up there on the bow and keep track of any debris that may cause damage to the boat. All you have to do is point which way I need to go to avoid floating objects, and I will adjust the boat accordingly. Then when we get to the pier, you will need to hand the bowlines to the attendant. Got it?" Julio nodded, desperately trying to control the excitement welling up inside—his freedom was just a channel away.

"Listen," Max continued, "we need to talk about this stop. It is for fuel only. We won't be leaving the boat. If we look suspicious and draw attention to ourselves, the coast guard may decide to board. If that happens, we go to jail. Do you understand?" Max paused and turned to face him. Julio just nodded. He didn't care about what Max was saying, he had his plan, and he wasn't planning on sticking around.

"There will be all kinds of things going on when we pull into port. We have to stay under the radar. Do you get my drift?" Julio nodded once again and turned toward the port side door. He felt a surge of deflation. Max's stare had been intense. Did he know? Glancing back gave him no solace. Max had turned away, busy with the ship to shore radio.

Finding a place to sit on the bow was not an easy task, and with the length of the channel, it could be a while before they reached the fuel dock. There was a barrel attached to the railing labeled "Life Raft." He climbed up. It was awkward, but the angle gave him a perfect view of the water below while keeping Max, in his sights, at the helm. He was confused at his purpose. With a depth finder and camera on board, he didn't see why his services were needed.

Watching the water go by was almost mesmerizing, making it hard to keep his brain awake and his mind focused. As the boat glided smoothly through the channel, his head swung up and down in line with the motion of the bow. He was losing his battle to stay awake.

As they neared the dock, he could see the fuel attendant waiting to meet them. Adrenaline rushed through his blood, awakening his senses. He surveyed his surroundings, looking for every possibility for escape, but what met his eyes left him in fear. Police lined the dock's only exit. They were searching a small craft just down the pier. He couldn't tell what their intent was or if they would be targeted next. What would happen to him if they were boarded? Julio barely noticed as Max skillfully pulled alongside the fuel pump; his gaze was locked on the line of blue uniforms. He heard a voice.

"Hey, throw me the line." Julio mindlessly climbed down off the life raft and handed the bowline to the fuel attendant.

"What's going on over there?" He heard his voice squeak.

The attendant looked up. "They found a dead body in that cruiser this morning. The police have been here all day. I expect the dock will be infested with them all week. Everyone is considered a suspect. You are lucky you're just in and out, or they would probably question you too. I just wish they would leave. They make our customers cranky." He moved toward the aft of the boat to take the stern lines from Max.

Julio couldn't take his eyes off the murder scene. How was he going to carry out his plan with the police blocking his exit? He stiffened as he heard footsteps behind him. "We need to stay on the bow of the boat in plain sight to minimize suspicion being drawn our way." This seemed strange to Julio, but he figured Max knew best in this situation.

"How long is it going to take?" He glanced at Max and back at the men in uniform. His heart ached—he was so close to freedom. All he wanted was his life back, but he knew it would only take one small act, and he would be calling a jail cell home. Would the FBI help him if he were arrested? This thought caused a moment of pause. No, they couldn't even save his mother. He was on his own. If he couldn't get off this boat before they left the fuel dock, then he would have to take it. That thought, though it gave him hope, also scared him. He was a stranger in a strange area, and his only source of transportation was a boat that he barely knew how to drive. Could he survive without Max in the vast ocean? He couldn't dwell on his misgivings. He had to focus on the present. He would watch for an opportunity to present itself, and he would be ready.

"About fifty minutes, give or take." Max's words made his mind search for the original question—fueling time, fifty minutes, right.

"While we wait, we can wash down the boat. I'll grab the water hose from the dock, and you go aft to the fishing locker and get the long-handled scrubbing brush. I'll rinse while you scrub. This is a good time to get all the bird crap and salt build up off the boat. Plus, if we look disinterested in what the police are doing, we won't draw unwanted attention our way, and we can get out of here without so much as a glance in our direction."

Max stepped across to the dock for the hose as Julio went in search of the brush. He looked at the storage compartments and tried to remember which one the fishing locker was. He decided to just start opening doors. The first one opened to a fire extinguisher and short-handled brushes. The next one was small, and it contained a tackle box. He moved on looking for the biggest one he could find, but it only housed life jackets. He closed that door and looked around. His eyes fell on a long metal storage bin attached to the transom. Inside, he found several long-handled fishing poles, a boat hook, and a gaff hook. There was even a small wooden bat used for bludgeoning fish. Along one side, there lay a long-handled, soft-bristled brush. He grabbed it and headed back toward the bow of the boat. Max was already spraying the boat to loosen up the bird guano when he returned. Though soaking the surface made it easier to scrub, it created a wet slick surface. It wasn't long before Julio was ditching his soggy shoes and going barefoot. Work often calmed him, and cleaning the boat was easing his stress.

Scrubbing the boat used muscles he hadn't used in a long time. The up-and-down motion sent aches and pains through his gripping hands, and his tired shoulders were rebelling at each rotation. However, the pain was keeping his mind focused and alert—it was therapeutic. It wasn't long before he was peeling off his wet T-shirt and basking in the warmth of the Florida sun. Memories flooded over him like a warm blanket. He was back at his apartment, stripped down to his shorts, with a hose in one hand spraying the sudsy soap off his baby, his Challenger—the car he would never see again. He felt sadness dampen his heart. Here he was, on a boat tied up to land, yet he was still a prisoner to fate. He glanced around, hoping for some change, some opportunity to escape. How long had it been since they'd arrived? Was there still time?

Catching sight of the dock and the police without drawing attention to his actions was difficult, but he worked it in with his stretching motions. He just needed the right moment, the perfect opportunity. He looked down as Max glanced at him. He had to hide any expression that might give away his hopes. He gripped tighter on the brush handle. He glanced down at his hands. Could this be what he needed—a weapon of opportunity? He smiled. All he needed was just the right movement, and Max would be swimming with the fishes or at least saying hi to them up close and personal. Julio silently laughed at his stupid joke.

The getting-away part of his plan wasn't quite coming together. He could try a diversion tactic of acting drunk or arguing playfully with Max, but he would have to do it without appearing suspicious. There was bound to be someone who would stop him and ask who he was, where he was going, and what happened. With this many police in the area, it would probably be them. It was definitely risky, but he didn't see another choice.

The cleaning project was coming to an end as they rounded the outboard side. This was the perfect place to put his plan in motion, with the boat acting as a barrier between them and the police presence. Julio knew it was now or never. He moved closer to his quarry. At that moment, Max stepped back and eyed him suspiciously. A voice from behind caused Julio to turn around, and there stood the fuel attendant. It was too late. He had missed his window of opportunity. His muscles drooped, his adrenaline released.

"Your tank is topped off, and as soon as you put my hose back, you can push off. I have people lined up waiting on fuel, so I need you to get underway as soon as possible. I'll be right back with your credit card and payment slip."

The attendant was turning to go as Max interrupted, "Could you add a pack of rum amaretto Corona, soaked?" He waved his acceptance of Max's words and disappeared.

"Don't even think about it, Julio. This isn't over. We'll deal with it later." Max turned and rinsed down the area they hadn't yet cleaned and followed the hose trail back to the dock. Julio realized what had just happened. Poised to strike, his moment had been stolen.

"Julio, get up by the bow to take in the line. As soon as the attendant returns, we're off." He could hear the distrust in Max's voice as it trailed behind him.

Julio let out the breath he had been holding. Glancing down at the brush still clenched in his hands, all he could feel was his heartbeat and his aching muscles. He walked to the rail and peered over the edge. Could he jump? Would he be able to get past the police? If they caught him, could he walk away? He knew if Perrone wanted him dead, there would be no place to hide. He needed to accept the fact that he would soon die. Whether by the sea or Max's hand, his life had an expiration date already determined. He was at the whim of his captor. His grip tightened on the brush handle as he broke it over his knee and threw the pieces into the water. Turning his back to the floating wood, he walked to the bow of the boat.

The attendant was handing Max a small paper bag and a receipt when he rounded the corner. The lines were quickly stowed, and the boat was pushed away from the pier. Julio was once again on debris duty, perched atop the life raft barrel repeating his earlier routine. He glanced back at the dock and couldn't believe that his freedom was slowly slipping away. He had lost his chance to avoid this horrid curse that was taking his life apart bit by bit. His mind and body groaned as he watched the Miami skyline diminish into thin air.

08

The Final Blow – Cay Sal

It wasn't long till they were out to sea and the waves were rocking the boat. Julio reached for the rail to steady himself as he headed for the galley to get something to eat. His simple breakfast had been over five hours ago, and with his physical activity and the dissipation of his adrenaline rush, he needed nourishment. The selection in the galley consisted of peanut butter, jelly, and a pantry stocked with various canned goods. Julio reached for the bread and peanut butter but stopped as his stomach recoiled. He turned toward the pantry. He was never one for eating food from a can, whether it was vegetables, soup, or beans, but he needed something different. He decided on a can of vegetable soup and quickly warmed it. Grabbing a spoon, he settled himself on the couch in the salon. He was thankful Max turned on the stabilizer to even out the rocking. It wasn't long until his body adjusted to the gentle sway. Nestled comfortably against the cushions, he dozed off as his empty bowl slid from his hands onto the floor.

It was the boat's horn that brought him out of his slumber. He reached for his phone, but it wasn't there. Startled, he jumped up and headed for the helm.

"What was that? What time is it? Have you seen my phone?"

Max jumped off the captain's chair. "It's your driving shift, Julio. I already called Juan to update our position and the storms status, so don't worry about that." Max's final words came from the salon as he slipped down the stairs to his stateroom.

Julio was not quite awake as he took the driver's seat. His sense of time was lost without his phone. How long he had been asleep or how long it had been since they left Miami was a mystery to him. His attention was drawn to the instrument panels as he searched for some indication of time. He noticed a small clock in the corner of the chart plotter that read "11:00." He glanced out at the sky, glimpsing colors of red and yellow as the sun peeked through the oncoming storm. The beautiful scene had him in a trance as he reached for his phone to snap a picture to show his mom. The memory of her and his hands' empty search brought his attention back to his nightmarish reality.

Max hadn't handed him back his phone. "Max, where's the phone?" There was no answer. That was strange. Why would Max call Perrone and then take the phone? Why was he in such a hurry?

Julio turned back to the chart plotter and corrected his course. His thoughts about the last several hours and how close he had come to knocking Max off and escaping in Miami filled his mind. Could he really have killed Max to regain his freedom? Now Max was on to him. And he has the phone. Had he reported to Perrone what happened at the dock?

"If only I could wake up from this nightmare. How did I get into this mess? Jason. Jason got me into this. Is he even looking for me? I bet he doesn't even care what happens to me. He probably thinks I took the money and ran. This FBI money has completely destroyed my life!"

Julio reached for the pouch on his leg; a quick panic rose in his chest until he realized he had taken the money off when he had showered. "It's hidden in my stateroom," he whispered, breathing a sigh of relief. Wait, had he really been going to knock Max in the water and run without any money? He had better get his head on straight. He was so tired, maybe just a quick nap. There was nothing in sight, just twenty minutes. He yawned and placed his head in his hands—he was out.

He jumped as the alarms from the weather radio woke him up. The noise helped focus his mind. How long had he been out? One glance at the monitors told him he was way off course. His hands were shaking as he carefully steered the boat back in line with the chart plotter, making careful turns so as to not disturb Max. His nerves were on edge. There was nothing like a dose of adrenaline to chase away the fog of exhaustion. He needed to use his time wisely, chart a new course, make a new plan—do something.

"Okay, okay, Miami didn't work out, but Max said something about K-Cell. Maybe I'll get another chance." Julio hit the zoom-out button on the chart plotter, looking for any sign of something called K-Cell. Ahead and to the right was a blue patch labeled "C-A-Y-S-A-L."

"Cay Sal. This must be the place. What did Max say he was going to do at Cay Sal, something about needing deep water?"

Julio thought back to his search of the boat, trying to figure out what Max would want to throw over the side. He couldn't think of anything unusual, like a package or an object that didn't belong. His mind was working hard to put together the pieces. Max worked for Perrone, and when Perrone wanted something buried deep in DC, he meant a body. Julio was the only extra body on board—there was no other explanation. Max was his executioner. So if he didn't come up with an escape plan soon, he would be sent to a watery grave. He sat up straight and looked around. He was out of time. There had to be a solution, a flaw in Max's plan. How much time did he have left?

"How does this stupid thing work?" His hands were still shaking as he put his fingers up to the chart plotter and whispered his thoughts out loud. "Here is Miami, and here is Cay Sal. It took us almost an hour to get to one finger length. So it should take us about two more hours to get to Cay Sal. If I am the cargo to be dumped, I may only have a couple of hours to live. There has to be a way out, something I can do."

Julio watched the monitors for a few minutes, hoping an answer would appear in front of him. His choices were few. He was in the middle of the ocean on a fast-moving boat. He knew he wouldn't last long if he just jumped into the water, his swimming skills weren't that good, and he would be at the mercy of a passing boat, if one came along. By then, he could die of thirst or get eaten by a shark. Plus, he hadn't seen any boats since they left Miami. Did they head in a different direction to avoid the storm? He only had Max's programed chart plotter for guidance.

He could knock Max out and tie him up and steal the boat. He would then need to find a place to get to shore, hoping he would have time to get away before Max was found and the police, FBI, and Perrone came after him. Could he really hide from Perrone? The only other choice was to kill Max, throw him overboard, and stay on this boat until he could find a place to go ashore without being noticed. He could then hide out with Juan's money. *Perhaps they would assume we both died at sea. But what if Max's body is found?* There were witnesses. If only the attendant on the fuel pier hadn't seen them together. One thing was for certain, if he pulled this off and Max was found, dead or alive, he would have a target on his back. Then what? Where would he go? What would he do?

"WAIT A MINUTE." His strong voice in the stillness of the helm made him jump and look behind him. He took a deep breath to compose himself. What was he about to say? "Oh, the money," he mouthed his thoughts. Where was Perrone's money? He thought back to his bag search. Was there someplace he hadn't looked? Was there any compartment he had missed? Julio's eyes were drawn to the odd-looking cooler with the lock in the corner of the helm. "Could the million dollars be in there? It would be just like Perrone to hide the money in plain sight."

Julio noticed that the boat was losing its stability. He heard a noise in the galley. It was too early for a driving change. He looked at the instrument panel to make sure everything was okay and they were on course. He never knew what to expect from Max. He had a way of talking softly to him one minute and threatening his life the next. With Max's quick exit earlier and his own impending death Julio didn't want to be an easy target for a tongue-lashing or a death blow. He was off the captain's chair when Max emerged from the salon. "I had it. You got it. Nothing changed." Then he hurried down the steps toward his stateroom.

He didn't know why Max had emerged early to retake the helm, but who was he to complain? He was so tired. All he wanted to do was fall on his bed and sleep for the next twelve hours.

"Julio, you better take your phone, so you don't miss your shift."

Julio heard Max but ignored him. He wasn't about to volunteer himself for his own execution. "You can call Perrone, you've done it before," he muttered under his breath.

The bed looked inviting as Julio entered his stateroom. He plopped down and reached to remove his shoes. They weren't there. Shocked to see his bare feet, his mind raced for an answer. It wasn't till that moment that he realized he hadn't put his shoes back on after the cleaning project. He played with the thought that they were waiting for him on the deck, but most likely, they were swept into the ocean with the wind and the rolling waves. "Feet, where are your shoes?" He laughed out loud.

He removed his shirt and started to remove his pants as he glanced down at his bare legs. Anxiety filled his veins. Where was the money? Where had he left it? He pulled up his pants and began searching his stateroom. He wanted to yell—to scream. What had he done? "Okay, Julio." He tried to calm his fears by interrogating himself. "Where did you hide the money?" He shrugged. "You idiot, when did you last see it?" This wasn't working. He took a deep breath and changed his tactic. "I need to think, to remember. I always take it off to shower, and I showered right before my last driving shift before we stopped for fuel. That wasn't that long ago. It has to be here somewhere."

Julio stood up and once again went through all the cabinets in his room—no money. He quickly moved across the hall to the head and searched through every nook and cranny. He went back to his stateroom and collapsed on his bed. "What have I done? Where could I have put the money?" His brain was so muddled, and he was so tired. "The money has to be here. I know I took it off here." He gave his room another look. It was useless. The money wasn't there.

He sat down. "If it isn't in my stateroom or the head, then where is it? Max and I are the only ones here. Max. Max has it! That's why he kept me on deck before we docked for fuel." Julio quietly opened his stateroom door and peered up at the salon to make sure the coast was clear. He inched toward Max's stateroom. Once inside, he carefully shut the door and searched every possible hiding place, both in the stateroom and in the head—nothing. The money was not there. Where could it be? Max. Max must have it on him.

Julio was furious by the time he made his way back to his stateroom. He couldn't stop pacing. Juan must have told Max about the money. Was that why he was still alive? Will his reprieve be over? He was at the mercy of one of Juan Perrone's henchmen. Did Max believe in mercy? He may have only hours left. His life was over. He felt the energy drain from every limb. He sat on his bed and dropped his head in his hands.

He wasn't sure what lifted the fog in his brain, perhaps it was his will to live, but as he arose and wiped the watery blur from his eyes, he felt new energy enter his willowy limbs. He wasn't dead yet, and he would not let his fate be determined by someone else, at least not without a fight.

Julio searched his room once again, this time for a weapon. "Too bad, I don't have my gun. If only the FBI hadn't kept it." Yet he wasn't sure he could actually take a life. In the past, when his neighbor was being a jerk, all it took was a few good swings with his bat, and he was much more reasonable. His job with Juan kept him behind the scenes and out of play. For that, he was grateful. But now he was front and center in the middle of the drama with no way out. He needed a weapon.

"If only I had my bat." Of course, this wasn't a case of a disgruntled neighbor—this was life or death. "Wait a minute." His head was screaming. "I saw a bat. Where was it? The transom—just lying there with the fishing gear."

He had to calm his nerves as he crept up the stairs and out the aft door. He raced for the fish locker as every creak and groan of the boat made his back stiffen and his pulse race. In the movies, this would be the moment the villain would sneak up behind him. But was Max the villain? He only had his assumptions to go on. He listened carefully and looked over his shoulder. Relief flooded his body as the black expanse of the looming storm met his eyes. He breathed deeply, coughing and choking on the damp sea air.

The hidden sunlight peeked through the clouds and illuminated the way as he reached into the fish locker and found the short wooden handle. With his hands gripped firmly around the bat, his legs buckled. He felt the slimy, wet surface of the deck through his jeans, and a wave of panic surged through his brain. Nausea overtook him, leaving the contents of his lunch to be washed away in the next splash of rain. It was time to take control. With the bat in hand and his nerves slowly releasing their knots, Julio determined his course of action. He would go back through the salon, sneak up behind the captain's chair, and bring the bat down on Max's skull.

He paced back and forth until his hands quit shaking. It was now or never. He slipped through the aft door, being careful not to make any noise that would give away his intentions. Something came over him. He was being pulled forward with an invisible cord, his mind in a virtual trance, as he neared his target. All concerns for his own safety were extinguished. It was kill or be killed. All concerns for Max's safety were dispelled – he was the enemy. The adrenaline was like euphoria surging through his veins. He felt so unaffected, as if he was watching himself on a movie screen. He wanted to laugh out loud, but that would alert Max to his presence. His senses where heightened as he made his way up the steps to the helm.

He was ready to bring the bat down when he noticed that the captain's chair was empty. As his brain tried to make sense of this new development, he looked up and saw Max through the open doorway, smoking one of his Dominican cigars. He moved forward, shaking like a leaf, with the bat resting on his shoulder as if he were poised to step up to the plate. His ecstasy increased with each movement.

Julio had forgotten that the starboard door frame had a step. The scream seemed to come from someone else, but the pain was real. Max's head turned toward the sound as Julio swung the bat around with the intensity of a major league hitter. To Julio, it was all in slow motion, like an instant replay. Max's expression was first stunned then fearful as his body folded and fell over the side of the boat, disappearing among the waves.

Julio was lost in time. He didn't know how long he stared down at the water before the throbbing pain in his foot engulfed his senses and awakened him from his trance. What had he done? He looked down at his mangled toe and the blood pool forming under his foot. With this kind of pain, he could only hope it was just his big toe that was broken. His mind was still filling in the pieces. Max was gone. He had knocked him overboard.

Julio looked back down at the gray water splashing up the side of the boat, bouncing off and forming white caps. It would have all been very beautiful in another time. Right now, he half expected to see Max's body floating by or to hear him yell for help, but all that was left was the silence of the storm's eye as it closed in on him like a dark shroud.

09

The Deep Blue – The Ocean Floor

It was his grip on the door frame that saved him from falling as Julio turned and gently placed his weight on his injured foot. Hopping to the captain's chair, he secured his stance and eased himself onto the seat. Taking a deep breath, he closed his eyes as the soothing sway of the boat and rhythmic sound of the waves calmed his stress and steadied his nerves. He was being lulled to sleep—sleep, much-needed sleep.

He wasn't sure just how long he sat there before he glanced through his half-opened eyes, catching sight of the instrument panel. Wait a minute. His senses were coming back to him. Who was driving the boat? Fear aroused his faculties as he searched for his bearing on the chart plotter. He was surprised to see that the boat was correcting its position and staying pretty much on course. The flashing green light in the corner attracted his attention. It read "A-U-T-O." He touched the display, and it flashed "Autopilot." So that's how Max was able to deliver boats for Perrone by himself. All those crazy diving shifts and all he had to do was find the autopilot button on the chart plotter.

He studied the display, carefully pushing each button along the side of the monitor. He found the MOB button—man overboard. He reached toward the monitor. *What was it Max said? I was to push it if he fell over the side of the boat.* He quickly pulled his hand back and let out a maniacal laugh. He would never push that button in a million years.

He had his life back, and he was going to find Juan's money and make a new start. He glanced across the room at the locked cooler.

It was getting dark. The sun was heading toward its resting place as the black storm clouds rolled in extinguishing its remaining light. Julio looked around at the vast darkness. He shuddered. In an instant, the sky was filled with explosive light followed by a deafening sound reminding him that his ordeal was not yet over.

Julio looked up at the sky and listened to the waves. He had heard about boats being lost in a storm at sea. He was barely able to drive this boat in good weather. The idea of stormy seas terrified him. He reached for the chart plotter and pushed "auto," causing the boat to wildly change direction. He pressed it again, and the boat corrected its course. He touched the "wypt" key, and it brought up a screen with a list of waypoints in order of distance from his current position. Scrolling down the list, he saw Key Largo, Florida. He moved the curser and highlighted it. He sighed. Could it be that simple? The boat could just take him to safety?

The blackness and the roar of the waves intensified. A burst of lightning highlighted the whitecaps rising around him. He could feel imminent danger. It was time to find land. He pressed enter on his course correction and was immediately tossed to the floor as the boat jerked then pitched to one side. Items slammed to the floor, causing a cacophony of sounds. It took him several minutes to realize that it was his programming change and not someone attacking him that threw him to the deck. The boat was merely turning around in the rough seas.

Julio got his bearings and crawled back to the captain's chair. His laborious movements confirmed that he had done major damage to his foot and movement would be hindered for some time. He was officially a one-legged pirate—he had killed someone, stolen a boat, and lost the use of one of his legs. "All I need is an eye patch, a wooden peg, and a parrot—a pirate, indeed. Argh!" His laugh was deep and howling.

Thunder rolled across the sky followed by a band of lightning, exposing the great waves in his distant path. Julio stared at the blackness left behind. A few minutes later, another shower of light followed by an even louder crack. The storm was getting closer, and his course change had placed him directly in its path. He sensed the pressure as the tempo of the waves quickened around him. Another flash descended, bringing even more angry beauty. Fear enveloped him, gripping his every nerve. He reached for the stabilizer button, hoping it would help, but upon pushing it, there was no change. The waves were just too strong.

An alarm went off, and he reached for his belt to silence his phone, but it wasn't there. He searched the helm for the direction of the noise and found the phone's glow. It was lying on the floor next to the locked cooler. Carefully, he lowered himself to the deck and crawled toward it. He knew what that alarm meant. He picked up the phone and stared at it, trying to decide what to do. If he called Perrone, it would buy him more time, but though he could manage the coordinates, he had no position detail to relay. It was time to disappear. He was done answering to Perrone and Vic. He grabbed the phone and slammed it on the cooler, but the noise persisted. Julio brought it down a second time but changed his direction to the lock, thinking to kill two birds with one stone. It was time to find out what secrets were hidden in this box. It took three hard blows to shatter the phone to pieces. He needed a stronger hammer to break the lock.

He had seen a hammer when he was looking for his travel bag. He sat back and mentally walked through his search—the engine room. He remembered a tool bag lying on the shelf. It would be there. He slowly inched his way down the stairs and back up to the helm with the tool bag in hand. The pain in his foot was a continuous throbbing sensation, but that wasn't what worried him. The thundering winds were stirring the waves and rocking the boat from side to side. He knew he had to work fast, find Juan's money, and get ashore, but would he survive the constant battering of the storm?

The hammer severed the hasp on the lock with the first blow. Excitement filled his body as he opened the lid. He was sure that he had found his treasure and his chance for a new start. The sight that greeted him took his breath away. Not only was there no money, but also the cooler was filled with handheld electronics. To Julio, they looked like fancy walkie-talkies he used to play with as a kid. He dropped the lid and looked around. He threw the hammer across the room, striking and breaking the latch on the helm door. The wind and the pitching boat whipped the door back and forth.

Julio put his head in his hands. Was this nightmare ever going to end? Couldn't he have one break? It was time to find Juan's money and find it now—even if that meant taking this boat apart piece by piece.

He reached in the tool bag and pulled out a screwdriver, a razor blade knife, and a pry bar. He eased his body off the floor using his one good leg and sat on the cooler for support. Turning to the first compartment, he removed the screws that held each door panel. It didn't take long for him to be elbow deep in wires, moving them aside to check every nook and cranny. By the time he had exhausted his search of the helm, he noticed that some of his displays had quit working, but he dismissed it as nonessential to his cause. He had to find that money. Without it, he might as well join Max.

Since the search of the helm was a bust, he moved to the salon. Working as fast as he could, he took apart any structure that obscured a possible hiding place. He came up empty once again.

The boat's movement was becoming more and more violent, making it difficult for Julio to get around. The storm was determining his timetable, and his time was running out.

Moving on, he made his way down to the staterooms and quickly shredded each pillow and mattress, scouring every inch.

He crawled up on the deck, tying a rope to himself to secure his connection to the boat, and inched his way along the surface to search each compartment—no luck. He loosened the life raft, tethering it to the bow to prepare for an emergency escape. All that was left was to locate Perrone's money.

He made his way back to the salon. Each movement seemed to drain his energy. His foot wasn't the problem, it was numb, but he was losing his will to fight, to live. He was exhausted, and with each rolling wave of the sea, the boat was taking on water. Did he have a chance? He sat with his back against the sofa, concentrating on his search. He had been in every room, compartment, and locker. He thought back to Perrone's instructions about other shipments but couldn't remember if any money compartment was mentioned. He briefly closed his eyes.

The boat pitched and sent him across the floor to the base of the helm's stairs. He climbed up to take a look. One glance at the chart plotter and he knew he was lost. All the instruments were dark, and the only illumination was from the frequent bolts of lightning. He glanced forward to the bow, and his heart sank. The tether holding his escape plan, his life raft, was gone. He slunk back in the salon to wait out the storm. His fate was no longer in his hands—he was at the mercy of the sea.

Scanning the room, he took in the devastation around him. The salon was covered with shredded foam, his own handiwork. He gathered what he could to create a nesting place to ride out the waves, praying that the boat would make it through the storm. He wasn't a praying man, but he remembered his mom's deep faith. If ever he needed a higher power in his life, it was now.

He was nesting, praying and pleading with God to spare him. Shock took over, cradling his fragile mind. The transition happened in the blink of an eye. His mind was saving him. He was thrown back in time. He was a child, existing on the memories of his happiest times. Julio had found his nirvana.

He saw his family together celebrating his tenth birthday, his parents, grandparents, and extended family sitting around the table talking of the old country, Cuba—their beloved homeland. He was there, reaching out to touch their faces. They were singing to him. It was his birthday. He was eating cake and laughing.

Something was happening. His memory was evolving. The ground was becoming a sea of rising water. He was running to his mom, but she was swept away in the waves. He turned toward his father, and he disappeared beneath a sea of foam. He heard screaming. He turned.

His grandfather was yelling at him, "I'm coming for you, Julio! Stay right there! I'll get you!"

He started to run toward him, but his grandfather's face was changing, morphing into his boss's face. He stopped. It was Perrone, not his grandfather, who was swimming toward him. Everything was falling apart—books and articles were flying through the air. His arms were over his head, deflecting objects. He felt pinned. Glancing down, he watched his child-sized feet begin growing to fill the small space. Items, in the form of furniture, were pushing him. He felt the earth beneath him shake, and he watched it start to collapse.

Was this reality? It was all happening in slow motion. He glanced up in time to witness a wall of water heading toward him. Everything was bending and falling in the water's path. How could he still be standing? Was he standing? He felt his body rise, surfing high on the wave's crest. The roar and crashing of the water became muffled as each precious breath resonated through his ears. The wall receded. He plummeted. Something snagged him. He was motionless watching the water rush past, taking what remained of the tattered vessel. The deep blue had claimed another offering.

Julio couldn't remove his eyes from the scene playing out before him. The mountainous water was eerie and viscous as it shredded its prey. He looked up and saw his savior. It was a portion of the fly bridge; a web had formed from bits and pieces of floating debris, pushing and pulling him away from the deathly scene. He was fighting for each precious breath between plunges in the crashing waves. He was in shock, his mind fluctuating in and out of his current state of awareness.

His mind had taken over. He was seventeen again, arguing with his mom about working for Juan instead of going to college. That day was the beginning of the end, and deep down, they both knew it. Their tension diluted over time, but his decision had placed both of them in the hands of his "benefactor." His mom had paid the ultimate price. Much like generations before him, he had misplaced his loyalties. His grandparents, aunts, and uncles escaped their beloved Cuba for freedom, only to be seduced back and imprisoned for their betrayal when they returned. Now here he was, waiting for his fate, only miles from her banks.

10

The Promise – Key Largo

"Good morning, Jack. Your breakfast is ready. How'd you sleep?"

"Rosa, what are you doing up this early?" He kissed her cheek and took his place at the table.

"The storm was pretty loud last night." She skirted the question and placed his plate on the table. "I thought, for sure, we were in for a category one." She watched him as he stared out the window at the rain. "Do you think it will stop soon?"

He turned toward her and forced himself to smile. "It looks like the worst of it has already passed." Turning back to the window, he watched as the streaks of water filtered down the glass pane. "It's time to take *Maria* out and take a look around."

"Couldn't you wait until the sun comes up?" Rosa knew her suggestion would fall on deaf ears, but she had to try, no matter how many times he ignored her pleas.

"The longer I wait, the stronger the possibility that someone else may be lost."

His tear was gone as quickly as it had appeared. Rosa didn't have to look to know it was there, just like she knew the only sleep he had last night was the catnap he took sitting in front of the television during *Wheel of Fortune*. Jack hadn't slept through a storm since that fateful night. Each wind gust, each lightning strike, each thundering sheet of rain brought back his worst nightmare—the one that changed his life forever, the night he lost his beloved Maria.

Jack stood up from the table and headed for the door. His thoughts were deep in the past. His Maria was gone, leaving him a shell of a man. Now all he had were her memories, the happy ones that appeared when he would hear a high-pitched laugh in the distance or a soft hum from a passerby. Then there were the haunting ones that came to him during each drop of rain, each bout of lightning, and each hurricane warning. Yet even in his darkest memories, her sunlit face would appear, and he would smile. She always knew how to find the good in every situation. She was his life, his breath—the other half of his soul. He functioned but just barely. When she died, she took his heart with her.

Jack met Maria at the country club. His parents were being honored for their contribution and service to the community, and he was their guest. He always felt out of sorts in such gatherings, but he knew his place, and this night it was next to his parents, being the ever-doting son. He was proud of them and their accomplishments. To him, they exemplified the American dream, building a business through hard work. Their small lawn service had blossomed into a successful property-management company with an upscale clientele, which included the very country club they were being honored in that night. Their success had opened up a whole new life with wonderful benefits allowing them to purchase a lovely home just a few doors down from where they stood.

Jack didn't grow up in such company. He felt out of place among the elite of society. If he could have sneaked out early, he would have gladly done so. It didn't take him long, however, to notice the graceful waitress with whom he would have eagerly traded places, and each would have felt more at ease. She was pleasant and charming with the ability to start and hold any conversation whether it was with the other wait staff or the community doctor. Jack was fascinated by her beauty and grace, watching as those she served would smile in her direction as she departed. He made several inquiries, but no one knew her or seemed to remember her from a previous event.

Jack was not one to make the first move when it came to dating. He was much more comfortable casually letting his friends set him up.

It took the pressure off and allowed him to stay in his comfort zone. So when this waitress affected him to the point of following her moves around the club, he felt unsure of how to approach her without coming off as a stalker.

It was at the conclusion of the event that he found her in the kitchen cleaning up. He walked into the sound of her humming, waiting for her to complete her song before he spoke.

"What was that you were humming? It's beautiful, but I don't think I've ever heard it before."

"Have you ever been to Cuba?" Maria's accent was strong, but he hardly noticed; his focus was riveted on her eyes.

"No, but if they have music like that, perhaps I should book a flight." He moved closer. It took everything he had to not take her in his arms and dance her around the kitchen to the beautiful tune that was playing over and over in his head.

"My name is Jack Winters. Did I hear someone call you Maria?"

"Nice to meet you Jack Winters." She wiped her hand on her dish towel and held it out as a formal greeting. "Yes, my name is Maria Sentry. Was that your parents being honored tonight?" Her attention was grabbed by one of the other servers walking through the door with another load of dishes. "Excuse me for a minute, Jack. It appears I am neglecting my duties." She walked over and took the rolling cart of dirty dishes and transferred them to the sink. "Thank you." She smiled at her departing coworker.

"Could I help with the dishes? I'm pretty good at drying. My mother always had me help her in the kitchen." Jack looked around and grabbed a dish towel and stepped up to the sink before she could refuse him. "Just put me to work."

Maria turned back to the sink, washed a bowl, and handed it to him. "Who am I to turn away help? It looks like it's going to be a long night filled with shriveled hands and tired feet. Not that I'm complaining, I'm used to it."

"If I might be so bold, this line of work doesn't seem like your regular profession. Are you filling in for someone?" He placed the bowl on the counter and turned to get another look at her bright face and dark eyes.

"I was a surgeon back in Cuba, long hours with very little pay but rewarding all the same." Maria seemed to gaze off in the distance. "That was until one of my patients needed care I couldn't provide. I knew if she didn't get to America, she would die, so I helped her find someone to get her across the waters. But her condition was so critical, she would certainly have died without medical help along the way." Tears were running down her cheeks. "I had to make a decision, let her go alone and take her chances or go with her and walk away from Cuba—never being able to return. I struggled with my decision, but my mother encouraged me to go. She told me that an opportunity like this would only come once in my lifetime, and I would regret not taking a leap of faith. She insisted by telling me, 'God will be with you, my dear, so trust his purpose for your life.'

"I could not knowingly send my patient to her death, so I trusted in my mother's wisdom and God's hand and secretly arranged passage for me on the boat. I said my goodbyes, and we left to cross the ocean. However, things did not turn out as I had hoped—the woman who became my good friend lost her life in an aggressive storm that took the lives of most of our small group. I buried her at sea next to a small Bahamian island, I later learned was called Cay Sal. It was ironic that she was the one that needed America to live, but I am the one that ended up living here. I still can't believe I made it, but I arrived in a foreign land that welcomed me. I lost everything, but I am not a quitter. God let me live for a reason, so I will do all I can to honor that gift. What you see in front of you is a college student on her way to becoming an American doctor who is willing to take any job that will pave the way. I have been blessed in my journey. This job has been good to me, and I have been able to meet so many wonderful people."

Maria turned to look at Jack, wondering how her life's story would affect him. Would he be understanding of the plight of her people? Most people whom she'd shared her story fell into one of two categories: sympathetic or bigoted. Being a Cuban immigrant had its price.

Returning home would mean a prison sentence for life. She needed her American experience to work. It was her future, her new beginning.

Jack couldn't keep his eyes off her as she spoke. He had truly lost his heart right there and then and would have spent the whole night with Maria if his presence wasn't requested back in the ballroom. He had a good understanding of both hard work and education, attributes he learned from his parents. Maria could have been the poster child for both. He knew he needed to get to know her better, and before the night was through, he had scheduled a date with the beautiful Cuban woman.

Their marriage came about quickly but not quickly enough for him. It was three months to the day when they were standing in that same country club exchanging their vows. He would have married her sooner if he'd known their time together was to be abridged. She was his life, the light that kept him going, especially on that fateful night when a drunk driver sealed his destiny on the eighteen mile stretch between Florida City and Key Largo. Losing a parent at any age is tough; losing both parents and stepping into their lives changed his forever. He had his education, he had his plans, and they didn't include living his parents' life. Yet fate set his course.

Running their business was harder than he thought. There were times he felt like giving up and walking away. It was good that he had a few loyal customers who kept him afloat as he struggled through, making it possible to make a nice home for Maria. Of course, he credited this to her. She comforted him through his angry demons: anger at death, anger at God. She would reach out and pray with him. She told him God had a plan, and he had been given a gift that someday he would be able to see. He found comfort in her embrace as she held him tight and let her spirit heal his soul. He always felt that she was that gift from God, sent to him to get him through his devastating tragedy. Then he lost her.

It happened three years into their marriage and two years after his parents' death. Jack and Maria were celebrating the anniversary of her crossing at Cay Sal. This was her tradition. It was Maria's time to remember her friend and the choice they had both made. It was at these times that she felt closest to her mother and her homeland. However, this trip would be different, a new beginning of sorts, the day that changed Jack's life forever.

It would be a quick trip. The sky was overcast, and the storm warnings were in play. They knew their time was limited, but they were determined to continue, regardless of the oncoming fray. They started out early in the morning and anchored just off Cay Sal.

During their brief window of sunshine that morning, Maria hurried on ahead to find the perfect spot. She had news she couldn't wait to share and a special luncheon to set up. She looked back to assure herself she had ample time to set her plan in motion. Her foot stumbled, flinging her body against the sandy shore. It was a simple fall, but with the twist of her body, her chest landed on a piece of storm debris. Jack saw her fall and ran to her, but she was barely breathing. Jack called the coast guard, and an emergency helicopter was dispatched. He held her in his arms, trying his best to stop the bleeding, but the puncture was to her heart. Maria was barely hanging on when the coast guard arrived. She was loaded on the helicopter and transported to a hospital in Key Largo. She didn't make the trip. There was just too much damage and blood loss. She was officially pronounced dead when she arrived at the hospital.

Jack had watched the helicopter carry his beloved Maria away. With the emergency personnel on board, there wasn't room for him to accompany her. He headed to Key Largo, piloting his boat through the crashing waves as the rain and lightning poured down from the sky. Jack knew when his beloved Maria took her last breath. She was with him. He felt her presence giving him stability, comforting him through his deep sobs. Jack had lost two that day, as the baby Maria was carrying had been too small to survive. It would have been so easy to give up and let the water take him to the depths of the sea. Together in life and together in death; he closed his eyes, and she was there. Her silhouette felt so real. He felt her love, her comfort, and that's when their conversations began.

"You can't give up on your life, Jack. Please don't grieve for me. Death cannot separate us. I'm here. Your life story has many more chapters, and we'll finish yours together. I will always be with you on your journey." He couldn't save her life, but even in death, she had just saved his.

From that moment on, Jack knew what he had to do. He had to live for Maria. He had to finish what they had started together. Her dreams were now his. She always told him he was her gift from God. He was the one who showed her a new world full of love, freedom, and possibilities, and she wanted that for her countrymen. Many of her fellow Cubans seeking freedom had died at sea. She knew, with the "wet foot, dry foot" policy in the United States, they need only make it to American soil, and they would be allowed to apply for residency a year later, being freed from tyranny. Her plan was to support those travelers on their journey, by leaving water and grab bags of supplies at Cay Sal. It was time to make her dream a reality. He christened his boat *Maria* in her memory, and the trips began. Each new morning following a storm, he would load fresh water and stash bags and head to Cay Sal. This was his new life, his promise to her, his tribute to his beloved Maria.

Jack's memories were always so fresh, especially after a storm. He wiped away his tears and turned around at the sound of Rosa's words. "Jack, there's a cooler by the door with food and water. Please, please be careful."

He put on his raincoat and turned a thankful smile toward her. "I can always count on you, Rosa." He picked up the cooler and disappeared into the blustery darkness.

11

Jack's Golden Goose – Cay Sal

Jack found his dock covered with palm fronds and debris. He cleared a path to the boat garage and loaded *Maria* with his cooler, stash bags, and other emergency supplies. The wind had lost some of its fury and the rain had all but stopped as he backed the boat from the dock and headed down the channel. Destruction was everywhere, and he knew that it would take weeks before it was cleaned up. For now, he would have to dodge the floating rubble.

Signs of morning began to appear as he watched each home come to life with lights dancing through the windows framing the silhouettes of joyful families. He was at peace. This was Maria's favorite time of the morning; in fact, he could almost feel her standing behind him pointing to each house, making up stories about the people inside. She was always with him on these rescue trips, like a warm blanket on a cold night, warming him with her laughter.

"Jack, look over there at that sweet mom with both her arms full. Someday that will be me."

"Including the tear-stained faces?" he would tease.

"Our children won't ever cry. They will be perfect." Her hopeful pride couldn't hide her mischievous smile and her wanting eyes.

Memories of what could have been were almost too much for Jack, but the images of her playful smile made him laugh. That was his

Maria, helping him laugh through each painful memory. He wiped his face and brought his mind back to dodging debris.

The clouds parted, lighting up the vast expanse before him. It was breathtaking with the cosmic array of colors glazing the morning sky. This was his haven, his serenity in the world. He was at peace. As he lost himself in the majesty, the boat began to lift and fall as it traversed the ocean waves. He broke his gaze and focused on his course. He maneuvered the boat and engaged the high-tech stabilizer he had installed for ocean travel and began his grid search. It was a slow and tedious process as he trolled along his selected route searching for anything that looked amiss.

It had been hours, but Cay Sal was finally in his sights. He could see her through his binoculars, and this put him on heightened alert. Would today be the day? He spied some bobbing wreckage in the distance and turned his boat toward the movement as his heart rate began to increase. He had taken this trip after each storm but, as of yet, hadn't been able to fulfill his promise to Maria. Could this be a Cuban refugee? Was he finally able to help someone?

The wreckage turned out to be a life raft from a boat. By its size, it looked like it was from a yacht. It was perfectly intact. He searched the raft and was somewhat relieved to only find pouches, which he assumed held food, water, and emergency money, but the number was odd—there were so many. His curiosity was piqued. To have a raft deployed like this usually meant there was a boat in distress. He picked up his binoculars and did a three-sixty, standing in the life raft, but there was no sign of another vessel. He finished loading the pouches onto *Maria* and deflated the raft, stowing it in a forward compartment.

He proceeded to open each pouch, looking for clues to his mystery. The first one filled with money was not surprising, but by the time he opened the fifth, he was shaking. What had he stumbled onto? A life raft full of money had to have been attached to a larger vessel. Where was its owner? There were ten pouches of money, plus a few more with water and food. He stowed them and returned his attention back to his search, weaving in and out of storm debris, looking for any sign of another craft. A half hour later, he spotted a cooler floating between two pieces of wood. One of the pieces could have been from a boat's helm, but the piece wasn't big enough to know for sure. He fished out the cooler and opened it. To his surprise, he found it filled with handheld GPS devices in waterproof bags. He placed them on a towel in the cabin and continued searching, but there was nothing. The waves crashed against the side of *Maria* as he brought his search to an end and headed to shore. Whatever happened here, he thought, may remain a mystery of the sea.

Anchoring off Cay Sal, he filled the cooler with the money pouches and floated it ashore. He walked around the little island trying to figure out what to do. He sat down next to the memorial marker he had placed to honor his beloved wife and opened one of the pouches to examine the money. He scrutinized each note carefully, looking for indication of counterfeiting, but they looked legit.

Nervously, he walked the island, again peering through his binoculars. Had he missed something? This thought left him unsettled. There was nothing, no sign of life other than his, and no other vessels in sight. He sat back down on the sandy beach and counted the money in the pouch in his hands—$100,000. With the ten pouches, there was a million dollars just sitting there in the cooler. He'd heard of people finding treasure in these waters, but that was Spanish galleons from ancient wrecks, not cash.

What was he going to do? Should he call the coast guard? They would be busy after the storm. Should he take it back and turn it into the police? Would they believe him or arrest him? There had been an issue of corruption in the Key Largo Police Department last year. Could they be trusted? What if the owner came back? Perhaps it was a couple who were caught in the storm, and this was their whole life savings. He had heard of people cashing in their retirement money, buying a boat, and living on the waters, away from civilization. Then there was the fact that the money was found in the Bahamas. What was the protocol in foreign waters?

"What should I do, Maria?" Jack looked up at the sky as a raindrop fell on his face. He turned his eyes toward the approaching clouds. "Well, I better decide quick. This storm isn't over." Jack looked at the cooler and turned to his wife's marker. "Maria, how about you keep it safe for me until I get some answers?" It didn't take long to seal the money back in the pouches and bury the cooler.

Jack headed back to the boat and pulled out one of the GPS units and created a waypoint for his buried treasure then stowed the device in his locked glove compartment. He took out another GPS and stored a waypoint for the Elliot Key ranger station. He placed the unit back in its waterproof bag and added it to the stash bag.

Elliott Key worked well as a stopping point for refugees because it was a remote island with the only permanent occupant being the ranger himself. Landing there qualified a refugee for the "wet foot, dry foot" policy. He had heard of Cubans landing on remote islands, barely reaching America, in makeshift floats, which vaguely resembled boats. Some stories of crossings consisted of inner tubes tied to wooden planks with ropes, while others told of wood-framed vessels with metal, from a tin roof, forming the skin—a vessel no one would want to take out of the harbor, let alone pilot across the ocean. He had to give these brave souls credit for seeking freedom in the midst of such personal danger.

Having a GPS unit to add to each stash bag was a great addition to the fresh water and food. Jack had chosen to place these bags at the ruins by the graffiti marker, tagging the word *agua*, Spanish for water, on a large area of the ruins so anyone floating by would notice and be able to find fresh water. He didn't know how many people he had helped by leaving these bags, but each time he came back, he had to replace the bags with new ones. In his mind, this part of the plan had been a success. If only one person escaped death, from their crossing, his efforts were not in vain.

The morning was ending quickly as he headed for home. Jack was unsure what to think about his morning's adventure. His imagination was running wild as he postulated different scenarios surrounding the origin of the money and the GPS units. Could they be from a drug deal or a hijacking gone wrong? Would someone be searching for their money? Could the money be cursed? Jack felt a chill go up his spine. Was his life in danger? "Snap out of it, Jack!" he chastised himself.

"Cursed? Really? I am probably just looking at this wrong. Perhaps today is my lucky day."

He had never felt lucky in his whole life. In fact, looking back, the only good thing that ever happened to him was meeting and marrying Maria, but finding a million dollars made him feel like Jack and the magic beans, which was, of course, his favorite kid's story since the hero was his namesake. So had he found his golden goose? What would he do with a million dollars? He was content with his life. Now, if his Maria were here and they had a family, perhaps he could find a use for such wealth, but as a lone bachelor, his business was enough to fulfill his needs.

"How about you, Maria? What would you do with a million dollars?" The answer came to him instantly. Maria would help others, especially those of her kindred who were crossing the treacherous waters. This was her dream, and she had handed it over to him.

"If I didn't know better," Jack thought, "I would think you sent this money to me so I would do what you asked. Is that what you did, Maria? Is this money your way of putting me to work?" Jack laughed. "It would be just like you to make sure, one way or another, that I keep my promise."

12

The Tree House – Palm Shores

As Jack docked *Maria*, he was grateful that the second storm had chosen another path. With the day's events and the sun peeking through the clouds, he was exhilarated. He wasn't sure if it was the money, the GPS units, or the vitamin D from the Florida sunshine that had caused the change in his demeanor, but it didn't matter. Today he felt he could take on the world.

He stepped onto the dock and took in the scene around him. Fallen limbs had covered the wooden surface and spilled into the harbor, but that only made him smile. Physical labor was good for the soul, and with the cleanup ahead, his soul would be well fed.

Jack put on his gloves and grabbed the closest branch. He dragged it to the front lawn for the city to mulch and haul away. It was at these times he thought of the loss of his child. Children were extensions of their parents, learning through training and example. Right now, he could have been working with his children; together, talking and laughing as they cleared the debris from the yard. Was it right to mourn what you never had? A pain tugged at his heart, but he brushed it away. Instead, he forced his mind toward the memory of his father, which brought a smile. His dad taught him how to work. He would always say, "A job is never done unless it's done right. So whatever it takes, make sure you do it right." And he did. In fact, Jack had become a perfectionist, much like his father.

He worked quickly and was near exhaustion when he picked up his last load and headed for the front lawn. He had already done a day's work, but he knew his day wouldn't officially begin until he walked through the back door of his house. This was a busy time of year for his company. There would be several clients needing debris removal. Plus, his neighbors all knew he had the equipment to remove large trees, so they would be calling on him as well. He didn't complain; the more jobs he had, the more people he could put to work. This was all thanks to Maria.

His beautiful Maria had been instrumental in finding him hard workers, who not only wanted a job, but also wanted a chance at a better life. She had arranged a connection with a nonprofit group that specialized in finding work for Cuban refugees. He put her in charge of hiring, and through her efforts, he was outfitted with a hardworking crew. She had set up an employment profile for his business, and each worker that was sent to him from that day on was easily transitioned into his employ.

Jack walked back toward the boat dock to store his tools. As he came around the corner, he heard voices coming from the neighbor's tree house. He didn't know much about the Choate family, but he knew the two teenagers had outgrown their tree house, and it was dilapidated and somewhat frightening. To think someone would be hiding out up there without permission made him nervous.

Paul and John Choate were your typical teenage boys whose lives were filled with sports, teenage high jinx, fast cars, and girls. They were always going somewhere and with very little supervision. Their behavior, at times, resembled a pack of wild animals you might see on a nature channel, taunting and goading each other into entanglements.

He knew very little about the boys' parents, except that they were overseas, leaving their brood in the care of an aunt who seemed to spend more time trolling for a rich husband at the country club than monitoring her charges.

There was a time, however, when Charles and Sara Choate were home with their boys, but that was before their company decided to expand overseas. What people were willing to sacrifice their families for always surprised him. He would have given up everything to have a little family like that.

Jack headed for the tree house to identify its occupants. As he approached, he heard two male voices talking about a bag they had fished out of the water.

"Hey! Who's up there?" All went quiet. Jack tried again. "Who's there? This is private property. Come out and show yourself."

"This is our business—not yours. Go away, old man," came a young voice.

"Is that you, John?" He had thought they were too old for that hideout. No answer.

Jack wasn't about to walk away without proof of identity. His own backyard backed up to this tree house, and it *was* his business.

He tried again.

"Paul and John Choate, if that's you, someone better answer me, or I'm coming up this ladder!"

Paul opened the door and climbed down to face him. "Who do you think you are? We have the right to be in our own yard without being harassed. Do we need to call the cops?"

"Go ahead." Jack turned to walk away. "But perhaps you need to find some manners before you talk to them. They don't like rude teenagers either."

Paul watched as Jack walked to his back door and stepped inside; he frowned then turned and climbed back up the ladder.

John seemed nervous as he peeked out the window to verify that they were, indeed, alone. "Do you think the money belongs to Jack?" Not waiting for a response from Paul, he continued, "Do you think he heard us talking about it?"

"I'm sure he heard something, but I'm not sure what. We need to be more careful." Paul opened the Velcro bag lying on the table and pulled out the money.

"How much do you think is in there?" John sat down on the bench across his brother.

"Well, JJ, there's only one way to find out. Count it."

John counted out a thousand dollars and laid it in a stack on the table. He continued counting and stacking until he had fifteen neatly stacked piles.

"Paul! We have $15,000!"

Paul picked up each stack as John would lay it down, recounting the money for verification.

"Yup. There's $15,000." He looked worried. "I wonder where it came from."

"What if it belongs to Jack? We did find it floating around his dock." John looked out the window toward his neighbor's house, making sure he was still inside.

"If it belonged to Jack, why would he leave it by his dock?" Paul reached down and picked up the bag to examine it.

"This bag is made to carry the money on your body, hidden away. Someone must have lost it in the ocean, and it washed in with the debris. We have no idea where it came from, who it belongs to, or if someone might be looking for it. Listen, JJ, we have to be very careful. No one can know about this. If someone finds out, we could be in real trouble. We have to keep a low profile, at least for now."

"What? We have $15,000, and we can't tell anyone or spend any of it?" John was visibly frustrated.

"I didn't say we couldn't spend it. We just can't tell anyone where we got it. For all we know, the money could be fake. We have to be smart about this and not draw attention to ourselves. We can't go out and buy a car or a motorcycle. Then there's Aunt Cindy. She can't find out, or she'll tell Mom and Dad, and they *will* make us turn it over to the cops. Then it's bye-bye, money." Paul's thoughts turned toward his parents. Would they really care?

"Okay, I'll keep quiet about the money," agreed John. "So what are we going to do with it? I mean, I've never had a thousand dollars, let alone fifteen thousand."

"Listen, JJ, let's each take $500 and hide the rest until we can decide what to do. Okay?"

"Sounds good to me. So where do we hide it without Aunt Cindy finding it?"

Paul thought for a moment. "When Dad built this tree house, he put in some hidden cubbies. I used them to hide things from you when we were kids. There's one in the back of the bench under the window and one under the table."

Paul went to the table, slid the panel on the underside, and pulled out a metal box. From the box, he retrieved a batman figure, a $2 bill, and a collection of baseball cards. "Here, JJ, you can have these back."

JJ opened his hand as Paul handed him the items. "Are you kidding me? You had these all along. You lied to Mom and Dad."

Paul ignored his little brother. "Hand me the money and let's see how much will fit in here."

JJ placed the treasures from his past in his pocket and handed Paul one stack at a time. The money was too much for the little box, so Paul moved to his other hiding place under the window. In this cubby, he pulled out a larger treasure box. This one, he opened quickly and put the items in his own pocket.

"What was in there?" John was watching closely for more of his lost childhood.

"These are mine and none of your business." Paul placed the additional money in the box and turned to face him. "These hiding places should work for now. We can hide the Velcro bag under the bench, and I'll get the padlock from my PE bag for the tree house door." John's eyes were fixed on Paul's pocket.

"What was in the box, Paul?"

"None of your business."

"Prove to me that those items are yours and not mine. I'm supposed to trust you, but you're not being honest with me about what's in the box."

"Fine." He reached in his pocket and pulled out a locket, a pile of letters, and a handful of candy.

"Who are those letters from? And why do you have a locket?"

Paul pulled out the top letter from the pile and handed it to him. "They're from Mom to us."

"Why did you hide them?" John looked up into the eyes of his big brother.

Paul turned to look out their little window. He wasn't sure how to explain how he felt about his parents' absence in his life. "I don't know. It just seemed right." He blinked away a tear.

"You miss them too, don't you?" JJ's voice was barely audible.

"Let's not talk about it right now. Besides, talking won't bring them home. I just wish they would have kept their promise." Paul headed for the door and then turned back. "Remember, don't tell anyone. We can only trust each other."

"And the locket?"

Paul looked down at the locket in his hand. "This locket is one that Grandma gave me before she died. Inside is a picture of her holding me as a baby. It seemed like a strange thing for a boy to have, so I hid it."

Paul opened the door and climbed down the ladder, barely holding on to his composure. He was supposed to be the tough one, the big brother. He just couldn't let JJ see him cry. Taking a deep breath to hold himself together, he headed for the house.

John sat looking at the letter in his hand, turning it over and over. He opened the envelope and pulled out the personalized stationery. It was definitely his mom's handwriting; she had graceful penmanship, making each letter distinctive and proper. His thoughts went back to her sitting at her desk in their study, writing. She loved to write letters. She called it a lost art in a world filled with instant messages and sloppy grammar. She would end each letter with a dab of perfume, adding her personal touch to her correspondence. John picked up the letter, unfolded it, and smelled the perfume—White Diamonds. He would know that scent anywhere. This dab may have come from his gift to her last Christmas.

He took a deep breath and began reading. The tears were there, silently squeezing out of the corner of his eyes and forming a trail down his face.

Dear Paul and JJ,

I can't believe it has already been a month since we embraced and said goodbye. I miss each of you dearly. I hope Aunt Cindy is taking good care of you. She only has good things to say when I call.

Paul, I am sorry we missed your birthday. Did you get the gift we sent? I hope it's what you asked for. I would love a picture. Has Aunt Cindy been videotaping your games? I don't want to miss a single play. How is Portia?

JJ, how are you doing? How was prom? I hope you are going to send me pictures. Was your date beautiful? I bet she was. I can't believe I am missing so much of your life.

I know it seems strange for me to write to you when we talk on the phone weekly, but I wanted you to have something special from me, and I can't think of anything more personal than a letter.

Only two more months and Dad and I will be home for a visit. I promise! I am counting the days!

Well, this is making me cry, so I will close. I want you both to know that I love you and will always be with you in spirit. I am only a phone call away.

Love,
MOM

John wiped the tears from his face and held the letter up to his nose, once again basking in the aroma of his mother's favorite perfume. He reread the letter then carefully folded it and placed it back in the envelope. He looked at the postmark. This letter was six months old. He thought back. His mom and dad hadn't been home since they left; something must have changed their plans. He couldn't remember what. But one thing was for sure, he wanted to read the rest of those letters.

Paul had kept them in his secret treasure box. Why hadn't he thought to do something like that? All he wanted, right now, was to have his parents' home. Why did they have to leave? He hugged his legs tightly against his chest, hoping to stop his heart from aching.

John hadn't allowed himself to feel any sadness at his parents' departure, and at times, when he felt abandoned or alone, he would surround himself with his friends' laughter but not this time. This time, he would allow himself to feel his sorrow.

His eyes were overflowing as he lowered his chin onto his folded arms. Tiny droplets of water ran down his cheeks, across his chin, dripping onto his faded blue jeans. His eyes were swollen from crying, and his arms were crusting from wiping his runny nose, but he didn't care. Right here, right now, sitting alone in this decaying tree house, he would allow himself to weep.

13

The Marina – Palm Shores

Rosa was happy to see Jack whistling as he walked through the door. Not daring to interrupt, she watched in silence as he hung up his raincoat and put the cooler by the kitchen sink. Jack didn't often return from his boat trips in such a mood. She didn't know if it was his lack of sleep through the stormy nights or his communications with Maria that frequently left him in a sullen mood. To see him clean the yard and then saunter through the back door whistling was a new and welcome change.

"I see you made it back safely. I assume all went well." Rosa was still staring at him.

He looked up and smiled at her. "It was a beautiful morning, and I have to admit I haven't felt this good for quite some time." He was almost giddy.

"Well, I'm glad you're back. It's been quite busy around here."

"What would I do without you, Rosa? You take care of my house, you watch over me, and I never have to worry about my business when I am away. You are a keeper."

"Who, me? You know I only know how to answer the phones. If I was in charge, we would both be living on the street." She winked at him and handed him his messages. "I hope you are here to give this poor old woman a break. The phone hasn't stopped ringing since eight this morning, and my list of chores are piling up as we speak."

"I think I can take it from here. I just need to wash up. You may go tackle your other tasks, but thank you for your help."

She stood up to leave. "Oh, by the way," Rosa turned, "Sal called, and I sent him to the jobs closest to him, and Louis called, and I sent him over to Marathon Key to take care of those properties, so I guess that leaves the ones around here for you." She turned toward the door as Jack took a quick glance at the pile of notes in his hand and shook his head. What would he do without Rosa? He laid his messages on the desk and headed for the washroom.

"I'll make you a sandwich and get you a Coke. I'm guessing you will be leaving soon." Rosa was in the kitchen and back with the food by the time Jack was ending his first call.

"It looks like they need me at the marina to inventory the damage and file the insurance claims. I'll forward the phone to my cell. The afternoon is yours." He gulped his soda down, and in four bites, his sandwich was gone as well. "This may be a late evening. I'll let you know about dinner."

"I'll leave you something in the refrigerator, just in case." She left him to work out his plans.

Rosa was well trained as a housekeeper, and knowing her place in someone else's home was important. She had learned early on not to get attached to her employers, and then she met Jack. She had lived with him long enough to know his character. She knew when it was okay to approach him and when he needed his personal space. That's when he confronted his personal demons. She knew just how much room to give him and when to stop him, and that's when her parenting would kick in.

She was like a mother hen wanting to take away her child's pain but knew it was all part of his healing. She didn't know how long he would mourn for his wife, but she hoped that someday he would allow his heart to love again. Her maternal side had adopted him. They were a family. He had won her heart at their very first meeting.

They met at the Key Largo Winn-Dixie grocery store. He was shopping as a lone bachelor, and she had just ended her employment for an Argentine executive who had been called home.

He was in the freezer section, trying to decide which frozen meal to purchase, when Rosa approached him. Jack, his head in the freezer, had a Mexican dinner in one hand and an Italian dinner in the other.

"Food like that will kill you, you know?"

A little stunned by her comment, he glanced over his shoulder and saw a small woman with a Spanish accent talking to him. He lowered his eyes, and in a barely audible voice, she heard him reply, "Promise?"

Rosa wasn't sure what to say. "Is-s everything okay?"

He stood up and turned toward her. "Sorry about that. I lost my wife recently." He forced a smile. "I do have to admit, the world would have been better off if she were here instead of me."

Rosa looked into his eyes for a brief moment and smiled. "When you lose someone you love, oftentimes a piece of you dies with them. I'm sorry for your loss." She reached around him and gave him a hug and stepped back. "Did you say you lost her recently?" She felt drawn to this man.

He cleared the constriction in his throat. "A couple of weeks ago."

"Well," she took a deep breath, "I'm sure she was a wonderful woman. I can't do anything to bring her back, but if you allow me, I can make sure you have a home-cooked meal—no one should have to live on frozen dinners." She smiled at him, hoping to lift his spirits. "My name is Rosa Guava, and I am a recently unemployed housekeeper. I have references and a recipe box full of family treasures. You, sir, look like you need my services."

He wiped his face on his sleeve and looked at this odd woman standing in front of him. "Are you Cuban?" There was something familiar about this woman, and his interest was piqued.

"Well, my parents were Cubanos, but they came to America before Castro came into power. They brought their traditions with them, and I was raised in a Cuban home . . . in America. Is that a problem?"

"My wife was Cuban," he said flatly and turned back to the freezer.

"Sounds like I am just what you need. Why don't you hire me on a temporary basis? If after a week you want me to leave, I will do so without incident."

He turned around once again. "Is this how you got your last job, talking to strange men in the grocery store?"

"What can I say? Strange men are my specialty." Rosa chuckled. "Actually, I usually get my jobs through a service, but for some reason, I felt drawn to you. Who am I to turn down a prompting from God?"

Jack smiled and looked up at the ceiling. The more she talked, the more she reminded him of his sweet Maria. "What if I can't afford your fee?" He watched her reaction to see if she was trying to pull a fast one.

"I'm sure we can come to an understanding that will work for both of us." She smiled at him. "Do we have a deal?"

"I'll give you your week, and I'll check your references, and we'll see how it goes from there. Deal?" He stuck out his hand.

"Deal." Rosa was happy to comply with this strange American tradition of sealing an agreement with a handshake, but it was followed by a warm Latin hug. She felt strongly about helping this man adjust to the loss of his wife. "May I ask your name?"

"Sorry about that. Where are my manners? My name is Jack Winters."

"Nice to meet you, Jack. Why don't we pick up some basics, and I'll make you that dinner?" That was Rosa, always ready for any challenge.

That was three years ago. She had been just what he'd needed to help him work through the anger and pain of grief, over and over, taking it one day at a time. Jack felt his sorrow deeply and struggled with acceptance, yet he seemed to be making progress. The frequency of his pain and anger had lessened in the last few months, and Rosa was beginning to see a new man emerge—one who smiled and laughed. She guessed it was the real Jack, the person he was before death became his unwelcome visitor, and it warmed her soul to watch him progress.

Jack finished his calls, sent out his local workforce, and headed for the marina. He knew the drill. After each storm, it was his job as property manager to assess the damage to the marina and the docks and write up the reports for the insurance company. As a service to the slip tenants, he would also document the condition of each of their boats by taking pictures and e-mailing them to the owners. This process made it possible to expedite the claims and the cleanup, minimizing delays from absentee owners.

The marina was only a couple of blocks down from Jack's home, but the roads were blocked with downed tree limbs. With the help of good neighbors, he spent most of an hour cutting a path to its entrance. His small community was good that way. They would pitch in to help one another out after each storm, especially monitoring the needs of the elderly in their subdivision.

Storms in Florida always caused quite a stir. Depending on their severity, life could be interrupted for days, weeks, or even months. Schools cancelled classes, businesses closed, grocery stores were cleaned out, gas lines became community hangouts, while patrons waited on gas trucks, and tree cutting parties advanced from one neighborhood to another.

Floridians would like this to be vacation time, but for the most part, it was physical labor as they worked to put life back in order. Many would meet their neighbors for the first time preparing for or cleaning up after these storms. It wasn't uncommon to see labor and ladders being shared in the work of installing hurricane shutters days or sometimes hours before a storm's arrival. Power loss was a common reality, and along with that came block party barbeques to use up freezer items before they spoiled. Odd as it seemed, the service needed before and after these storms helped communities come together.

By the time Jack arrived, it was pushing late afternoon. With the summer sunsets running out the clock, he was given the daylight he needed to complete his assessment. Jack walked the property taking pictures to document the damaged boats and the carnage left behind.

Each storm left its mark depending on the severity of the winds and the number of tornados it brought. These tempests often amazed him. One might miss your property, leaving devastation next door; whereas another would destroy your home but leave your neighbors untouched. Although his home merely had downed limbs and palm fronds, the marina, only a few blocks away, had damaged buildings and docks. The pictures told the tale; the marina had felt the storm's fury.

Jack finished taking the pictures and headed for the office to download and send them to the boats' owners and insurance companies. This process was time-consuming in and of itself, but this time Jack had other matters on his mind. As he documented each boat and its condition, he checked it for a missing life raft, hoping to find the origin of the mysterious life raft he had found at Cay Sal. He checked the records to make sure all the boats assigned to slips were present. Although many were battered and broken, he could account for all the vessels berthed at the marina. He figured his search would lack fruition because of docking schedules, but he felt deflated, nonetheless.

He turned to the Internet next. The marina office was without power when Jack arrived, but he quickly hooked up the generator and connected to the satellite emergency Internet system. This allowed him to finish his reports and turn to the Notice to Mariners (NTM) website to check for any distressed boats out of the Miami or Key West area. There had been a few fishing vessels in trouble but nothing unresolved and no report of a missing yacht. This was perplexing, on the one hand, yet left him somewhat relieved, on the other.

The money was still a mystery. He continued to search the Internet for any clue of a missing or damaged boat. He opened one link to a report of a dead body found at a Miami fuel dock, but the time frame and boat size weren't right, so he saved that one for future inquiry.

He sat back in his chair. What if he never found a connection to the money? He did find the cash in Bahamian waters; perhaps it wasn't even an American yacht. He had to accept the possibility that this mystery may never be solved.

Jack hadn't slept much in the last twenty-four hours, and he was thoroughly exhausted as he packed up and headed for home. It was after midnight when he entered his kitchen and pulled dinner out of the fridge. He needed some sustenance, a shower, and a bed, and he was grateful he could count on Rosa to take care of his hunger. He opened up the container and found a note:

Jack,

I knew you would be late and most likely fall asleep if you had to wait on the microwave, so I just made you a sandwich. Get some rest, and I'll see you in the morning.

Rosa

Jack smiled at the note. Rosa knew him too well. He was lucky to have her in his life. He took his sandwich and headed for the shower.

14

The Spending Spree – Key Largo

"Hurry up, JJ, or I'll leave without you!" Paul yelled.

It had been a long day of chores and cleanup projects, followed by video games, waiting for Aunt Cindy to leave for the club. But what they really wanted was to go to town and spend the money that was burning a hole in their pockets. It was about 3:00 p.m. before she finally grabbed her purse and headed for the door.

"I'm going to see if they need any help cleaning up at the club. I'll see you boys in a few hours." And she was gone.

With the storm recently ending and the lateness of the afternoon, Paul didn't know if their favorite dive shop would be open, but after being tied to the house all day, he didn't care—he just wanted out. School had been cancelled. This fact made him even more claustrophobic, and since Aunt Cindy was too inquisitive or too interested in their private business, he could only hope that she would spend the rest of the day at the club.

It wasn't that he didn't love his mother's sister, but she had become clingy as of late. Take last week, for instance; he and JJ had a couple of friends over to play Guitar Hero. It was when they had stopped for pizza that she arrived on the scene and started with the questions. She wouldn't leave them alone until they told her every aspect of their lives. When had their families moved into the Palm Shores area? What did their parents do for a living? Have they traveled overseas lately? And were their parents married or single? Then she moved onto what they knew about their neighbors. It was too much and too embarrassing—she had crossed the line.

"JJ, let's go!" Paul was sitting in his dad's red convertible Mustang in the driveway, honking the horn and yelling at the top of his lungs. "Hurry up, JJ, I need to get outta here now!"

"I'm right here!" John ran out the door and jumped into the passenger side. "Are we going to the dive shop first?"

"If it's still open, but we have to get out of the housing area. Tanner said the back exit was unmanned and the streets had been cleared as far as the marina. Beyond that, we're on our own." Paul gunned the engine and backed out of the driveway.

"Are we picking up Tanner and Taylor?"

John and Paul were good friends with Tanner, and he was the third in their Three Musketeers world. Tanner was sixteen, between their ages, and he lived by the back gate. His mom was the manager of the association, and she had keys to every business in their little community. With Tanner's access and their ideas, there was not much they hadn't done or tried; however, he was also their conscience. He kept them out of any major trouble and was often the glue that fixed their quarrels.

Taylor, on the other hand, seemed more mature in a lot of ways, always questioning the safety of their pranks and fun. He had recently moved in next door to Tanner and was six months older than Paul but built like a linebacker. He struggled at first with fitting in, arriving at the beginning of his senior year. It didn't take long for Tanner to include him in their activities. With Tanner's endorsement, the brothers accepted Taylor into their pack. Paul and Taylor became fast friends. They were very seldom seen apart from each other.

"I think we need to leave them out of this for now. We don't even know if the shop will take the money or if it's counterfeit. Once we know it's legit, then we can spend it in front of anyone we want." Paul turned his eyes back to the road in time to dodge some trash cans rolling around in the street. He was grateful that the cans were his only obstacles as he approached the marina. From there, it got tricky, and he had to drive carefully, maneuvering around downed trees. He started to relax when he saw the back gate ahead. However, his adventure wasn't over as he drove the local roads heading to town. He found himself zigzagging up and downside streets to miss the large branches blocking traffic. They both sighed with relief as they pulled up to find an "open" sign on the dive shop door.

The local dive shop was bustling with tourists rescheduling their cancelled charters. Paul and John were ready to spend their money. They searched up and down the aisles, pricing the camouflage wet suits and dive skins. Blue seemed to be the popular color with their friends, but the shop only had one hanging on the rack—a medium. They both reached for it, causing a tussle. There was an abundance of green and gray, but neither wanted to concede their color choice.

Portia, a short dark-haired beauty that Paul had a crush on, approached the pair. "Hi, Paul. Hi, JJ. Tanner texted that you were heading to town. I can't believe you made it. I heard it was a mess out there."

Both boys turned at the sound of her voice. "Oh hi, Portia, you're working today? I didn't see you when we came in." Paul blushed. His feelings for her were shown on his face.

"Well, we made it, that's all that matters. Of course, a few less downed tree branches would have helped." He smiled down at her, releasing his hand from the hanging wet suit.

"We're here to buy wet suits. Is this the only one you have left?" John took the blue camouflaged one and hugged it to his chest.

"Well, since all these are the same kind, I am assuming you both want the last blue one, right?" She smiled up at Paul. "Let me look in the back and see if there's anymore." She headed for the back door. "You want another medium or a large?"

"I guess we should try them on. One of each would be great." Paul took the suit from John and held it up in front of him.

Portia turned back. "I'll try, but they are very popular, and I can't promise anything." With that, she was gone.

"Are you going to ask her out on a real date or just keep giving her that goofy grin every time you see her?" Paul dropped his smile and punched his brother in the shoulder.

"Like you are any better with Kasidy. When was the dance, six months ago? You know you turn sixteen next month. Mom and Dad may even let you go without a chaperone." John grabbed the suit and headed for the changing room.

"I'm trying this one on!" he yelled back as he shut the door.

Paul had time to browse a few aisles before Portia returned with two blue camouflage wet suits—one large and one medium.

"Here you go. We got a whole new shipment in just before the storm, but we haven't had time to put them on display." She handed the suits to Paul. "Personally, I don't understand the big deal about the blue ones, I like the gray ones, but no one seems to buy them. As you can see, we have a full rack."

"I never thought about the gray ones. I'll try on both." Portia smiled as she reached into the gray rack and pulled out a large and a medium and handed them to Paul. He headed toward the changing rooms.

"How did it fit, JJ?" Portia walked up behind John as he stepped out.

"It fit great. I'll take this one. Now I need a new mask, snorkel, and fins." He handed her the suit as he headed for the back of the store.

Portia turned toward the noise of the squeaking door as Paul walked out wearing a gray camouflage wet suit.

"What size is that one?"

"Large." He lunged forward to stretch the suit to gage his flexibility in the neoprene. It didn't hurt that he got to show off in front of Portia.

"This one will work great, and you were right, the color is really different, almost a metallic silver. I'll take it." Portia smiled. She loved it when guys listened to her suggestions, especially Paul. Paul headed back into the changing room.

The boys took longer than expected to find their masks, snorkels, and fins they had been eyeing for months. Tourist season always left the store somewhat disheveled. John found the blue one he wanted to match his wet suit underneath a pile of fins, and Paul found a white one, which complimented his suit, on a rack of dive computers. Dive computers were also on their list, but after checking the price, they made a mental note to come back in a few days. It felt safer to spread out their purchases.

After waiting in line for what seemed like hours, they finally met back up with Portia at the cash register, and she rang them up. On their way out, Paul turned back to her and casually asked, "Why don't you meet us at the sub shop when you get off?"

"Sounds like fun. Order me a turkey on wheat. I'll see you in a half hour."

The sub shop was a small local hangout that also had an arcade. It was always busy, but with the storm and all the excursions cancelled because of the storm, it was overflowing with teenagers. They went in, anyway, because they knew that most tourists went back to their families for dinner around five thirty or six, and that would thin out the crowd.

A table opened up in the back corner, and they quickly claimed it. Paul headed to the counter to order his meatball sub, Portia's turkey on wheat, and a roast beef for John. It took nearly twenty minutes to get their sandwiches, but they didn't mind; that gave them time to talk before Portia arrived.

"They didn't even question the hundred-dollar bills when I paid at the dive shop or for the subs either." Paul sat down at the table across John.

"They're probably used to them from the tourists, but why use a hundred, here? Why not use the change from the dive shop?"

"I wanted to use as many of the hundreds as possible while we're in town, so I don't have any in my wallet. I caught Aunt Cindy in my room the other day. I asked her what she was doing. She tried to tell me she was putting laundry away. She didn't even have a basket with her, just her purse over her shoulder as if she was leaving. It gave me the creeps, so I checked my wallet on the dresser to see if any money was missing. The funny thing is I only carry a few tens in my wallet. I keep the rest in my front pocket in the money clip Dad gave me for Christmas last year."

"Did she take any money?" John was checking his wallet to see if he had any money missing. Before Paul could respond, he said, "Wait a minute. We each had $500, right?" Paul nodded. "And the dive stuff came to over six hundred and something, right?" He nodded again. "Okay, so that was seven $100 bills, and then you used another one just now, here at the sub shop." He looked up at Paul's concerned face.

"Yes, we've used eight $100 bills, and that leaves two. I've used all of mine, and you should have two left, so what's your point?" Paul glanced down at John's wallet, opened in his hands.

"Paul, I only have one left in my wallet." Paul hurried and pulled out his money clip to double-check.

"Looks like you've been robbed." Paul reached across and took the last hundred and placed it in his money clip and secured it in his pants pocket. "I guess Aunt Cindy didn't just look in my wallet for spending money. This proves my suspicions. Now she knows about the money. So much for being discrete." Paul was banging his fists on the table and causing others to turn in their direction as he heard his name over the loudspeaker. He stood up and headed for the counter to pick up their order.

John took a minute and rechecked his pockets and his wallet. Sure enough, he was missing a hundred-dollar bill. He would have to be more careful in the future, but what about now? What did Aunt Cindy think when she found hundreds of dollars in his wallet? What were they going to do?

Paul sat down their order and retook his seat. "We need to come up with a story to tell Aunt Cindy if she asks where the money came from."

"I can tell her it's from my savings account."

"Okay, that sounds reasonable for you, and if she questions me, I can say I got a part-time job that pays me in cash. She knows I'm not a saver." Paul smiled.

"True. We all know that. But who would you work for? She'll want to know." Both boys stared off into space as they considered their dilemma.

"How about our neighbor Jack? There's no love lost between him and Aunt Cindy, and besides, they never speak to each other. Plus, using Jack, she'll never check it out." John looked into Paul's face for acceptance of his idea.

Paul's mind went back to the yelling that had woken him up early one morning. He couldn't see much from his bedroom window, but he could make out his aunt's voice yelling at their neighbor.

Jack first met Cindy at a dinner party that Charles and Sara Choate had thrown to introduce her as the boy's caregiver while they were overseas. Cindy was polite and friendly but seemed to size a person up and categorize them based on their wallet size, and since Jack wasn't a wealthy man, she was polite but dismissive toward him.

Not long after their parents' departure, Cindy had returned from a date at 5:00 a.m. Jack had been preparing to take his boat out when a loud BMW drove up, and an inebriated Cindy climbed out. Amid the noise and confusion, Jack appeared in the front yard to investigate. It was her behavior and her coming home at that early-morning hour that caused him to question her ability to look after her nephews. He had threatened to call their parents, but alas, it was an empty threat since he didn't have their number. The contention continued between the two. He wasn't shy about telling Cindy what he thought about her, and she said some choice words in return. The conflict caused a deep rift between them, and they agreed to stay out of each other's business. Jack walked away but not before warning her to do her job or he would call the authorities. Paul always felt the threats were empty, but they were enough to intimidate her. This rift, he thought, could work to their advantage.

"That's true. The way she talks about Jack, she'd never ask him, and besides, he hires people all the time to do odd jobs all over the housing area. We can say that he asked us to clean the boats at the marina and paid us in cash, but we have to get our story straight and be convincing. The last thing we need is for Aunt Cindy to get suspicious."

The roar in the room had quieted, and Paul looked up as he heard the bell on the door and saw Portia walking toward them. "We'll talk about this later. Portia's here."

"Hi, guys. Sorry I'm late. It's been a crazy day, and I'm starving." Paul scooted over to clear a chair for her as John divvied up the sandwiches. "Thanks for ordering for me. What do I owe you?"

"We'll just call it your tip for helping us with our wet suits." He smiled a sheepish grin and picked up his sandwich. John just shook his head and picked up his own. He couldn't believe how his brother acted around this girl—he was so embarrassing.

Their conversation quickly turned to Portia's day dealing with the tourists at the dive shop. She vented between bites. "You wouldn't believe how many angry people came in today and demanded that we take them on their snorkeling excursion even though it wasn't safe. Don't people have brains? Then when we were rescheduling, they were fighting over the times. It was nuts."

Paul was barely listening. He was staring out the window behind his brother.

"It makes me wish I lived out where you guys do instead of within walking distance of the shop. Then I could've stayed home today." Portia caught Paul's attention with her last comment.

"Personally, we left our house as soon as we could get away. I can't stand feeling trapped, and that's how these stormy days make me feel." Portia turned and looked at him as he returned to the scene outside.

"I feel that way sometimes too, especially when we get the category storms and everyone's heading for Miami for safety. I hate the bumper-to-bumper traffic and the chaos. Plus, part of me is worried about being caught in a tornado and getting wiped off the map."

Paul just nodded and changed the subject. "How about a game of air hockey before we have to head home?"

He didn't want to think about death, storms, or uncertainty anymore. He had enough of that in his life between the lack of communication from his parents, his aunt going through their wallets and stealing money, and now $15,000 dropped into their laps. That doesn't include the overwhelming responsibility he felt for his brother's care and the fact that he was about to graduate and become an actual adult. If only his parents were here instead of halfway around the world.

A feeling of anxiety had been building in him. No matter how he tried, the lack of letters and phone calls from his parents for the last two months was setting off a firestorm of worry and fear. Aunt Cindy kept trying to tell him that everything was fine, but she was acting different lately. She was lying about everything. It wasn't just the stolen money. She was insisting their mother was making regular phone calls. Oddly enough, the boys were always absent when those phone calls came through.

With no letters or calls, his imagination was taking over. He had started calling his parents' emergency numbers, only to be left with endless ringing and more unanswered questions. He didn't dare share his worries with JJ or their friends until he was certain there was something to worry about. However, as each day came and went with no word, his brooding was growing darker.

"Score!" Portia did a little dance with her paddle that made Paul laugh. Her light heartedness and joy were just what he needed to change his mood.

"One more point, and she's going to beat you."

John was enjoying watching his competitive brother being beaten by a girl, especially this one. Of course, Paul would say that he let her win to save face, but John knew how he really played, and she was beating him fair and square.

Portia wasn't the type to gloat over winning, but with her crush on Paul, it was just another way to get his attention. She danced around the table and sidled up next to him, hugging him tighter and longer than what might seem appropriate for a winning display, but she didn't care about the win, she was where she wanted to be.

She had crushed on Paul since the eighth grade, but it wasn't until recently that he started flirting with her. She was willing to return his advances and had accepted his offer to prom, but since then, he had become distant. He was affectionate, but his mind seemed a million miles away. She knew it had to be something with his parents, so she didn't pry, but she tried as often as she could to lighten his spirits and make him smile, like he was doing right now, holding her in his arms.

15

Sierra's Plight – DC

Sierra was exhausted. Her world had been turned upside down in the last five days. First, Jason was found dead in the parking garage, then Julio's car had turned up abandoned at the docks, and now she was reading over a report of a home invasion that left Mary Torres, Julio's mother, dead. The report was simple and vague, leaving many unanswered questions. Any other time, she wouldn't have given it a second glance, but following on the heels of Jason's demise and Julio's disappearance, it was suspect. It could have been punishment for Julio's deception.

Sierra had pushed for information from Juan's men who frequented the bar where she had spent the last year working undercover, but no one was talking. Even with the unpaid overtime she was putting in, she left empty-handed each night. Her lack of sleep and her personal interest in this case was draining her physically and emotionally. She had fallen for these two men, and though she tried to justify her feelings, she had crossed the line, and that fact was harder for her to accept than their loss.

Sierra met Jason the first day she walked into the Washington DC office. He was talking to a tall distinguished man whom she later learned was her new boss, Director Smith. Jason seemed to notice her right away and abruptly ended his discussion and walked over to greet her. She was both flattered and somewhat annoyed at his arrogance. After introductions all around, she felt more at ease with both men. As time went on, Jason seemed to single her out whenever they were in a room together. She couldn't remember how many times he had asked her out, and she had turned him down before she finally said yes. They had a great time together, but their assignments hadn't allowed for a relationship to blossom. But she would make an effort to talk to him during agency meetings. He was her first thought when she set Julio up as an informant. He seemed happy to take him on.

Julio was her assignment. She was to flirt with him and get him to trust her. It took a lot to get Julio to accept her into his confidences, but once she did, he began to share instances about his childhood, his boss, and his work. She felt sorry for him. If only she could save him from his poor choices. Their time together became much like dating. He would sit in her area at the bar, and she would find time each night to sit with him, so they could talk. In many ways, she loved him. But what that really meant, she wasn't sure. Saving him was her priority. At times she was torn. She knew bringing him in as an informant would put him in more danger, but it was the only way to get him away from Perrone.

No one knew about Julio's arrangement, except her and Jason; and she was sure Jason took his knowledge to the grave. That left Julio as the weak link. Did he get Jason shot? No, not the Julio she knew—it couldn't be. She was missing something. There had to be a leak somewhere in the department, perhaps an overheard phone call or a paper trail. But who? Who else knew about this operation? She had to find out. She needed answers. Those were her last thoughts as she faded off to sleep.

Her phone rang. It was 2:00 a.m. She sleepily answered it. "Hello? Who is this? Oh, Director. Sir, yes, this is Special Agent Cortez. How are you? Yes, I can come to your office first thing in the morning. What time? Five thirty, it is. What was that, sir? Be invisible? Yes, sir . . . Good night, sir."

Sierra lay back and tried to calm her racing mind. Sleep was impossible now. She got up and went through her notes from the meetings with Jason and Julio. She wanted to be prepared for whatever

Director Smith asked. He was a thorough man who expected the best of his agents. If he wanted to see her, she needed to be prepared.

She met Director Smith on their first day in the Washington DC Office. He had been transferred from Chicago, and she was fresh out of Quantico. They had gone through bureau orientation classes together, which allowed her time to get to know him. He was a likeable guy who seemed to care about his work and his staff. He talked about undercover agents and how deep some had to go to accomplish their assignments. He talked about the takedown of Nicholas Bastos in Chicago and how it took good agents to pull it off, but he almost lost one. Director Smith had been promoted and given his choice of offices after that. He had chosen DC for personal reasons, though he never explained further. Sierra just assumed it was marital in nature.

It was 4:00 a.m. when the alarm on her phone sounded, and she sat bolt upright. She had managed to squeeze out an hour of sleep on the couch, but she would need real sleep soon. She dressed quickly, grabbed her notes, and headed downtown. Director Smith was a stickler about being on time, and she knew he chose this early hour to avoid her being seen. She entered the building dressed as the cleaning staff and headed for the stairwell where she removed her disguise and ran up the stairs to the fifth floor.

"Nice to see you, Special Agent Cortez. Follow me, please."

She was winded from her quick climb, so she just nodded and followed him down the hall. When she could speak without panting, she asked, "Sir, where are we going? Isn't your office back there?"

"I'll explain in a minute. Does anyone else know you're here?"

"No, sir, I took the stairs, and they were empty."

"Good. Come this way, and when you leave, go out that door at the end of the hall and head down the back stairs."

Sierra followed her boss into a secluded conference room that was used to process witness-protection candidates. This room was perfect for private business since it was swept for bugs on a regular basis. Cameras, recording devices, and two-way mirrors were also banned in this room for security reasons.

"Have a seat, Agent Cortez." Sierra looked around the room and took a seat across the table from Director Smith . "Now I know this seems cloak and dagger, but I needed to talk to you privately. What do you know about Special Agent Jason Kirtland's murder?"

"Well, sir, I'm sorry to say, absolutely nothing. I hooked him up with an informant named Julio Torres who worked for Juan Perrone. Agent Kirtland outlined a plan for him to switch out some money on one of Perrone's boat shipments leaving last Monday. The initial meeting seemed to go well, but that was the last I heard until . . ." She lowered her head as her voice choked. Director Smith looked away to give her time to compose herself. She took a deep breath and lifted her chin for courage and continued, "I've listened and flirted with most of the patrons at the bar, but if someone knows anything, they aren't talking. I'm so frustrated with the whole mess. There's Agent Kirtland's death, Julio's disappearance, and now I've learned that Julio's mother has been shot in a supposed home invasion gone wrong. I went over all my notes last night, and I'm sorry to say, sir, that I have absolutely nothing new to report, except . . ." Her voice was quivering. "I feel, sir, that Jason's and Julio's blood may be on my hands."

"Why is that? You didn't kill them, did you?"

"Not in the pull-the-trigger sense, sir. But I'm the one that set Julio up to be turned and gave him to Agent Kirtland as his informant, and now he's dead, and Julio may be dead as well. Then there's Julio's mother."

"Listen, Special Agent Cortez, I am sure you've heard this before, but you are not responsible for what an informant does or doesn't do. First of all, Jason knew the risks, and this Julio made his decision of his own free will. He knew what was at stake when he signed on with the FBI, and he knew the consequences of his actions. You did your job. You are not responsible for the outcome. Besides, you don't know all the facts, so don't take it out on yourself. That being said, I do believe we have a leak somewhere. This has all been too quiet, too clean. We should have heard something by now. An FBI agent's death usually starts ripples or rumors. I've put out feelers, but no one's heard a thing." He paused, taking a deep breath. "Cortez, we have to be careful on this one, so keep your head down, your ears open, and watch your back. You're on your own out there, with no backup. One slipup and I have another body in the morgue. We have other undercover agents in different parts of this investigation, so this is not all on your shoulders. Be smart, and be careful."

Sierra looked into his eyes and nodded. She understood what he was saying, but she needed answers to lessen the guilt she felt inside.

"That being said, what do you know about Juan's second-in-command Victor Ramos? Have you heard anything about him from Juan's men?"

"Well, they call him Vic, and other than that, not many nice words are said about him. My impression is that he is trying to take over his boss's interests. The boys at the bar are pretty protective of their comments. They're always looking around for stray ears, but I get bits and pieces here and there. When his name is said, the crowd hushes, and it's always followed by a change of subject. I sense that they are more afraid of him then Perrone."

Director Smith smiled and stood up and walked across the room, turning his back on Sierra. "So you would say he seems to be positioning himself well in the organization?"

"Something like that. All I know is that the men are touchy when it comes to him." She paused and looked down at her folded hands. "Sir, do you think Victor Ramos was the one that killed Jason, Julio, and Mary Torres?"

"Mary Torres—I don't know anything about her death. Agent Kirtland's death, I would say that is possible, but Julio may not be dead. All we know about him is that his car was abandoned and torn apart at the dock. You know, there's always the possibility that he ended up on the boat with the shipment. We had a sighting yesterday in Miami of a boat that fueled up with one of Perrone's flagged accounts. There were two men on board. One was definitely Juan's partner, known as Captain Max. We have his signature on the receipt, but the other occupant is an unknown. Our Miami bureau is working with Miami Police Department to get a copy of any video that the dock may have captured. There was a murder being investigated at the docks that day.

A woman was found dead in a personal watercraft tied up to one of the fueling piers. Sam, the fuel attendant, when questioned, mentioned the yacht with the two men on board in his statement to the police. He said they asked about the police presence, and there was definitely tension between them. They seemed nervous about something." He paused and looked at the wall across the room. "Right now, it is speculation, but we are pursuing this case as if Julio is missing, not dead, until there is indication otherwise."

Sierra couldn't help but smile at the thought that Julio might still be alive. "Sir, if you can keep me in the loop about Julio, I would really appreciate it. As for now, I'm exhausted. So if there isn't anything further, I could use some sleep before my evening shift at the bar. I have to admit I haven't slept much lately."

"Sure. Listen, Sierra, on a personal note, your safety comes first. We don't know what is really going on inside Perrone's crew, and I can't stress enough for you to be careful. This is a tenuous case, and we've already lost one of our own. Make sure you are taking safety precautions for your own welfare. Now, if you discover anything further, you know how to reach me." He walked to the door and held it open for her.

Sierra hurried out the back door, down the stairs, and through the parking garage, making her way to her car across the street. The morning buzz was just getting started downtown, and she was happy to be heading in the opposite direction. She had done the whole work in the city and commute thing for several years, and she didn't miss the chaos.

Working for the FBI had been an interesting career choice for her after graduating from Creighton University in Omaha. Although her degree was in criminal justice, she figured she would continue on to law school. One Saturday afternoon, that all changed. Sierra went shopping at Westroads Mall. It was a normal day. The mall was filled with moms pushing strollers and teenagers hanging out at the food court. But then in walked a gunman, and he started shooting. Screams filled the air. Many patrons hid as others found an alternate exit. Sierra hid herself among the clothing racks and observed the gunman's demeanor throughout the ordeal. There was something about law enforcement's game plan that bothered her. It wasn't long till the boy, not more than fifteen years of age, was soon lying on a stretcher headed to the morgue. The incident affected her deeply. She had sleepless nights for weeks. Perhaps it was a form of PTSD, post-traumatic stress disorder, though she never went for counseling. The odd part was that she never felt like a victim. She wanted to create a new outcome—give this young man another chance on life. When she slept, she would play it over and over in her head, critiquing law enforcement's decision. At these times, she pictured herself running things, talking down the gunman. He would emerge into the arms of his waiting parents, and with counseling, he would be whole.

After that, Sierra couldn't settle for just litigating cases, she wanted to be the one on the front lines. She applied to the FBI, and with her professor's help, she was accepted to Quantico. Now here she was, working undercover on a case that she had allowed to get personal. She had wondered how long-term undercover assignments affected her colleagues. As an innocent bystander, everything seemed so straight forward, but now she was in the game, and the twists and turns kept coming.

Sierra could hardly keep her eyes open as she approached her home. The relief that Julio may still be alive helped release her tension. She was not responsible for two deaths, only one—Jason. Had she sent a killer his way? Could Julio have killed Jason? Either way, Jason's death was on her watch. Could she ever forgive herself? Forgive Julio? These were her last thoughts as her tired aching body rested on her unmade bed. Sleep, much-needed sleep, came quickly.

16

Bar Tales – DC

It had been a slow night, and Sierra was ready to pack it in when a group of Perrone's men walked in. The mood in the bar changed with their demeanor. They were not happy, and that usually meant there would be fists flying by last call.

After a couple of rounds to drown their sorrows, it was Carlos who got grabby. He reached for Sierra and pulled her into his lap. Normally, she would have resisted and called the bouncer for help, but this time she wanted information. She played along with his advances, hoping to get something new.

"What's with all the downed faces tonight?" Sierra pushed, but it was going to take more.

"Come on and tell Sierra what's got the lot of you looking like someone died?"

"Nothing to worry your pretty little head about, but if you want to make me feel better, I'm sure we can think of something."

"How about I get yawl another round? On me." She stood up quickly before he could stop her and headed for the bar. When she returned with the drinks, she purposely changed her delivery to the other side of the table, far from Carlos's reach. As she approached, she heard Vic's name coming from one of the other men. She slowed her progress as not to appear to be listening.

"Why is Vic punishing us? Are they sure it was Julio?"

"Mondo, I know you're frustrated, but you know better than to talk business outside the warehouse." Carlos looked nervous as he glanced around.

"Fine. But how can he come in and rip us a new one when we haven't done anything wrong?"

Carlos looked again, scrutinizing the patrons carefully, before he spoke. "Listen, Mondo, Julio split with unknown amounts of money, and because of him, we'll always be guilty in Vic's eyes. We just have to do our jobs and hope that he will cut us a break."

"I know that's what it looks like. But why is he in charge? I thought we were only supposed to take orders from Juan or Julio—" He stopped, realizing what he was about to say.

"Think of Vic as the new Julio, if that helps, and shut up!"

"Here you go." All eyes turned to Sierra as she approached.

"What do you say, Sierra, are you ready to experience a real man?" Carlos ended any more discussion and turned the subject back to her.

She winked at him and walked back toward the bar. Her shift was over, and she was ready to leave. She had heard enough. It had sounded like Victor Ramos was taking over the warehouse, and Julio had been set up for stealing from the mob. So even if he was still alive now, he wouldn't be for long.

She had everything she was going to get from this place. Her mind was made up. Tomorrow she would pack her bags and follow her only lead—she was going to Miami, Florida, for answers.

17

The Boss – DC

Juan Perrone had been born into a mob family—it was in his blood. He was the third generation of Perrones to run the DC underground. It was his town, like his fathers and grandfathers before him.

From the outside, his brood looked like any other upscale suburban family with a big house, two children, and a dog. His wife Dharma was your typical soccer mom and president of the PTA. Juan himself was well placed socially with his philanthropy and community-action groups. It was their political connections that gave them their status. Many United States dignitaries had been introduced to the Washington elite in their home. But deep inside, they had their hands in all aspects of the city's dirty underworld. This was the business that paid for their BMWs, private schools, and country clubs.

Juan relished in his life. He was the boss, and he owned Washington, but the winds were changing, and that made him very nervous. Would it all come crashing down? Victor Ramos had shown up from Chicago to warn him that the FBI had infiltrated his peers across the United States. This bit of information, though it was interesting, only caused him more anxiety. After hearing of the death of his good friend and supplier Nicholas Bastos, he had no problem believing Ramos's information. Was he next? If the government could take down an organization as strong as Bastos's, could he survive? He needed this shipment to Saint

Maartens to succeed. This new supplier was key. Everything was riding on Max and this initial offering.

It's not that he didn't trust his old friend, but the calls had stopped. It had been twenty-four hours since he had heard from Max or Julio, and the data from the GPS unit had stopped transmitting. He knew they had docked in Miami, and both men were alive and well. That small piece of information wasn't necessarily comforting. Max was supposed to kill Julio as soon as they hit the ocean, and he had fallen short on his assigned task; however, he did promise that he would take care of it before they reached Saint Maartens.

Could he trust him to kill Julio?

Max was adamant about this being his last transport. He wanted to retire. What did that mean? It's not like he was getting a pension from the company. Putting Julio on that boat with Max in such a state may not have been the best idea.

The stress of the whole thing was exhausting. With securing the new associate and waiting for word of Julio's death, Juan's anxiety was heightened with each passing hour.

Why Julio had decided to betray him? He couldn't understand. He had prided himself on his carefully crafted organization, each individual precisely placed like pieces of a jigsaw puzzle. Julio was a major piece, chosen for his ability to use his intelligence to think things through. He was articulate and demanding when it came to the rules of the warehouse, identifying errors in shipping that would have cost more than money.

It had taken many meetings with the young man to convince him to stay and work for his crew instead of going off to college, but his efforts had paid off. He was an unusual hire. Julio had turned up one morning on his doorstep, asking for a job. He said Soni had introduced them at a party, but he didn't remember all those his recruiter brought to meet him. But Julio was quick to learn the business, and he never had a problem trusting him until now—that was, until the FBI got to him and turned him. All the time and effort he had put into that young man and he was only left with betrayal.

It was Victor Ramos who heard from an acquaintance inside the FBI that he had a mole in his midst, but to find out that Julio had turned on him seemed implausible at first. Sure, he didn't want to get into the blood and guts of the organization, but he had always been loyal. If it were anyone else, he wouldn't have been surprised, but he had come to trust that boy like a son. But regardless of his feelings for him, betrayal of any sort could not be tolerated. It was a hard lesson but not one he would ever repeat. A cleansing had to take place with each one of his crew thoroughly scrutinized, and with Ramos's help, the process turned out to be quick and efficient.

Victor Ramos was still somewhat of a mystery to him. He seemed almost too perfect. In any given situation, he had the answer. If he hadn't come from Nicholas Bastos's employ, Juan would have figured him for a plant. Vic had explained that his contact in the FBI hadn't given him enough warning to save Bastos. So when Bastos was killed in the raid, he left Chicago and headed for DC to warn his boss's friend. Juan was tentative about trusting him at first, but he had proven his worth and turned out to be a valuable second.

It was Victor who brought Julio's deception to light and arranged for his treachery to be repaid in kind. He also stepped up and took over the warehouse, culling the deadwood and traitors from the group. Victor Ramos also calmed his fears of an FBI takedown, knowing he had someone looking out for his family's interests. Of course, killing Mary Torres was a little over the top, and he let him know he would not tolerate such actions in the future, but sadly, she had to be silenced. There was evidence found of her involvement. The woman did have FBI money in her home—the very money Julio was going to use as a traitor against him.

Money did strange things to people, and Julio had been caught in its trap. Juan had hoped that he was actually innocent since there was no money in his car or his apartment, but Ramos produced the bills found in Mary Torres's home.

That sealed it, Julio had stabbed him in the back, and if Max was serious about leaving his employ, the deed fell to him. However, as of yesterday, Julio was still alive, and that knowledge alone was causing him to second-guess his decision to trust this job to Max or to send Julio with the boat. Where were they?

With Ramos running the warehouse and handling the men, Juan was left with too much time to worry. He couldn't shake the feeling that something was very wrong. He would push the nagging thoughts aside, but they didn't retreat far enough to allow him peace. His short-term plan of replacing the Chicago supplier with available couriers was taxing. The shipments were too small, and soon he would fall short of demand. He needed this new supplier, and he needed Max to succeed. He had a million dollars and a boat worth twice that somewhere in the Atlantic Ocean—blind to him. The only information he had was the fuel-dock sighting in Miami—courtesy of Victor Ramos's friend in the FBI, a credit card charge for fuel, and the last voice mail message from Max with coordinates—then nothing. Was Max on track? Was Julio dead? Did they outrun the storm? He had to find out.

A man like him had to be careful how he approached each situation. Though he had government officials at his disposal, they protected his interests to secure their own. DC was full of deceitful players working angles to get what they wanted. With many of his contacts, he had to watch his back while finalizing deals with handshakes. No one was really trustworthy. Most times it came down to who had the most to hide. Then there was the FBI; they were his worst enemy until Victor Ramos came along. Ramos had insider help, which cleared many paths. This knowledge should've calmed his nightmares. But something didn't feel right. Was it the killing of Bastos, Julio's betrayal, or Max's silence? Perhaps it was a combination of the three. Whatever it was, it was stealing his peace.

It was after he awoke in a sweat that he decided he had to prepare for the worst. He needed to be ready to act if there was any indication that the boat didn't make it through. He needed a plan and a crew he trusted to send to Florida for answers. There were only a handful of men he knew well enough to send on this assignment. Victor Ramos had weeded out the betrayers and replaced them with men he knew. But though Victor trusted them, they were too new for Juan to be certain of their loyalty. He needed input from his second-in-command. He needed to talk to Victor Ramos.

18

Lead at the Dock – Miami

Sierra slept later than she'd planned. It was the first real night's sleep she'd had since she heard of Jason's death. Feeling rested, she went to work arranging her flight. The earliest one she could find was early evening. It seems the weather in Florida was causing delays and cancellations at Miami International. She used the time to book her hotel, pack, and update her case file with the new information she had learned from Director Smith.

With her neighbor set up to keep an eye on her apartment and water her plants, she anxiously awaited her arranged taxi. The earliest flight she could get out of Ronald Reagan National was at 4:00 p.m. with arrival in Miami at 10:00 p.m. Her nerves were on edge as she replayed in her head Director Smith's information. She needed answers, not only to Julio's disappearance, but also to Jason's murder. Right now, Florida was her only lead.

The arrival of her ride turned her attention to the task at hand. She handed the taxi driver her bag to stow in the trunk, and she slid into her place in the back seat. It was pleasing to find that her ride smelled almost pleasant. She was happy to see the old cabs had been retired and replaced with new, more comfortable versions, but they were smaller. Having one or two passengers seemed fine, but if you had three or four, it could be quite uncomfortable, to say the least. She gave the cabbie her destination and terminal number and turned her focus on the traffic. The streets were congested, though it was early afternoon, but her taxi seemed to know all the shortcuts to get her there without delay.

The departure lane was bustling with activity, so her cab dropped her at a crosswalk amid horns and yells in their direction. She quickly grabbed her bag and hurried inside out of the traffic flow. Sierra checked the overhead monitors and found her flight delayed a half hour then headed to the ticket counter to declare her weapon. They noted her gun in their manifest and prepared the necessary form for her to take through TSA priority screening. She never knew what to expect going through TSA; sometimes she could get in and out quickly and other times it was hours. Each new security threat caused longer lines and higher tensions as travelers did their best to hide their frustrations as they processed through.

The terrorists, when they crashed into the Twin Towers and the Pentagon in 2001, didn't destroy America, but they did leave her in fear; the kind of fear that makes you look over your shoulder more often when you are in a crowded airport, the kind of fear that allows more intrusion in your private life as it whittles away at your freedoms, the kind of fear that changes America and slowly weakens her.

Sierra had seen this behavior through her job. There had been more suspicious-character reports that were called into the FBI by anxious citizens demanding that the government do something, anything; even if it meant giving up their rights in the process. This behavior often disturbed her. She had joined the FBI with the intention of safeguarding the United States of America with their rule of law, each state governing itself, combined under one Constitution, but more and more power was being taken from the states, and the federal government was becoming a powerful albatross. This was making her question if our very Constitution would survive so much fear. Were our enemies without or were they taking over our government from within? Would the U.S. Constitution stand amid so much corruption?

Sierra had seen a shift in the minds of the people, allowing those who were power-hungry, in the name of security, to step up and take the reins; power players under the guise of the Robin Hood syndrome taking from the rich and giving to the poor, creating an entitlement generation that would feed off government and vote for those who would continue their sustenance.

She had also seen it in the FBI. Agents she worked with had given up the fight and given in to the "dark side," as she called it; many joining the very crime bosses they were assigned to infiltrate because of a promise of wealth and security. It was sad to see so many giving up. For her, each criminal caught was one less preying on the public. She stood for justice with a little mercy thrown in to keep her humble.

As she stood in line, she glanced up at the TSA screeners, watching as they took each individual through the various security monitors. She observed the distress on many faces as they undressed themselves, laying their shoes, belts, jackets, and other items that they were able to remove from their person on a conveyer belt for screening; then walk through a detector setup to show their transparent body on a monitor. This allowed for body screening for illegal surgically-implanted items.

Her gaze moved to a couple of screeners hand-checking a woman pushing a young child in a wheelchair. The child was crying as the agent felt down his body and around in the chair for any object of concern. His mother was being checked as well, and her tear-filled eyes told her story as the agent placed her hands down her body, touching her most private areas. She turned her focus to the man who was with them, waiting for the screening to end. He was opening and closing his fists as he watched his little family being fondled. She saw his face tighten and his eyes water as he stood helpless to spare his loved ones from their trauma.

Sierra lowered her gaze and turned back to her line. She approached her screener with her badge, her ticket, and her weapon-declaration form. He took the form and ushered her behind the priority passenger screen. She removed her shoulder holster and handed the agent her gun then proceeded to take off her shoes, jacket, and belt and place them on the conveyer belt. He handed her back her shoulder holster and gun, observing, as she put it securely on her person. She picked up her belongings and hurried to her assigned gate.

Sierra checked in with the gate agent to verify her seat and to let them know she was an FBI agent traveling with a gun. They offered her a first-class seat as an upgrade and then called over a gentleman and introduced her to the air marshal assigned to the flight. He was pleasant but direct as he stressed the boundaries and procedures he expected her to follow. They boarded the plane together, finalizing their discussion on the ramp. It didn't take long for Sierra to get settled in her seat and doze off as the plane taxied to the runway for takeoff.

The stewardess awakened her as they were preparing for landing in Miami. Sierra couldn't remember the last time she had slept through a whole flight, but she wasn't surprised at her fatigue. The plane landed smoothly, but the pilot had to wait for a gate to clear. Sierra didn't mind, it gave her time to wake up and get her thoughts together before she disembarked...

Sierra checked into the Courtyard Marriott on Second Avenue, close to the port of Miami. She liked the chain of hotels under the Marriott banner because of their "no smoking" policy and their business center. Unpacking enough to complete her bedtime routine, it wasn't long till she was fast asleep.

Morning came early as she awoke to the sun streaming through her hotel window. If only she had time to enjoy the beauty of the beaches around her. She still needed to call Agent Terry at the Treasury Department's fund-monitoring unit to see if there was any reported activity on the marked money. If any of the bills had come in, that would give her another lead to follow. For now, Sam at the Miami seaport's fuel dock was her only chance for information. She also needed to eat. Sierra took the elevator downstairs to the restaurant and ordered breakfast. Since she slept through the food service on the plane and hadn't eaten since lunch the previous day, she was famished, and a headache was forming.

Sierra settled into her booth and ordered her food, placing a call to Agent Terry while she waited. It only took one ring before he answered, "Hey, you reached Agent Terry. What can I do you for?"

Sierra hadn't met him in person, but she was told that he could answer any question about banking or financial transactions. Other agents had nicknamed him "The Smart Southerner." She was bothered by the suggestion that "Southerners," who had a slow Southern drawl, were dumb. She knew better. She had many friends who grew up Down South, and they were on the top of their field.

"Agent Terry, this is Special Agent Sierra Cortez. I am calling about Special Agent Jason Kirtland's file on Julio Torres."

"Special Agent Kirtland? Oh, the agent who was killed last week, right? I was sorry to hear about that."

"Yes, that's him." Sierra talked through the lump in her throat. "As you can see, I am the backup agent on the file, and my contact information should be listed next to my name."

"You have the cell phone number ending in 5-4-5-4?" he enunciated each number.

"Yes, that's right. So do you have anything for me?"

"As a matter of fact," he said in his slow precise speech, "there was a bank in Key Largo that flagged seven $100 bills this morning that came in from a local dive shop and another $100 bill from a local sub shop. The bank is double-checking each bill to make sure there was no mistake. They had an incident last year that caused quite a stir when counterfeit money was deposited from the sheriff's department, and before they were through, there was a local deputy doing time. So they are being extra careful on this one."

Sierra couldn't believe what she was hearing. "Agent Terry, are you saying Special Agent Kirtland's marked bills have turned up in Key Largo, Florida, at a local dive shop?"

"That's the way it appears, but I will get back to you in about an hour and let you know if these flagged bills are a definite match for Special Agent Kirkland's funds."

"I'll await your call. Agent Terry, I also need to tell you that there is a possible leak in the department that may have led to Special Agent Kirtland's death. So for now, I am the only contact you can trust on this case. Do you understand?"

"No problem. I'll talk to yaw later, Special Agent Cortez." Agent Terry hung up the phone.

Sierra looked at her phone as she contemplated this new development. Key Largo, Florida—she opened her map program on her smart phone and calculated the distance from Miami to Key Largo, just over sixty miles. She finished her breakfast, grabbed her purse, and headed to her car. She would wait for Agent Terry's call to make the trip Down South, but she needed to get more information from the dock attendant at the fueling pier. She was taking a big chance that he was actually working today, but since he was her only lead, she felt that her answers were there.

Sierra looked up the Miami seaport on her phone and put the address into her GPS. It took her longer than she thought to get through traffic and find a parking spot. She approached the dock asking for directions to the fueling pier from a passerby. He pointed to a blue building at the end of the pier. She maneuvered her way down the walkways until she reached the building.

Harry was working the fueling station, and he was busy talking to a customer when she approached. She took the time to look around and see where the cameras were placed and what angle they would capture. She was staring up at the camera, deep in thought, when he noticed her.

"Can I help you?"

"I hope so. My name is Special Agent Cortez, and I am looking for Sam. Is he working today?" She looked Harry straight in the eyes to gage his reaction to her question.

"Can I see some ID?" She showed him her badge. "Sam should be here anytime. He takes over for me. Has he got himself in some trouble? Just a second, I need to finish this. I'll be right back."

Harry walked over to the yacht that was fueling up and unhooked the hose. "Will that be all, sir?" he asked the gentleman as he was handed a credit card for payment.

"Could you add a box of Davidoff Millennium Blend?" Harry just nodded and disappeared into the office, processed the payment, and reappeared handing his waiting customer, standing on the bow of his boat, a brown paper bag, his receipt, and his credit card.

As Sierra watched the process, another young man walked past her and headed for the building. She watched him for a minute and then followed.

"Are you Sam?" He had a set of earbuds in his ears and couldn't hear her. She tried again, only this time she tapped his shoulder. "Hello. Are you Sam?" She startled him, and he jumped.

"Can I help you?" he mumbled at her, though his voice was quivering.

"I hope so. My name is Special Agent Cortez, and I am an agent for the FBI." She showed him her badge. "I would like to talk to you about a yacht that was here two days ago getting fuel. There would have been two men on this yacht who may have seemed nervous that the police were here investigating a murder. They may have been looking over their shoulders a lot. This yacht filled up with fuel, on an out-of-state credit card."

"Are you talking about the one that the cops came and took the video card for? You know, they never gave it back, and I had to replace that memory card with my own money. So much for helping the police. My boss was furious that I talked to them, so he won't be happy that you are here asking questions."

Sierra ignored his complaint. "That's the one. Can you remember anything else about the two men—perhaps describe them for me?" Sierra smiled at the young man.

"Okay, but then you will leave us alone?" He looked at her with probing eyes, and she nodded. "Well, I'll never forget that boat. There were two men. One was obviously in charge, and he liked giving orders, even to me. They pulled up, asked for fuel, and then proceeded to use my water hose without even asking. The man in charge told the other one to go get a brush. It took him a while to come back, and then they started scrubbing down the outside of their boat. That might be okay somewhere else, but we are a fueling pier, not a maintenance pier, if you know what I mean. The second guy was very nervous, he reminded me of a caged animal. Every few seconds, he would look over at the police walking around their murder scene. He worked hard, even kicking off his shoes when they got soaked. This guy was wearing a T-shirt and long pants that looked like they had been slept in, and he could have used a razor. The strange part was when I approached them to get my hose back and tell them they were done and they needed to leave, it looked like they were on edge. I think I stopped an attack. The second guy, with the broom in his hands, had just turned toward the other guy, like he was going to hit him, but he stopped when I came around the stern of the boat. They were both pleasant as they put my hose back, and I gave them their receipt, and then they pulled out and left, which I was very happy to see. The last thing we needed was the police to investigate another boat on the fuel docks. It's bad for business, yaw know. That's all I know. So are we done?"

Sierra took her phone out and showed Sam a picture of Julio. "Is this one of the two men?"

He looked hard at the photo. "Maybe? This could be the man with the broom. He was younger than the other man. But if this is him, he has lost some weight and grown some facial hair."

She thanked him for his information and walked back to her car. She sat there for a few minutes watching as one boat left and another one pulled up for fuel. It was interesting how much this young man Sam had observed. So Julio was unkempt and was desperate to get off the yacht. She needed to get a look at that video. It sounded like he wasn't there of his own free will. He was put on that boat, probably by Perrone, with no change of clothes, and he was obviously in fear of his life. He must have thought Miami was his only chance for escape, and if he went as far as the fuel attendant said, he may not have made it much farther along their route.

She dug out her map of Florida and looked to see where a boat would travel from Miami to Key Largo. It was definitely out of the way for a route to Saint Maartens. Could they have driven close enough to land for Julio to jump off and swim ashore with the marked money? Not on this route. Something had to happen to throw this boat so far off course. Perhaps it was the storm. If he made it to land, he had to know that spending the money would flag the FBI. Perhaps he was signaling for help.

Sierra pulled out her phone and looked up the local police station. She called and asked for the detective assigned to the murder case at the fuel dock. She was forwarded to a Detective Cruz, who answered her call on the first ring.

"This is Detective Cruz."

"Hello, Detective, this is FBI Special Agent Cortez. I would like to meet with you today and go over a video that you took from the Miami seaport a few days ago, during a murder investigation."

"Special Agent Cortez, is it? May I ask what connection the FBI has with the young women found dead at the docks?"

"I would be happy to meet with you and explain my request. Are you at Fifth Street and NW Second Ave?"

"I will be soon. I'm on my way to the station right now and will be there for the next few hours. If you want to meet with me, it would have to be during that time."

"Sounds good. I'll be there in about fifteen minutes, depending on traffic. See you then." They politely said their good-byes and hung up.

Sierra reached the police station in less time than she expected and was seated in the audiovisual room before she even met Detective Cruz. She was watching the footage as he walked through the door.

"Sorry for my tardiness. You didn't tell me you were *bonito*." Sierra paused the recording and stood up to formally introduce herself. She always felt that showing respect to the person you were talking to was important, especially if you were asking for a favor. She needed him to not only respect her but also see her as a colleague.

"Detective Cruz, I'm Special Agent Cortez. Thanks for setting this up for me."

"All business then. Okay. I'm curious to see what the FBI has to do with a dead hooker found in an unregistered boat abandoned at the fuel pier." He had set aside his flirtation and leaned against the back wall. He wanted answers as to why the FBI was poking around in his case.

"Actually, I'm not interested in the dead hooker or the unregistered boat but what else this video may have captured that day."

"Well, then I'll leave you to your viewing, but first, may I see your ID. You know, we don't let just anyone in here." Sierra pulled out her badge and ID and showed him. "This must be a pretty important video."

"About that, I am actually undercover, following a lead for a missing yacht. Do you think you can keep my identity under wraps for now?"

"Perhaps you should have said something during our phone conversation, Special Agent Cortez. I'm afraid I have already cleared your name with our FBI liaison."

"So the local FBI knows I'm in Miami?"

"I'm not sure about your internal procedures, but our FBI contact is aware that you have requested to view our 'murder at the docks' video."

"May I speak to your FBI liaison?"

"Sure." Detective Cruz pulled out his phone and placed a call to Special Agent Medina.

"Special Agent Medina, this is Detective Cruz. Yes, we just spoke. I have Special Agent Cortez here, and she would like to talk to you." He handed the phone to Sierra.

"Hello, Special Agent Medina. This is Special Agent Cortez. Can you hold on for a second, please?" Sierra placed her hand over the phone and turned to Detective Cruz. "Can you excuse us for a minute, Detective?"

"Sure, I'll be right outside."

She waited until he exited the room before she continued, "Medina, I am sorry about that, but I am working undercover on an assignment from DC. I am here in Miami to follow up on a lead that was captured on a video of another crime scene. Detective Cruz said he cleared my name through you."

"Yes, he called about an hour ago and asked if you were FBI. You haven't checked in with the Miami office?"

"No, I wasn't going to check in with the Miami office. I know it's procedure, but there is a leak in our department, and I don't know how far it reaches. I would like to ask you to keep my existence and identity under wraps for now."

"It's too late for that. When Detective Cruz called me, I called my supervisor for clarification since I don't know you and the detective didn't have your badge number."

"Who did you call to verify my credentials?"

"Supervisory Special Agent Macdonald, and he put me on hold and called Washington."

"So Macdonald and his contact at the DC office know I'm here. So much for undercover work. Do you happen to know who his contact is?"

"No, but perhaps you should call him and get this worked out, especially if you are worried about leaked information. You do realize a simple courtesy call would have saved both of us from this mess."

"Perhaps. Could you give me Macdonald's phone number?"

"Well, you're in luck. He just walked in." Medina handed his phone to Macdonald, and there was a pause with background whispering.

"Special Agent Cortez, what a pleasure. Do you plan on stopping by and introducing yourself?"

"To be honest, sir, I wasn't planning on letting anyone know I was in town. I am undercover, and I am trying to keep it that way."

"Let me guess, you are following a lead, and you are here of your own choice and not by assignment, I respect that, but if you want us to back you up, you have to let us know you're in town."

"I understand, sir, but for right now, could you tell me who you cleared my name with in DC and what information was shared? There is a leak in the department that is affecting my case, and I need to know who is aware of my presence in Miami."

"I called Director Smith's office, and his assistant verified your status. I explained that you requested access to a Miami PD video, and they were clearing your credentials with us."

"Was my presence in Miami discussed in any way?"

"No, just that you wanted to see the video. I take it you don't want Director Smith to know you are here?"

"Director Smith told me not to trust anyone. Even telling you this is going outside those boundaries."

"Director Smith won't know you're here from me if you stop by before you leave the area or unless you do something that I have to bring to his attention, deal?"

"Deal." Sierra got Macdonald's cell phone number and ended her conversation. She opened the door and handed Detective Cruz his phone.

"Did you get everything worked out?"

"Yes, thanks, I appreciate your help." She smiled at him and closed the door. He nodded in her direction and went back to his desk.

She was happy to get back to work. There were hours of video still to go through. It was tedious, but her efforts paid off. The recording was good, and the angle was just enough that she could see the two men quite well. Sam was right—the younger one looked like he was wearing clothes he had slept in on more than one occasion, and he had at least a week's stubble growth on his face. The weight loss was evident, and with the dark recesses under his eyes, she surmised that he hadn't slept much. Sierra watched as the two men disappeared around the side of the boat. This must have been the time of the almost attack. They were lost from view until they came back around to hand over the water hose. The older man was handed a bag from Sam. The younger one helped with the lines as they pulled away from the dock. It didn't take long for the boat to be out of the camera's frame. Her last glimpse showed the younger man forlorn and sitting on the bow of the boat.

She backed up the recording and refocused her mind to look for any small detail that might give some clue as to what happened after they left, but there wasn't anything new. She looked around her for any prying eyes as she pulled out a jump drive, made a copy of the video file, picked up her purse, and slipped away from the police station without further notice. As she walked to her car, she went over in her mind what she had learned thus far. She could tell through his appearance that the young man on the tape was Julio. Julio was definitely on the boat, he was alive when they left Miami, there was a tension between him and Max, and the marked money may be sixty miles south of where she was.

Sierra pulled out her phone to check the time and noticed her message indicator light was on. She was unsure how she had missed a call, but she dialed her voice mail and listened as Agent Terry, in his slow Southern drawl, confirmed that $800 of the marked FBI money had indeed turned up in Key Largo, Florida, and that the money was definitely connected to Special Agent Kirtland's file. She hung up and headed for her hotel. It was too late to drive Down South tonight, but first thing in the morning, she was going to the Florida Keys.

19

Rescue – Cay Sal

It was Sunday morning, and Jack was anxious to head back to Cay Sal to check on the money he had buried and to look for clues to his mysterious find. The money's origin had haunted him with thoughts of boat parts and people floating in the ocean. It was all he could think about as he was clearing trees and cleaning up debris from the storm. A million dollars had fallen into his hands, and that just didn't happen every day. There was a back story that left a shadow across his windfall, and he needed answers.

It had been two full days since the storm had hit the Keys, and now the sky was full of bright sunshine. The heat and humidity in the air had left the days hot and sticky, but his crew had managed to complete their work orders in a timely manner. With the marina repairs coming to a screeching halt, pending settlement of insurance claims, and with his management properties cleaned up and awaiting tree replacements to arrive, Jack was ready to take *Maria* back to Cay Sal and troll the area to see if he had missed anything.

It was five thirty as he walked into the lit kitchen and sat down to his already-prepared breakfast. It was baffling to him how Rosa knew his schedule even before he did.

She welcomed him with her usual smile. "Off to Cay Sal, today?" She turned and leaned her back against the sink.

"A much-needed oasis." Jack took a bite of his breakfast like a starving teenager.

Rosa smiled at his hearty appetite. It warmed her heart to see him in such high spirits. She mouthed a silent prayer, thanking God, and turned back to Jack. "Well, enjoy your day."

Seeing him like this calmed her fears. She finished washing the pans and utensils, leaving them to air dry. She then dried her hands and sat down to breakfast, pausing to say a silent blessing over her own food.

"I will." Jack hesitated. "Wait, what did you say?" He almost spit scrambled egg as he stumbled over his words.

"I said 'enjoy your day.' Oh, and there's a cooler of water and one of food by the door. Do you expect to be home for dinner?"

He looked up at her as she sat calm and collected across him. Isn't this where she warned him to be careful? Should he question her or just go with it? With women, he never knew. He decided to embrace her positive nature.

"I'll plan on being home for dinner, if you will take most of the day off and have some fun. It has been a busy weekend, and we both deserve a little vacation."

He knew she would make sure all her work was finished before allowing herself some personal time, but he hoped she would heed his advice.

"Sounds like a deal. I'll see you tonight." Rosa flashed him a smile as he placed his plate in the sink, loaded his arms with the coolers, and headed for the door.

As he was storing his supplies on the boat, he noticed a bright light shining through the little window of the tree house. He wasn't sure whether he should investigate further, but his curiosity got the better of him. He walked to the tree and climbed the ladder, preparing to knock on the child-size door when he heard a phone ringing.

He put his ear against the door and listened. There was a series of four rings and then a recording. "You have reached a number that has been disconnected or is no longer in service. If you feel you have reached this recording in error, please check the number and try again." There was a pause, more ringing, then, "If you'd like to make a call, please hang up, and try again. If you need help, please hang up, and call the operator." Then silence. He wasn't sure, but he thought he heard a sob. He held his breath and strained his ears.

He heard rattled breathing followed by a raspy whispering voice. "Where are you, Mom? Where are you, Dad? Has something happened to you? Why don't you call me? It has been two months! I can't believe you would call Aunt Cindy and not JJ or me. She has to be lying! You have my cell phone number. Why not call me? It costs the same." Paul took a deep breath, and through his sobs, he continued, "Where are you? Why don't you answer your emergency number?" Then more ringing.

"If you'd like to make a call, please hang up, and try again. If you need help—" Followed by more silence, except for the occasional sob. Then more ringing.

"You have reached a number that has been disconnected or is no longer in service—" Then silence followed by a low-battery beeping sound.

Jack took a deep breath, backed down the ladder, and headed to his boat. Paul must not know that he had heard this vulnerable moment. A young man's future is often carved out of the shavings of his boyhood.

It was a calm serene morning as Jack headed out to sea. This was his favorite time of the day, both for the beauty and his personal time with his beloved Maria. The sun was preparing to rise, and the color reflecting off the water normally gave his soul peace, but today his mind was lost in the voices he had just heard from the tree house. He knew his neighbors had been gone for quite some time, but he didn't know that they had abandoned their boys.

"No wonder those two always seem to have a chip on their shoulder. I'm not sure what to make out of this, Maria," he voiced his concerns to his deceased wife as he made his way through the choppy waters.

"Maria, what is going on with our neighbors? Do you think they're okay? What kind of parents go halfway around the world and then don't communicate with their children? And why would their aunt lie to them about their parents? I know she can be odd at times, but what she's doing is downright cruel."

Jack was quiet for a minute as he tried to find a solution.

"Maria, do you remember anything about this job that Charles took? I have to admit I am at a loss. Listening to a young man Paul's age crying over his parents' absence is almost too much. Part of me wanted to open the door and hug him, and the other part wanted to let him grieve in peace." He paused, thinking about his actions. "I guess the later won." He wiped at the tears forming in his eyes.

"Was I wrong to walk away, Maria? Do you think there is anything I can do to help?"

He looked up at the dramatic colors forming a picturesque sunrise on the horizon. He felt energy from such a lovely formation—proof to him of God's presence. He would not give in to despair. Perhaps it was time for him to trust in God again.

Jack stalled his boat and knelt. "Please help me, God. If there is anything I can do to help Paul, please, God, show me the way. In Jesus's name. Amen." He felt peace come over him. He basked in the sensation for a few minutes then started the boat and moved on. He had his answer. God was with him; he would let him lead.

Jack set his course for the Bahamian island of Cay Sal. His mind stayed busy trying to solve the three mysteries that had recently landed in his lap. First, there was the abandoned life raft. This was most likely from a yacht damaged during the storm, but the question was, what happened to the boat and its occupant? He understood that this may never be solved, but this life raft brought with it the second mystery—the origin of the money.

Could someone or some company really lose a million dollars and not care what happened to it? There could be danger down the road with such a boon. Then there was the mystery of Paul's parents. Jack had lost his parents recently, and he would love to spare the neighbor boys from that kind of pain at such a young age. He didn't know how he could help but starting today he would make sure he was kinder to those boys.

As he approached Cay Sal, he went to the lighthouse first. The supply bag was untouched. He refreshed the water and headed to the big island of the chain. Anchoring out, he swam to shore, dragging his cooler of food. He checked his burial spot and found the money from the life raft undisturbed. He reburied it and laid out his lunch.

He enjoyed his picnic sitting beside Maria's memorial marker. She was always with him here. Here, he could step out of his reality even if only for a short time. He could never explain this part of his life to those around him. They just wouldn't understand.

He had just polished off his last morsel and had concluded his diatribe of his weekly events to Maria when he thought he heard a faint groan. He stood up and looked around, squinting against the sun's brilliance, but nothing materialized. He was confused. What had he heard? He pulled out his binoculars, doing a full circle sweep of the area. Off in the distance, he could see what looked like a reflection coming from a mirror. He blinked his eyes and silenced his breathing, straining his ears for clarification. Another muted noise reached him. He loaded his lunch cooler and swam back to the boat. The mirror had vanished from view. He maneuvered through the choppy waves to his calculation of its last known position. He trolled the waters for upward of an hour. It was not an easy cipher.

Jack was just about to give up when he spotted a fragmented compilation of boards. He maneuvered closer. There was a raft of sorts. Lying there was a half-naked man dyed red from the sun's rays. He anchored, took a life preserver, and attached it to a rope. Hooking it to the boat's transom, he swam to the raft. Checking the body for signs of life, he felt signs of a pulse. It was faint. He checked for breathing. He was alive.

It took some effort, but Jack was able to swim to his vessel and draw the raft close enough to transfer the battered body from the dilapidated craft to his boat. It took all the energy he could muster and the little he could attain from his charge to accomplish this feat. Jack laid him down in the cabin and administered droplets of water. With much coaxing and patience, the young man finally accepted small sips from a water bottle. When Jack felt he had done all he could for this stranger, he unhooked the raft and headed for home. His ward needed more help than he could give. It was time to take him to Rosa.

It was evening when they arrived back at the dock. Jack wasn't sure how he would manage to get this young man into his home, but as he parked, he was shocked to see his neighbor Paul Choate pass by on a Jet Ski. Jack flagged him down and asked him for help.

"Paul, do you think you can park your Jet Ski and help me for a minute?"

Paul looked like he was struggling between saying a smart remark and his curiosity for what his neighbor wanted. Since finding the Velcro bag at the dock, they questioned how much Jack may or may not know about the money. Perhaps he could find out. He parked the Jet Ski on the end of the dock and walked over to the boat.

"What can I do?"

"Thanks, Paul." Jack used a soft tone, trying to show a friendlier attitude. "My friend is hurt, and I could use your help getting him into the house."

Paul took one look at the sunburned body lying in the cabin of Jack's boat and asked, "What happened to him? He looks almost burned to a crisp."

"He had boat trouble and has been floating out in the ocean. Could you take that side?"

They worked together and walked him across the yard and into Jack's home. Rosa saw them coming and met them at the door, directing them to the guest room. They carefully placed him on the bed, and Paul removed himself from the cramped quarters. Jack briefly explained what he knew of the young man's situation and left him in Rosa's care.

Paul was standing with his back to the picture window looking at the wall hangings displayed around the room.

"Is he going to be okay?" he asked as Jack walked in.

"I think so. If anyone can pull him through, it would be Rosa. She is a miracle worker in her own right. She's certainly done wonders for me."

Jack glanced back at the closed door to the bedroom. Paul turned around and stared out the big window, catching the view of his backyard and Jack's boat dock.

"I remember this room. When I was little, my babysitter used to live here. She was great. I remember finger painting over there." Paul pointed to the kitchen table. "JJ and I would watch TV over there." He gestured to the left side of the living room. He turned back to the picture window in deep thought. "And I remember playing on the tire swing that used to hang from our tree before my dad—" He sniffed, and his hand went up to his eye. "Before my dad built the tree house." He forced a smile on his lips as he pointed to the small section of the big tree he could see from the picture window. "Back then, I think I spent more time here than I did at home." He paused for a minute. His eyes moved to Jack's reflection in the big window. "You know, Mr. Winters, it doesn't matter how much we want life to stay the same. Time keeps moving forward."

Jack turned his full attention to the troubled young man standing in his living room. "Well, Paul, you're right about one thing—this is a good house filled with wonderful memories. And this room probably hasn't changed much. My parents weren't much for change, and though my Maria was in the process of redecorating, she passed before we got much done, and I haven't had the heart to change a thing."

Paul looked at the man whose eyes were taking in every inch of his surroundings. It wasn't hard to feel sympathy for his neighbor, realizing just how much loss he had experienced in the last several years. He wondered how Jack managed not to give up on life. He turned his gaze back to the window and saw in the reflection of the glass that Jack was watching him.

"Well, I guess I better get the Jet Ski back to the marina before I'm charged for another day." He turned and headed for the door, hesitated, then turned back. "Let me know if you need any more help." Jack nodded, and he was gone.

He watched Paul exit his home and wondered how he could help this young man. He thought for a moment that he was going to open up and confide in him, then again, why would he? Their relationship, thus far, had consisted of waves and yells. Perhaps he would take Paul up on his offer of assistance, even if he had to invent uses for his services. It was time for him to really get to know the young Choate.

He headed to the dock and unloaded *Maria*. Tidying up the cabin, he stored all evidence of the life raft and his new guest under the bench seat. He wished he knew where this young man had come from and if he was connected to the GPS units or the million dollars. His answer would have to wait. He felt the stickiness of the sand and saltwater clinging to his skin. It was time for a shower. By the time he reentered his home, Rosa had his dinner waiting for him on the table, but she was obviously tending to her patient. He quickly washed up, ate, and headed for the shower.

It didn't take long for his housekeeper to have their guest sipping soup from her spoon. She had assessed his burns and had placed salve and bandages on his most damaged sores. He was responding well to her care.

"How's our patient?" Jack commented as he walked into the guest room.

In Spanish, Rosa asked the young man to lie down and rest. She gently nudged Jack toward the door and out into the living room.

"Can you tell me again where you found this young Cuban man?" She was studying his face as she continued, "You do realize it's a felony to bring undocumented aliens into this country."

"Rosa, I didn't have a choice, he was dying—I had to help him." He hurried on before she could respond. "Once he is feeling better, we'll just have to figure something out. Besides, I promised Maria I would help her countryman, and this young man is the first one I have been able to help cross the waters. Do you know how good it feels to finally keep that promise?"

"I understand what you are saying, Jack, and I rejoice that you feel drawn to this noble cause, whether for a promise or just good will, but if you are put in jail, you can't help anyone. We need to keep his presence here a secret, and since the neighbor boy knows about him, that will be almost impossible. Our only hope is for him to heal enough to travel. Then perhaps you can take him someplace close enough to shore where he can arrive by himself and officially take part in the 'wet foot, dry foot' policy." She paused as they both stared across the room, thinking.

"I hope you brought his raft with you. He will need some form of dilapidated vessel if we are to make his journey believable."

Jack thought about that for a minute. He realized he didn't think this through. After he just saved his life, he didn't want this young man to have to go back to Cuba.

"Listen, Rosa, you get him well enough to travel and explain to him what we are doing, and I'll figure out the rest of the logistics. The last thing I want to do is send him to his death or Cuban prison for trying to escape tyranny. I don't think that Paul is questioning his nationality, but I will stop any rumors that may go that way. It'll be okay. When do you think he will be able to travel?"

"Well, he is eating some, so if he has a good night, he may be able to go as early as tomorrow afternoon." She glanced at the bedroom door and forced her words to have strength.

Jack moved toward the door as he spoke. "If that's the case, I'll head to the garage right now and build our guest a broken-down raft. I knew that keeping all those rusty nails and weathered boards would come in handy one day." He laughed as he exited through the back door and headed for the garage.

Jack heard his neighbor's Mustang pull up in front of their house as he turned on the light. He figured it was Paul coming back from returning the Jet Ski. This put his mind back on the tree house and the private moment he had interrupted that morning.

He was deep in thought when he heard a voice from behind him. "How's your friend? I hope he's going to be okay."

Jack turned to see Paul standing in the doorway. "He's doing much better, he plans on going home tomorrow."

"That's good to hear. When I first saw him, I thought he was dead."

Jack turned toward Paul with his hammer in one hand. "I know what you mean, I had the same thought. By the way, thanks for your help."

"To tell you the truth, I wasn't going to at first, but I felt I should make up for the way JJ and I treated you Friday at the tree house. We were pretty rude." Paul looked like a little boy confessing to his father for breaking the neighbor's window.

Jack almost laughed but caught himself and changed it to a simple smile. "All is forgiven and forgotten."

Paul smiled and watched Jack reach for a board. "So what are you working on this late at night?"

"Just a project to clear my mind. I find peace in working with my hands." He reached for another board and laid them side by side on the workbench. There was a can of rusty nails sitting there next to his project, and he took a couple in his hand. "I guess you made it back to the marina in time to return the Jet Ski?"

"Yah, it was closed when I got there, but Tanner was waiting for me. He checked me in." Jack just shook his head.

The boys in this neighborhood had the run of the place, but Tanner was the one with the real power with his mom's keys that he "borrowed" often. He mostly kept them out of trouble. However, the community didn't get too upset when the boys helped themselves unless damage was done.

Paul walked over to the workbench to observe what his neighbor was doing. "Why are you using rusty nails? You have a bottle of new ones right over there."

Jack thought for a minute. "This is just a prototype, so I don't want to waste the good nails until I am ready to build the real thing."

"That makes sense, so what are you building?" This question was the one that Jack didn't want to answer, but he didn't want to push Paul away either.

"Well, I'll tell yah. I'm testing raft theories. I'm wondering how dilapidated a raft can be and still float? I figured I would put a quick one together tonight and test it in the morning." He took a deep breath and was thrilled that the truth actually worked in his favor.

"Sounds like fun. Can I test it in the morning for you?"

"I don't see why not. Why don't you bring those old boards over here, and you can help me build it."

Paul walked over, loaded his arms with boards, and carried them across the room.

"Place half of them on that work bench over there, and the other half, give to me. Then grab a hammer from the toolbox behind you, and let's build this thing."

They worked for about half an hour when Paul turned around and looked at Jack for a minute then asked, "Mr. Winters, do you know how to check an international phone line to see who it belongs to?"

"Why, did you get some exotic beauty to give you her number and you forgot her name?"

Paul smiled. "I wish, but no. I can't seem to reach my parents. They are working overseas, and the phone number they gave me is disconnected. Plus, the other number they gave me for emergencies says it's out of service. What do you think that means?"

Jack was hoping he could help this young man, but now that he had asked, he didn't know how he could. He didn't have any connections overseas or knew anyone who did. All he could do was to listen and try to decipher some clues from Paul's information.

"How long has it been since their phone numbers worked?"

"I didn't start trying to call until I hadn't heard from them for over a month, so all I can say is their phone numbers haven't worked for about a month. Before that, it's anyone's guess."

"When was the last time you heard your mom's or dad's voice on the phone?" Jack was careful how he asked this question. He wanted to skip the stuff about the aunt. He heard a sniff, but he wasn't trying to be cruel, he was trying to help.

"I think it was the Fourth of July. Mom was so excited because they were talking about being home the end of August before school started. They had arranged to be home for my senior year in high school. That was the last time I heard her voice. Aunt Cindy keeps saying that Mom calls her every week, and they are getting closer to coming home every day. But if that were true, why would they call and talk to her and not JJ and me? And why don't the phone numbers my mom gave me work?"

Jack could hear the tender catch in Paul's voice as he spoke. He knew this wasn't easy for this seventeen-year-old young man to expose his feelings to a neighbor he didn't really know. It was good that his back was to him, allowing Paul a safe barrier for his openness.

He had misjudged Charles and Sara Choate. It seems they were missing their boys and were trying to arrange their lives to be home for this very important year for their son. But what had happened to change their mind or perhaps their plans? Why had they stopped communicating, and why were their phone numbers not working? Death was the word that came to his mind, but he couldn't even think to go there. For Paul's sake, there had to be a different reason, and he wanted to help him find the answer. He stopped hammering and turned around. This pretense between them needed to be breached. This young man was feeling helpless, and he would do what he could to help.

"If it was that important for your mom to be home for your senior year, you have to know she is doing everything she can to get here. As far as the phone numbers go, why don't you give them to me, and I will see what I can find out. What can you tell me about your parents' business overseas?" Jack didn't know the first thing about who to ask, but he figured he would start with the FBI.

"The last postmark on my mom's letters came from Djibouti, Africa, but that was over two months ago."

"Wow!" Jack turned and looked at Paul. "What are they doing in Africa? I mean, it's not top secret or something, right?"

"I don't know. I heard my dad on the phone once talking about shipping something, but my parents don't tell us much about their work."

"Djibouti, Africa, does have a major shipping port. I bet they have some interesting stories. I'm going to have to get to know them better when they get back." Jack turned back to his project.

"I don't know anything about Djibouti. I liked it when they were working in Miami, at the seaport. At least then, they only took an occasional trip, and that wasn't more than a week at a time." Paul turned back to his project, feeling comfortable with this new dynamic with his neighbor.

"When they left, I thought it would be great. I mean, what teenager doesn't want their parents to move halfway around the world? I thought it would be fun making my own decisions and doing what I wanted. I didn't realize how much I would miss them. What I wouldn't give to hear them yell at me for doing something that I knew was wrong or lecturing me on being safe. Mom would always try to act so mad, but I could always tell that she wanted to either laugh at me or cry because I wasn't going to be around much longer for her to worry about. My mom is a lot stricter than Aunt Cindy, but for some reason, that doesn't seem to matter anymore." Paul took a deep breath. "I just want my parents to come home. Mr. Winters, do you think something has happened to them?"

Jack made a motion to wipe his brow as he brushed a tear from his eye. He had already envisioned the worst and knew the pain that came from grief. He didn't want this young man to feel that kind of pain unless it was actually warranted. He had to keep him focused on hope and stay positive.

"First of all, why don't you call me Jack? Everyone I know does. And second, I don't know why your parents have quit communicating, but giving up is premature. Why don't you keep trying those numbers and let me see what I can find out about them this week. In the meantime, I suggest we use the advice of my sweet *Maria* and turn to God for help. Are you a praying man, Paul?"

Paul looked over at Jack. "I have to admit the only praying I have ever done was around the table during Christmas and Easter dinner. I always felt God had more important things to do than listen to a complainer like me."

Paul lowered his head and hammered in a nail, which bent over on the first strike, and it took him more than a few hits to drive it through the wood. Hammering was therapeutic.

Jack sat his hammer down and turned to watch Paul. God and religion were always tricky topics. Some people were close to God, attending church regularly and trusting that everything had a purpose and all would work out with God's help. They would thank God for everything, blessings and trials, and often talked about keeping a prayer in their hearts. His Maria was like that.

Then there were others who went to church a couple of times a year, Christmas and Easter. The rest of the time, they figured things out on their own, only praying to God in times of despair and tragedy—this was him before he met Maria. The third group, he put in the atheists' category—the nonbelievers. These always bothered him. It wasn't that they didn't have beliefs, but they seemed to put their faith in man or materials or science. He had seen enough miracles in his life to know that there was a God. How much this God took an interest in his life, he wasn't sure. He had even yelled at him for taking his parents and Maria away, but he had come to believe, as Maria did, that things did happen for a reason; and if he needed to be a better person on earth to be with his Maria in heaven, he would. Right now, he felt strongly that he needed to help Paul believe, if for no other reason than to give him hope of a higher purpose and a watchful caretaker.

"Paul, I don't know if you knew my Maria, but you would have liked her." Jack wiped another tear from his eye. "She was such a good person with the deepest faith I have ever seen. The funny part was that her life was full of tragedy and loss, but she understood that God was real, and he touched every aspect of her life. She taught me to believe, and when I lost her, I knew it was because she was ready to meet her God. I know he has prepared a place for a beautiful soul like hers. However, what I learned from her, more than anything, was that God sees all and knows all, and when we go to him in our prayers, we are his children asking for help from a loving parent. If anyone can help solve your parents' mystery, it will be God, and the way to get help from him is to pray. Now that's all I have to say on the subject." He turned back to his makeshift raft and continued hammering.

Paul, deep in thought, stared at Jack's back for a moment. Perhaps God was whom he needed to talk to right now. Keeping his pain and worry inside was tearing him apart. He wasn't sure why he had trusted his personal feelings to Jack, but he did feel better. He turned back to his hammering and picked up his finished portion of the raft. He carried it over to Jack, and they combined their halves and stepped back to observe their finished product.

"Well, it seems structurally sound. Not sure I would want to trust it on a long journey, but I have to admit we did good." Jack slapped Paul on the back.

"It's done, right? It looks horrible but interesting. I'm not sure there's enough there to hold me out of the water." Paul placed it on the floor and sat on it. "I guess it'll work. Do you think it'll float?"

"We'll find out in the morning. Meet me at the dock around six?" Jack laid the raft on the work bench and followed Paul to the door.

"Six o'clock? I don't leave for school until eight." He looked at Jack's big smile. "Okay, I guess I can pry myself out of bed that early."

Jack had to admit he enjoyed watching this teenager complain about getting out of bed early in the morning. A pain crossed his heart as he thought about the child Maria was carrying when she died—his child. Had he lost his chance to be a father?

Paul turned to walk away then turned back. "Jack, thanks for listening to me tonight."

"Listen, Paul, one thing I have learned is that we are not alone unless we choose to be. You can talk to me anytime. I'm not sure how much help I'll be, but I will listen. Get me those phone numbers, and I'll see what I can do."

Jack walked into his still house after he locked up the garage. He peeked into the guest bedroom and found Rosa holding the hand of their guest and singing quietly to him in Spanish. The young Cuban's chest seemed to rise and fall in the slow rhythmic pattern of someone who was at peace and sleeping soundly. He smiled at the pair and headed off to bed.

20

Social Work – Key Largo

The sun's rays peeked through the partially-drawn curtain as Sierra pulled herself out of bed and headed for the shower. She didn't remember the last time she had felt so rested, and sleeping-in was a luxury she missed. Although she was one who rode the anxiety of a situation, not allowing herself to crash till the end, yesterday had given her enough to quiet her mind and allow her body to slumber. She had physically seen Julio alive on that video, and she was hanging on to that reality. Still, the questions lingered. She could see his face, standing there on the boat, helpless and scared. Time was not her friend. It had been over forty-eight hours since the sighting on the fuel pier. She couldn't dwell on the negative possibilities; she had to work the clues and follow the trail—even if he was dead. That thought heightened her trepidation. She pushed it away. She refused to grieve the unknown.

There were many hidden truths when it came to investigations, but the pathways always amazed her. It was hard to believe that someone's story could contain so many twists and turns. How else could she explain the FBI money leaving on a boat in DC, heading for Saint Maartens, ending up so off course at a dive shop in Key Largo, Florida?

It was the unknown of the storm that she was using to fill in the missing pieces to her puzzle. Was it possible for the boat to have been blown off course and land in Key Largo? If so, was Julio still alive? Or was it Max? She couldn't rule any of these possibilities out. She needed more information. Her only lead was the money. She could visit the dive shop and sub shop, hoping someone remembered who may have paid for their wares with $100 bills, but beyond that, her hands were tied until the bank opened on Monday. Of course, the money could have been spent in singles or a lump sum. It may have its own web to unravel. She feared her work was just getting started. It was time to head South.

It didn't take her long to dress and head downstairs for the hotel's continental breakfast. The room was bustling with children being corralled by their parents. She hoped one day to be one of those parents, but for now, her life didn't have room for a family. She filled her plate with scrambled eggs and a bagel, and she grabbed a yogurt and headed back to the quiet of her room.

She needed to compile her notes and organize her thoughts. She knew that Jason met with Julio the night he was killed from his phone call asking her out; perhaps she should have accepted. This thought made her miss him. She bit her lip to stop any tears before they formed and continued going through her notes. She knew Julio was on the boat headed for Saint Maartens—the video confirmed he was still alive when they docked for fuel. She also knew that the FBI money had been flagged in Key Largo. That took care of most of her information, except there was the little matter of a mole inside the FBI. This would limit any sharing of information with colleagues and possible backup. She was alone.

It didn't take her long to pack her things into her rental car. She was grateful that Florida rental companies had installed SunPass units so she could drive through the express lanes on the turnpike. She made good time and within an hour was driving the eighteen-mile stretch between Florida City and Key Largo. This was her first time in the Keys, and though she had heard about the drive, it shocked her that it was a highway between two bodies of water, the ocean on one side and the everglades on the other. It was beautiful. The drive seemed slow and cumbersome, filled with bumper-to-bumper traffic. She mused how one accident could shut it down for hours and hoped she would be spared that ordeal. Seeing the old draw bridge ahead was a symbol that she had finally arrived in Key Largo.

She typed "Diving the Keys" into her GPS and followed the directions. It was a quaint little store in the midst of Downtown Key Largo with a combined sandwich and arcade shop next door called The Sub-Base. This was the place.

As she entered, she was surprised to see it bustling with activity. There were many customers booking excursions and browsing through the aisles.

Sierra walked around and observed the workers. There was an older gentleman behind the counter whom she assumed was the owner or manager, a younger man running one of the cash registers whom could have been the elder's son, and a young girl who was waiting on customers and going in and out of the back room.

Sierra walked up to the register and joined the line of patrons waiting for service. When she approached the elder gentleman, she introduced herself as a private detective working on a case. He introduced himself as Nick Summers, owner of the dive shop. He seemed to freely share information but didn't remember anyone acting unusual or spending seven $100 bills in one purchase the day after the storm. He informed her that most of his business was billed through credit cards. However, there was an influx of customers that day, and he did remember there was quite a bit of cash in the deposit. He suggested she talk to his employees, and then he motioned to the next person in line. She didn't fault him his abruptness, they were busy, and she wasn't a paying customer. She stepped aside and turned her attention to the young girl exiting the backroom, walking in her direction. She had just handed a dive suit to a young man and motioned him toward the changing rooms.

The young girl approached Sierra. "Welcome to Diving the Keys. My name is Portia. Can I help you?"

"I hope so. My name is Sierra. The owner Nick said I could ask you some questions about some purchases that were made last Friday. Were you working that day?" Sierra observed the reaction of this young girl.

She seemed pleasant to the clientele yet seemed to show annoyance at her job.

Portia took a deep breath and answered, "Nick, he's my uncle, and I live close by, so when the storm hit and all the excursions were canceled, they called me in to help. It was crazy in here with all the angry people. Did you know that people act stupid when they're angry? Or maybe they were always stupid. I don't know, but it was pretty crazy. I was ready to quit, but then my boyfriend came in. He always knows how to make me smile." She blushed. Sierra smiled at the girl.

"Boyfriends are good for that. However, I was wondering if you remembered any large transactions that day, say around $700?"

Portia seemed to think for a minute. "There were several excursions that cost that much and more. Nick schedules those, but we were refunding more than we were booking that day. As for me, I sold fins and snorkels mainly. Those are usually under a hundred, but I did sell some diving equipment to my boyfriend and his brother. That was just over $600."

Sierra's interest piqued. "Did these friends of yours pay with hundred-dollar bills?"

Portia's eyes shifted to the far wall. "Let's see." She turned back. "I remember they bought dive suits. Paul looked so cute in the silver one. He wanted a blue one, and I told him I like the silver one better, so he bought the silver one. I laughed so hard after they left. Boys are so easy, but don't tell them I told you that. Anyway, they also bought fins and snorkels and said they were coming back in a few days for dive computers. Yes, they paid with hundred-dollar bills. Paul says his part-time job pays him in cash."

"Where is this part-time job?"

"I think he does odd jobs for his neighbor. He's the manager at the marina where they live. He also gets money from his aunt. She's in charge while their parents are overseas. I can ask him who gave him the money at school tomorrow, if you like." She glanced around the room. "I need to get back to work, my uncle is starting to give me that look, unless you want to buy something."

"No, but thanks for the help, Portia. You don't need to worry about the money. If I need more information, I can ask Paul myself." Portia smiled and headed for the changing rooms where the boy she handed the dive suit was exiting.

"Portia, may I ask you one more question?" Sierra was instep behind her.

"If you hurry, as much as I hate this job, I do like my paychecks."

"I'll be quick. Can you give me Paul's last name?"

Portia stopped and turned around. "Is Paul in some kind of trouble? He has been so sad lately. I think it has something to do with his parents. Is that what this is about? Are they okay?"

Sierra didn't know anything about Paul's parents, and she was raising too much suspicion. "I'm afraid I don't know anything about his parents. I'm just following up on some paperwork. Don't worry, I'm sure everything's fine."

Portia stared at Sierra for a few moments, trying to decide what to do. She took a deep breath and supplied. "Choate, their last name is Choate, C-H-O-A-T-E." With that, she turned on her heels and walked away.

Sierra watched her saunter off to help another customer. She couldn't believe what she had just heard. Her culprits could be two local teenage boys. Was she on the right track? Could these boys be helping Julio? If so, their lives could be in danger. She took one last look around the shop and headed for the door.

When Sierra exited, she walked over to The Sub-Base, the sandwich shop next door. She entered the small structure, looked around, and headed for the counter. Behind the register, were two teenage boys laughing and mocking each other as they talked. She observed their interaction while waiting for their attention. One of the young men turned, saw her, and smiled.

"What can I get yaw?" he asked.

The smell of fresh bread made her stomach growl. It had only been three hours since breakfast, but she ordered anyway. "How about a turkey club and a bottle of Diet Coke?"

He relayed her order and took her money. She glanced at his name tag.

"KC, I was wondering if you could help me. Can I ask you a question about this sub shop?" She smiled, and he blushed.

"Sure, what do you want to know?"

"Were you working the day after the storm?"

"I'm here every day. My dad owns the place, so I pretty much work when he's here and when he's not."

She ignored his complaint. "Were you busy that day?" She smiled at him to regain his attention.

"The day after the storm? You bet. It was wall-to-wall people in here. Whenever the beaches are closed and the dive shop cancels excursions, this place is packed."

"Sounds like good business for you."

"Dad likes it."

"Did you have many big spenders that day? You know, paying with hundred-dollar bills?"

"You would think so, but usually, we deal with small bills. However, we did have a few hundreds come in that day. I was working the register, and there was a family of five kids and two parents that ordered sandwiches and tokens. It came to over $200, and I remember he gave me two $100 bills and change."

"Was that the only ones that paid with hundreds that day?" Sierra was pushing for some kind of connection she could use.

"Well, there was Paul and JJ Choate. They came in around five and bought food and drinks. Paul paid with a hundred-dollar bill. I remember thinking it was overkill for $30 worth of food. Most of the guys we get in here pay with tens or twenties, but the Choates are kind of different. Yaw never know with them."

"So do these Choate boys often pay with hundred-dollar bills?"

KC thought for a minute. "No, they usually pay with twenties. That must be why it stood out."

"KC, quit hit'n on her. Her sandwich is up!" Brian yelled from the kitchen.

KC handed Sierra her sandwich and Coke and thanked her then turned toward the kitchen to deal with Brian.

Sierra found a quiet table in the corner and watched the boys goofing with each other. So the Choate boys were in both places and paid with hundred-dollar bills in each. It sounded like she needed to find these boys. She took out her notepad and wrote down what she had learned. *Paul and JJ Choate, high school students, parents were currently out of the country, possibly on business, spent eight $100 bills in two shops the day after a major storm hit the area, have an aunt who is their guardian.* It also sounded like the two were free spirits and perhaps a little wild, at least from KC's perspective, though she sensed some jealousy in his assumptions.

Sierra pondered on her information as she ate. How could FBI money on a boat bound for Saint Maartens wind up in the hands of teenagers in Key Largo? She had seen the route on a map, and for the boat to stop here, it would be way off course. Could a storm really push a boat this far West against the current? If so, where were Max and Julio? If they are here, why are teenagers spending the money and not them? Could the boys be hiding one or both of them? She needed answers, and the Choate brothers were her only lead—she had to find them. If the boat is here, Perrone won't be far behind. If these boys are mixed up in this, their lives are in danger.

She finished her sandwich, threw her trash away, and walked back up to the counter. KC saw her immediately and hurried toward her.

"Still hungry?"

"No, but my sandwich was very good, thank you."

"You're welcome." It was Brian from the kitchen. She turned a smile his way.

She turned back to KC. "I was wondering, could you tell me how to find Paul and JJ Choate?"

He dropped his smile. "Why do you need them?"

"I work for the bank, and we are following up on some questionable activity after the storm. It's kind of hush-hush, but I'm sure you'll keep it under wraps for me, right?" Sierra whispered, putting on a serious look.

He leaned forward and whispered back, "Are they in trouble?"

"Not officially."

"Oh okay." He looked downhearted. "Well, they live over in the Palm Shores Subdivision, but I don't know where. They will be at school tomorrow though. Believe it or not, it's easier to talk to them at school than to get into their housing area. You have to be on a list." She could tell this was a sore spot with him. There was an obvious history between these boys. She smiled, thanked him for his help, and left the shop.

For the next few hours, she drove around the area checking out public marinas for any unusual activity. Her search came up empty. Although there were damaged crafts from the storm, none of them fit the description of Perrone's yacht.

She drove by the Palm Shores Subdivision, even asked for admittance, but KC was right, she needed to be on a list to gain access. She wasn't ready to use her status as an FBI agent and alerting the Choate family of her presence this early in the game, could do more harm than good. She located the bank and the local high school, which was twenty minutes from the housing area. She was out of things she could do on a Sunday.

She turned her focus to Monday morning, trying to put together a plan that could keep her identity under wraps but still get the information she needed. The bank would be easy. She could show them her ID and get possession of the bills. If Terry kept his word and kept her mission secret. The high school, on the other hand, would be tricky. She would need access to the brothers in order to interview them. She needed a cover story.

Sierra drove back to town and found a local motel, checked in, and ordered a pizza. She called a real estate company, asking to see any apartments for rent in the Palm Shores Subdivision, making an appointment to meet Carol at a duplex the next afternoon, using the name Sierra Skinner, activating one of her aliases. This allowed her to complete her background check and rental application online. Carol assured her this would expedite the process, permitting her to move in immediately.

Tomorrow she would need a way to get into the school to talk to the Choate boys. Since Portia and KC knew what she looked like and knew she was asking about them, she needed a disguise. Sierra opened her suitcase, and after inventorying her options, she decided to run to the local pharmacy for supplies. She needed hair dye, eye makeup, and bold earrings. She also picked up tanning cream and sandals.

Morning started at six o'clock. She showered, dyed her hair, applied her tanning cream, and dressed to fit her new role. She decided to meet the principal as a social worker checking up on the Choate boys. Her goal was to look overworked but presentable. She chose her least tidy business attire, leaving off the jacket, and added fake glasses. She completed her outfit with casual shoes. Her eye makeup and earrings would be added later. She looked in the mirror and was quite pleased with her finished appearance. Now, to complete her facade, she sat down at the desk in her room and put together a file folder marked Paul and JJ Choate.

There was a knock at the door. She looked through the peep hole to see a courier. She opened the door and signed for her package. Her new identification had arrived, and she was ready. Her first stop was the bank to get possession of the marked bills. For this, she needed to present the list of serial numbers Terry had left on her voice mail and her ID. Her next stop would be Monroe County family services in Marathon Key, a forty-five-minute drive. Here, she needed to establish her identity for verification purposes.

From there, she would back track to Coral Shores High School, hoping to get an audience with Paul and JJ. Depending on how long that took, she planned to visit a few more marinas, eat lunch, and check out of her room before she headed to the Palm Shores Subdivision to meet the realtor Carol who had lined up a duplex for her to see.

Sierra removed her glasses and stored them in her purse. She tied her hair back and added her blazer for a more professional appearance. As she entered the bank, she saw a few tellers and a gentleman sitting in a glass-enclosed office. The atmosphere was quiet and still. She hesitated briefly and noticed all eyes had turned in her direction. She smiled and sauntered toward the office labeled Jose Santana - Bank Manager. The gentleman inside saw her approach and met her at the door. "May I help you?"

Sierra displayed her FBI badge and ID. "Mr. Santana, my name is Special Agent Cortez, and I believe you have some money for me to pick up." Sierra handed him the list of serial numbers.

He offered her a seat. "Please excuse me for a moment. I'll be right back."

It was all too easy. He brought her forms to sign and handed over the bills. Of course, she had to replace them. That was $800 she hoped to get back from the bureau when she filed her expense report. Sierra quickly finished her business and headed south to Marathon Key. She needed a legitimate family services business card she could duplicate for her new identity. She also wanted to establish her persona in case someone needed confirmation of her identity.

It was fall in Southern Florida, but the beautiful landscapes that framed her drive were timeless. It was morning and the temperature was already seventy degrees with a high forecasted to be ninety. She understood the draw to this oasis with its warm days and balmy nights surrounded by the soothing sound of the ocean. It was the tourists that seemed to bring the rapid heartbeat with their commotion spilling over the locals who seemed unconcerned about the interruption. If only she could live such a life, but her life was back in DC, where everything was boisterous and bold, many lives thrown together in chaos.

In Marathon, Sierra stopped at a gas station and applied heavy makeup, adorned her glasses, and put on her large hoop earrings. She was ready. Pulling up in front of the office, she grabbed her file folders, checked her appearance one more time, and stepped into the office. To her surprise, what she found was an unmanned desk. She could hear voices emanating from the back, but no one was within eyesight. After taking a visual inventory of the reception area and finding no recording devices, she picked up a business card and went back to her car. There, she quickly scanned in the card, doctored it, and printed a half dozen personal business cards with the name Sierra Skinner. Within a few minutes, she walked back into the office and made enough noise to be noticed.

"Can I help you?" came a voice from the meeting room doorway.

Sierra stuck her hand out with her business card and quickly walked toward the voice.

"Hi, my name is Sierra Skinner." She handed over the card. "It looks like you are busy, but I just wanted to stop in and introduce myself. I am here from the Tallahassee office. However, I am actually in town on vacation. Of course, I don't think we actually get those." She smiled, and the other lady returned the gesture. "You see, one of my former families lives here now, and I was instructed to do a surprise inspection as a final follow up."

"You're from Tallahassee, and they want you to check on a family here? Why didn't they just call us and ask us to follow up with them?" She glanced down at the card. "Sierra, is it?"

"That's right. I'm sorry. I didn't catch your name." The family service worker looked at Sierra's face. "My name is Maura, Maura Fields. I am the manager of this office." Sierra leaned in and gave Maura the double-cheek kiss, a customary Latin greeting. They both smiled.

"Nice to meet you, Maura. I have to admit that follow-up was my idea since I was going to be here anyway. I asked my manager if that was okay. She said I needed to notify you of my presence but that it was my choice to do it myself or hand it off to you. So since I have history with the family, I felt I would finalize this file and save us both some paperwork. Besides, this one touched my heart. You know, one of those that gets under your skin and touches your heart." Maura and all the women in the room behind her nodded. It was the curse of the case worker—caring too much.

"Well, Sierra, I hope you have a nice vacation, and I hope everything is okay. However, if you find an issue, you need to go through this office. Here's my card if you need anything." Maura put the Sierra card in her pocket and pulled out one of her own.

"I will certainly do that, and thanks." Sierra turned and made her way to the exit. She quietly slipped out as she heard the meeting room door close in the background. She sat in her car for a few minutes and caught her breath. She never knew if one of her made up personas would pass the muster. She hoped no one would call and question her identity, but if they did, she at least put a face with a name so it would be easier for anyone in the office to confirm that she was in the area.

The school was quiet as she made her way from the front door to the office. She hadn't been surprised by the obvious addition of the intercom and buzz-in procedure. Schools in America had to adapt to keep ahead of the increased violence. Parents were being pressed to work two and three jobs, keeping them away from their offspring to the detriment of their children. In their absence, their children have plugged into a violent virtual world often emboldening them to act out their curiosity and frustrations on their fellow students.

Kyra Spielman was in her office as Sierra walked up to the secretary's desk, introduced herself, and asked for an audience with the principal. After a brief phone call, she was shown into the inner office. Kyra met her halfway across the room and offered her hand in greeting. "Hi, I'm Kyra Spielman, the principal here at Coral Shores High School. What can I do for you today?"

Sierra handed her one of her Sierra Skinner cards and politely asked for a confidential conference. Kyra motioned her toward a chair, closed and locked her office door, pulled the blinds between the two offices, signaling that she would like some privacy, and returned to her desk.

"Sierra, is it?" She studied the card in her hand, raising her eyes for a response.

"Yes, ma'am." Sierra used the formal Southern response that she heard in many Southern states, and since Tallahassee was close to the Georgia border, she felt comfortable adding it to her new identity.

"I see you're from Tallahassee. Aren't you a ways out of your purview?" This question was expected from a professional educator, but she felt confident she left a deep-enough trail to pass the screening attempt.

"Well, it's kind of a long story, but the short version is that I am here to follow up on an old case that involves two of your students, a Paul and JJ Choate. My job is to evaluate the local office's procedures. Our process is to choose an old case and follow it from beginning to end to see if all measures were followed correctly. Then we interview the teenage or adult child involved with the case. I'm sorry to take up your time or the time of your students, but I promise it will only take a few minutes, and you can sit in on the interview, if you'd like. Normally, I would do these with the parents, but I understand that these boys' parents are currently out of the country on business." Sierra opened one of the mock folders she prepared to simulate verifying her information.

Kyra watched her for a moment and then picked up the phone to her outer office.

"You don't mind if I call the local office and check on your identity before I allow you access to someone else's children, do you?" She turned her attention to the phone and asked her secretary to connect her to the local children and family services office. Sierra just smiled.

The intercom buzzed, and the secretary's voice came over the line.

"Maura Field from children and family services on line one." Kyra picked up the phone. "Hello, this is Kyra Spielman, principal at Choral Shores High school. Am I speaking to Maura Field?" She smiled into the phone. "Thank you, Ms. Fields. I was wondering if you could verify a case worker from the state that's in my office asking to speak with a couple of my students. Yes, a Sierra Skinner, from Tallahassee . . . Okay, thanks . . . No, we can't be too careful . . . You too . . . Goodbye." She placed the phone back on its cradle and turned her attention back to Sierra.

"Just so we understand each other, I will allow you to speak to my students, but I want you to know that interrupting their schooling is highly frowned on. High school years can be fragile for our youth. It is important to keep their days as structured and uneventful as possible."

21

The Mole – DC

It was just after 5:00 a.m. as Director Smith sat at his desk with a stack of case files awaiting review. As was his routine, he had arrived two hours earlier than the rest of the staff to assess the progress reports from the previous week. Though often he was buried in paperwork early in the morning, he enjoyed the solitude the predawn hours offered him. His agents knew the unwritten rule that during this time, only emergencies would be allowed to permeate the director's door. But once his assistant walked off the elevator, the morning would officially begin.

He was halfway through the pile when he spotted a form marked CONFIDENTIAL from the desk of Special Agent Terry at the Treasury Department's Fund Monitoring Unit. It was a brief form detailing that the funds from Special Agent Kirtland's "Julio Torres" file was traced to a bank in Key Largo, Florida, and that Agent Sierra Cortez was en route to investigate and retrieve the funds.

He leaned back in his chair and stared at the form. He set it aside and looked through his pile of phone messages—nothing from Sierra. His mind went back to their last meeting and how upset she was about Agent Kirtland's death and the unknown whereabouts of Julio Torres. So Sierra wasn't going to sit on the sidelines after all. Should he be worried?

His cell phone beeped. He glanced down, hoping that it was her checking in. He read the coded message displayed on the screen. Of all people, why was Victor Ramos contacting him now? He glanced at the clock and sent back his coded reply and readied himself for the meet. He quickly scanned over the rest of the file folders in front of him, stacking them by priority for his return, hoping not to miss any pertinent information. Locking his door, he headed down the back stairs.

The lot was empty as he backed into a shaded parking stall. He figured they had about half an hour, tops, before the manager would show up to open the hardware store. He glanced around spotting the red Corvette heading in his direction. He knew it was Special Agent Ramos without even seeing the driver's face. He always liked to make an entrance, and a car like that just left a presence. Of course, that kind of attention is not what they needed right now. This spot was chosen because of the company's security system, but the way Ramos was coming, his car would be seen by the camera—he knew better.

Victor parked the Corvette and joined Director Smith in his car. Stiff pleasantries were briefly exchanged, moving into the meat of the conversation.

"What can I do for you, Victor?" The edge in his voice was clear.

Victor turned and looked into the director's eyes. "I think there is a way of bringing down Perrone, but I need to know if there has been any new information on Julio Torres?"

Director Smith blinked and looked out the front window, taking in the vastness of the parking area. He seemed to wrestle with himself. "I've already told you about the fuel pier. Now I need something from you."

He glanced over at Special Agent Ramos. "For all we know, he is dead out in the ocean somewhere. Has Perrone heard from him since Miami?"

Victor Ramos looked straight ahead, keeping his expression blank. Anyone seeing the pair would have guessed they were in a poker game to the death. He blinked and allowed his features to soften to lighten the mood. He needed information from an old friend, not an opponent. He pasted on a smile and answered, "He was receiving periodic calls, but they have stopped. We don't know if their communication has been damaged, if Captain Max has stolen the boat and or the money, or if he and Julio are on the bottom of the ocean. They were supposed to land in Saint Maartens sometime between Friday and Sunday. They didn't meet their rendezvous with the buyer. Perrone is pretty pissed, but he doesn't know where to look for answers. Have you heard anything about the boat or the money from any intelligence sources?"

The look on Victor's face was one of concern and hope, but Director Smith still wasn't sure how much information he should share now that Sierra inserted herself in the investigation. If it came right down to it, could Ramos be trusted to spare her life? There were still inquires in the bureau about the Chicago takedown and Victor's lack of intelligence.

"Listen, Victor, I know that the intel I have given you in the past has enabled you to gain Perrone's trust, but you must understand that any information I give you now may put other agents' lives in danger. If I give you what I know and you act on this information, you have to promise me that you will do your best to protect my agents."

Victor turned and looked out the window. His blank look was back, hiding his inner amusement. His plan had worked. Director Smith still trusted him. He put on his most concerned look and turned back.

"Director, I promise I will do everything in my power to minimize the harm to any agent or civilian. My goal is to remove Juan Perrone from his empire. Which is what the FBI wants, right?"

Director Smith looked deeply into Victor's eyes, hoping to find a sense of duty, but all he could see was a hole—an inner void. What had this job done to this man? Could he still trust him? Victor Ramos had always been a pro at hiding his emotions. One had to be a chameleon in undercover work. One wrong move and it could get you killed. Was he hiding something now? The director held Ramos's gaze longer than was comfortable for each man. There was no proof that Victor Ramos was anything more than a deep undercover agent, and he needed to trust him even though his brain was screaming stop. Breaking eye contact, Director Smith pushed aside his inner warning and took a deep breath.

"Well, I don't have much to share, but I did receive word from the Treasury that some of the marked funds that were in Julio Torres's possession when he left on that boat have turned up at the First State Bank of the Florida Keys in Key Largo."

"Really. That changes things. That means that Julio or Max or the boat is in Key Largo. That will definitely give me a place to start." Victor reached for the door handle and stopped as he felt a hand on his shoulder. He turned back.

"Victor, we have been friends for a long time. We have lived lifetimes together. You have been imbedded with the worst of the worst. Perhaps . . . you may consider retiring after this one." Victor shook his head and rolled down the window. He stepped out of the car, shut the door, and leaned in through the opening.

"Director, I can honestly tell you that this is the last time I plan on working undercover for the FBI." He climbed into his car and sped away. As he exited the parking lot, he passed the hardware store manager, pulling into his marked spot.

As Director Smith sat in his shaded hideaway, watching the store manager, he replayed the meeting with Victor Ramos in his head. Something about Ramos had unnerved him. He had changed. Though his energy had returned, his loyalty was still in question. Was he wrong to trust him with confidential information? He sensed that the man he worked with in Chicago wasn't the same scarred man who just left. Did Victor have it in him to be a part of another takedown?

Chicago turned out to be a mess from beginning to end. Thank goodness for Bastos's girlfriend turning on him. Special Agent Ramos had been in a position to take down the crime boss but hadn't stepped up. Most of his information in the last few years had been worthless. He seemed to lack energy and motivation to complete the task. The decision to pull him out had been squashed. It had taken years to work his way into Bastos's trusted circle, and the bureau wasn't going to pull an inside agent. Both of their jobs had been connected with Ramos's insertion in Bastos's organization. Had Ramos and Bastos become too close? Would he have ended up in the warehouse takedown if the FBI hadn't moved up their timeline? Smith had noticed a picture of Victor Ramos looking quite upset in the group of onlookers that night. He destroyed it. That picture would have ruined Victor Ramos's employ with the FBI. He would have gone from lead agent on an assignment to desk duty or the unemployment line. In hindsight, perhaps the best thing for Ramos would have been to let the chips fall where they may.

As director, he would make sure Special Agent Ramos was true to his word—this would be his last case. Director Smith started his car and inched along the fringe of the parking lot, exiting west, back to his office.

***

It took half the morning, filled with meetings and phone calls, before Director Smith could get back to his stack of files and phone messages from the weekend. He wasn't sure how he had missed it the first time through, but there lay on his desk a memo from Supervisory Special Agent Macdonald, Miami field office, asking for confirmation that a Special Agent Sierra Cortez was indeed connected with the Washington DC office. Was this her way of contacting him discretely? If so, it was a failure on her part. She should have had them call his private number, not process it through his assistant. Until the leak is found, everyone is suspect, and with a mole in the department, she had allowed her whereabouts to be exposed.

He picked up the phone and dialed Miami.

"Hello. This is Special Agent Medina. How can I help you?"

"This is Director Smith from the DC office. Please patch me through to Supervisory Special Agent Macdonald."

"Yes, sir."

It was a quick connection.

"Hello. This is Supervisory Special Agent Macdonald."

"Macdonald, this is Director Smith. What can you tell me about your meeting with Special Agent Sierra Cortez?"

"Good morning, Director. I see you got a copy of my inquiry. I called on Saturday to verify Special Agent Cortez's status requested by Miami PD. She had asked to view a video at their precinct, and they have a 'verify all FBI' policy. They called, and since she wasn't connected to any of our active cases in the area, I placed them on hold and called your office. Your assistant said you were out of the office for the weekend and would be back on Monday. He looked up her name and verified her active status. We passed along her credentials to a Detective Cruz from Miami PD."

"Did you speak to anyone else about her whereabouts?"

"No. She told me she was undercover, and there may be a leak in the department with regard to her case. So is that what this is all about?"

"I'm afraid so. Macdonald, I need you to keep her name out of any conversation or paperwork. Also, tell anyone in your office who may have heard her name or talked to her to keep it hush-hush. Do you know where she headed after she viewed the video?"

"Don't worry, sir, we'll keep her presence under wraps. I don't know where she went, but she did say she would stop in and introduce herself before she left the area. If she is true to her word, she is still down here. I gave her my number in case she needs anything. So unless she calls, she is on her own."

"Well, she's a smart agent. We'll see how this plays out. Please call me directly on my private line if you hear anything from her. I'll send it to you over secure e-mail."

"Director, I have to ask, can you tell me anything about her case? It's kind of hard to back her up if I don't know what she's working on."

"No. I'm afraid I can't share any details right now. If that changes, I will update you. Please keep me informed."

Macdonald sat his receiver down on its cradle and walked through his office door.

"Medina, I want a copy of that video that Special Agent Cortez viewed. Call Detective Cruz and tell him you are on your way to pick up a copy—ASAP. When the director is holding back that many secrets on one case, I think we need to know more about what Agent Cortez is doing in Miami." He turned to go back to his office and stopped.

"Oh, and this case needs to be top secret. No word of this can leave this office—names or videos. Understand?"

"Yes, sir." Special Agent Medina picked up the phone as Macdonald disappeared behind his office door.

22

Answers – Palm Shores

It was Monday morning, and Paul, dressed in his new wet suit, was anxiously waiting at the dock. Jack approached, dragging the makeshift raft. Together, they placed the structure in the water and tied it to the dock. Before Paul climbed on, he handed Jack a piece of paper with an international phone number and a cell phone number.

"Thanks, Jack" was all he said as he stepped carefully onto the raft's rickety surface. Once he was stabilized, Jack unhooked the knot and pushed him off from the dock, keeping the rope secured.

It turned out to be quite the dance as Paul had to rotate his body to stay aboard and keep the raft above water. They tried using bricks to determine the right balance as they simulated waves to see how it would react to the ocean current. It was decided that brace pieces would need to be added for stability. They were out there for almost an hour when Paul realized he had to get ready for school or he would be late. Jack thanked him for his help and sent him home.

It took twenty minutes to drive to school with minimum traffic, and he knew JJ, Taylor, and Tanner would all want a ride. He had to hurry with his shower and breakfast. JJ opened the door as Paul ran past him to the shower.

"Where have you been? We need to leave in ten minutes, or we'll be late."

Despite the storm, school was open. This bit of news didn't please the boys. Though they enjoyed the social part of school, they looked forward to the unscheduled days off hurricane season gave them each year. It was the minimal damage, the new metal roof, and the installed backup generator that made it possible to open on Monday, making Friday their only day of escape.

Paul and JJ had been warned about their tardiness, and it was still early in the year. So they had made a pact not be late the rest of the semester. This wasn't easy since they were not good at policing themselves and Aunt Cindy was not one to wake them up or make sure they got to school on time. They had learned the first month that it was their responsibility, and Paul knew his senior year was not the time to mess around with his graduation requirements. He showered and dressed quickly, grabbed some breakfast bars, and headed for the car with JJ following close behind with one ear attached to his cell phone.

"We'll be there in less than two minutes, Tanner. You and Taylor need to meet us at the curb so we won't be late."

The screech of the tires faded into the distance as Paul backed his dad's convertible out of the driveway.

Jack took the raft back to the garage and added the bracing pieces, then took it back to the dock to test it again. He used some bricks and did his best to simulate the conditions of the ocean, but he missed having Paul's help. He had done everything his muscles would allow, and the raft seemed to float no matter how the weight was distributed, so he felt it was ready. He tied it to his boat and headed for the house.

***

Rosa was sitting by the young man's bed, talking in Spanish. As he entered the bedroom, she looked up at him.

"His name is Roberto, and he was separated from his family." Jack shook his hand and called him by name as Rosa continued.

"He doesn't know what happened to them." She dropped her eyes to hide her expression as she spoke, and Jack nodded. He hoped that this man's family would be okay, but right now, he had to worry about the task at hand.

Rosa had fed Roberto, removed his bandages, and dressed him in his torn and tattered clothing. She had already explained to him what they were doing and why and told him what he needed to do once he reached land. She also had him memorize Jack's phone number and told him once he was processed, he could call him for a job. He thanked her and stood on his still-shaky legs as she guided him to the back door where Jack took over.

Roberto was still struggling, but he was well enough to walk to the boat with Jack's help. It wasn't long before they were loaded and pulling away from the dock.

Jack knew just the right spot to leave him so he could complete this journey on his own. He felt he had done all he could as he drove away, watching him float alone in the ocean, and he knew it was for the best; besides, it was good that he did this last part on his own. There was something about the human spirit that needed to succeed to survive. Those who felt the exhilaration of success understood why the trial is part of the experience. Those who have relied on other accomplishments struggle with a defined purpose in their own existence, often expecting others to pave their way.

As Jack pulled away, his spirit was soaring; he said a silent prayer for Roberto and his family's safety. Maria wanted him to rescue those who were faltering in their journey, and in the last twenty-four hours, two such souls had come into his life. He had done all he could for Roberto, but what more could he do for Paul? Had their parents abandoned their boys? Where were Charles and Sara Choate? He needed answers. Paul needed answers.

He pulled out his cell phone and searched his contact list for one name—Louis Medina, his college roommate. He wasn't sure where he had ended up once he joined the FBI or if he was still with them. In their last conversation, he was heading to Quantico, while Jack was heading back to Miami to run his dad's business.

It was a triple bypass that encouraged his parents' move to Palm Shores, a lifestyle that allowed them to lighten their load and lessen their ss. If he had only known it would be less than five years later that he would lose both of them in a senseless car accident, he would have appreciated the extra time he had with them. He felt the same remorse flowing from Paul. He had to help him find answers. He scrolled down the list finding "Medina, Louis" and pushed send. All he could do was hope that his old cell number would still be active.

The third ring came and went before a small voice answered. "Hulo."

"Hello. This is Jack Winters, and I'm trying to reach Louis Medina. Is he there?"

"No. Sorry. This is his grandmother. He gave me this phone last time he was here."

"So, you are his *abuela*. He spoke of you often. You see, Louis was my roommate at Florida State."

"Did you say your name was Jack? I remember him mentioning a friend named Jack."

"Louis was a dear friend of mine, but I am sorry to say I haven't kept in touch, but now he may be the only one who can help me solve a mystery. Do you have another phone number for him?"

"He left me his number. Just a moment . . . Here it is . . . 305-400-7223."

"Thank you, Abuela."

"Take care of yourself, Jack, and tell my grandson to call his *abuela* more." Jack smiled as he hung up the phone and dialed. So Louis has a Miami number all this time, and he was just up the road.

***

Agent Medina had just stepped out of his car as his cell buzzed in his pocket. He pulled it out and looked at the unfamiliar number. He wasn't sure if he should answer it, but his curiosity got the better of him.

"Hello?"

"Hi. This is Jack Winters, and I'm trying—"

"Wow, Jack, is that really you?"

"That depends. Am I talking to Louis Medina?"

"Well, actually, it's Special Agent Louis Medina."

"Believe it or not, Special Agent Louis Medina is who I need right now."

"Is everything okay? I heard about your wife. I'm sorry for your loss. Is this about her death?"

"Thanks, but no. I'm calling about another matter concerning my neighbor's parents. I don't have much information, but I was wondering if you could use your connection with the FBI to check on a Charles and Sara Choate from Key Largo, Florida. Their teenage sons haven't heard from them for a couple of months, and they're worried. I told them I would help them try to find some answers. Do you think you could check their names and see if anything comes up?"

"Jack, I would love to help you, but you realize it is a long shot at best. Where were they when the boys last heard from them?

"Djibouti, Africa. They own a shipping business out of Miami. I'm not sure what their business was in Africa though?"

"Well, Jack, I don't want to alarm you, but that area of the world is hard to predict. There are ongoing abductions for ransom, and I'm sure you've heard about the piracy. Have the family received any ransom letters or calls?"

"Not that I've heard. Could you see what you can find out and get back to me as soon as possible? I can try to get more info from the boy's guardian. Of course, she doesn't like me much, but that's another story."

"I'll run their names when I get back to the office, and let you know if I find anything. That was C-H-O-A-T-E. Charles and—is it Sarah with an H, or S-A-R-A?"

"It's Sara, no H. Thanks a lot for doing this. I didn't know who else to call."

"Well, now that you have my number, and I have yours, we'll have to get together for old times' sake."

"I'll be looking forward to that, and by the way, your abuela says hi. She gave me your number."

"My sweet abuela. She needed an emergency phone, so when the bureau issued me one, I gave her mine. I'm glad you still have the number. It was great to hear from you, Jack."

Medina ended the conversation as he walked into Miami PD and asked for Detective Cruz.

***

Jack saved his friend's new number and headed for the marina. He needed to check again for missing yachts that would explain his bounty at Cay Sal, and he had several meetings lined up with boat owners who were deciding what to do with their insurance claims: fix their boats or replace them. Either way, they needed to be pulled from the water. Once the boats were removed, he could get his workers in there to repair the damaged docks and get the marina back in business.

He just walked into the office when the phone rang. It was Rosa. "How did it go this morning? Did our friend get off okay?" It took every effort to keep her voice level and calm.

"Yes, he did, and it looks like a nice day out on the water, so he should make good time."

"Are you going to be busy at the marina today?"

"I have four different owners coming in to assess their boat damage and schedule their removal so I can fix the damaged dock. If there is a decision made today, we could be lifting one out this afternoon."

"Have you heard from the Cutlers?"

"They are scheduled to arrive the end of the week. Their boat is down on the end. We have to move several others before we can get to theirs."

"Sounds like you will be home late. I'll bring dinner to the marina for you before five."

"Sounds great. Have a good day, Rosa."

Rosa hung up the phone. She couldn't remember the last time she had been this scared. She was worried about Roberto, or should she call him by his first name Julio? She hated to lie to Jack. Perhaps it wasn't a lie, more of a stretching of the truth. Was it wrong to let him think he had rescued a Cuban refugee? So Roberto wasn't escaping from Cuba. He was escaping from a different tyranny—a mob boss who had killed his mother and sent him to his death.

Julio Roberto Torres had confided in her, and at least for now, she felt she needed to hide his identity, even from Jack. He told her his story about his abduction, at least that's what she called it since he wasn't given a choice. She was scared for his safety. There had to be someone looking for that boat and its occupants. He was so frightened, and he had good reason. His boss wanted him dead, and the police would surely arrest him for murdering the boat's captain. She had to keep him safe and help him change his identity, if that is what it took. Juan Perrone must think Julio Torres was dead, that he went down with the ship during the storm.

It was close to five when Rosa returned from visiting her friend Roma. It was arranged; they would allow her guest to stay in their boat until it was removed from the marina. The boat was stocked with food and clothing, and Roma would make sure she gave her plenty of notice to move him before the crane lifted the boat out of the water. By then, they could figure out another place for him to stay. Rosa grabbed the food bundles she had packed earlier and headed for the marina. As she pulled into the parking lot, she maneuvered her car to the far side of the building, hidden behind Jack's truck.

She entered the office and handed Jack his dinner, waiting for him to take time to eat. This allowed her to question his progress.

"Thanks, Rosa, I'm starving, and it looks like I'll be here awhile longer finishing up paperwork."

"Did all your owners make it today?"

Jack answered between bites. "No, we had Donnelly and Jacobsen, but Turner and Rodriquez rescheduled for tomorrow. And Cutler said he won't be able to come till Monday. That may not be an issue if everyone else drags their feet. Well, actually, it's probably for the best. It can be a drawn-out process, depending on the damage, the crane, and the tow truck. It may be the middle of next week before we get this place cleared enough to repair the docks."

"One thing I've learned over the years is to take it as it comes." She smiled. This gave her and Julio more time than they had previously planned.

Rosa said her goodbyes and took her empty dishes to the car. She picked up the second bundle and turned toward the marked beach path, whistling as she walked. She moved slowly at first until she was hidden in the tree line. She then took the fork in the trail to the picnic area. She figured it was too early to meet up with Julio, but the suspense was killing her. She had to know. Rosa rounded the last tree and saw a figure sitting at one of the picnic tables. He turned as he heard her whistle. His familiarity made her smile.

Julio had been just as happy to see her as she was to see him. He knew that if it wasn't for Rosa and her friend Jack, he would be dead. He would find a way to repay them for their kindness, but right now, he needed to stay out of sight for a while. If Juan knew he was there, he would send someone after him. He would never have guessed his ancestry would save him. Posing as a Cuban refugee just might be the ticket, he needed to get a new life. According to Rosa, he could get a job right here working for Jack. Key Largo just might be his salvation.

23

Sending in the Mob – DC

Victor Ramos knew that the information he had just attained was the final piece to his plan. He couldn't contain his enthusiasm as he walked into Perrone's office.

"I've got it!"

Juan looked up from his desk. "You've got what?"

Victor eyed his boss and noted his tired eyes and inebriated condition. "Are you okay, sir?"

"Yes, yes." Victor's attention to his appearance annoyed him. "What do you have?"

"Well, my source just told me that the FBI money, that little snitch Julio made off with, just turned up in Key Largo, Florida."

Juan lowered the papers in his hands and looked at his second-in-command. "Key Largo, Florida?"

"That's right. The serial numbers match. We've got him, sir!"

Juan was up, pacing. He stopped and leaned on the front of his desk. "Are you sure this information is reliable?" He looked up as Victor nodded. "So what you're telling me is an inexperienced seaman overpowered Max and took my boat to Key Largo?" It seemed unlikely with the currents and the storm. Juan looked at Victor whose assurance shown in his big smile—no words were necessary. "I know you have confidence in your friend's information, but that doesn't explain why the last coordinates from Max weren't anywhere near Key Largo. Something's off." He took a deep breath.

Victor Ramos had been with Juan long enough to know that if he didn't give him time to personally process information, he would be asked to leave, and he needed to be there at just the right moment to set his plan in motion.

Juan turned his gaze downward at the papers in his hands. He had shipments coming in and orders to fill. He had no time or patience for this.

"Something happened. It had to be Julio. This is his doing. If Max would have killed him when they reached the ocean, none of this would have happened. For that matter, I should have killed that boy myself." The anger was changing his face.

"Max—where is Max? Could he have made a deal or killed Julio and disappeared with my boat? He talked about this trip being his last. I should have monitored him closer. Or they were in on it together. That's why he spared him. Max made a deal with Julio and took the boat to shore himself." His face was going through all different contortions. He looked like he would burst.

Victor broke the silence. "Do you really think they would have done it together?"

Juan's depressive mood was setting in. Victor had him right where he wanted him. It was time to make his move.

"If you would have asked me that on any other shipment, I would have defended Max, but he was pretty mad at me when I told him he had to not only take Julio but also dispose of his body along the way. Max has been with me from the beginning, yet I have never asked him to kill anyone—some people just don't have the stomach to take a life."

"Well, sir . . ." Victor was choosing his words carefully. He had to steer Juan in just the right way. "I can grab a few men and head to Florida and get some answers. Unless . . ." He paused just long enough for Juan to look up at him. "Unless you want to take care of Max and Julio yourself."

He took a minute. This was the very decision that was keeping him up at night. He had wanted Victor's input on which of his men he should send to Florida to check out the sighting at the Miami fuel pier. That seemed insignificant now. Victor was right. This required a heavy hand. Between locating the boat and taking care of Julio and Max, it had to be one of them, and Vic was a take-no-prisoners man. If he wanted answers from Max, this one he should handle himself. He glanced down once again, at his work orders, and then at the man standing in front of him. Could he leave his organization in Victor Ramos's hands? He eyed him from head to toe and paused to look deeply into his eyes.

Victor stood silently by, letting his boss process his decision. He sensed his uncertainty. He was a man possessed, not with ghosts or demons, but with anxiety and apprehension. With lies and shadow puppets, he had managed to infiltrate and shatter Perrone's foundation. It was a broken man standing before him.

It was easy, eliminating some of his favorite men by convincing him of possible traders in his organization then replacing them with his own picks. The fact that Julio turned out to be dirty made it much more believable. Giving Max a heads up that Juan was going to have him killed on this next run at the bar last week fit in perfectly with the last-minute addition of Julio to the trip. So now it was time for him to finish the process. All he needed was for Juan to leave his empire in his hands. Had he destroyed him enough? It was time to find out.

"I could take Mondo and Carlos and catch the next flight to Miami. Just say the word."

Juan looked into Victor's face. It was time to make a decision. He was the boss, and he needed to inspire the same eagerness and hope he was witnessing in Victor Ramos's eyes.

"I'll take Mondo and Carlos and take care of this myself." He picked up the phone and called his secretary to make the travel arrangements.

Victor could hardly contain his exhilaration. It worked. Juan was going to leave his organization in his hands. He was ready.

"Victor, I need to go over some things with you. Have a seat."

24

Passing the Bucks Around – Key Largo

Paul and JJ exited the school building almost in a trance. It was the conversation with Sierra Skinner that rattled them. She had connected them with the hundred-dollar bills. They hoped she bought their story about being paid with hundred-dollar bills from their marina job. They needed to cover their tracks. It was time to go see their neighbor and get a job.

They hurried to their car, Tanner and Taylor racing to catch up or lose their ride.

"Why were you guys called to the office?" Taylor asked.

"Oh, it was nothing," Paul quickly replied and glanced at his younger brother, but JJ didn't seem to get the hint.

"What do you mean, Paul? That Sierra Skinner woman, though she was hot, was pretty scary."

"Scary? Hot? Who is she, and what did she want with the two of you?" Taylor leaned close and seemed overly intent on their answer.

Paul tried to jump in before JJ could expound further. "She was just some woman wanting to know how to get a hold of our parents."

JJ straddled his seat to face his friends, barely containing his excitement. "No, she wasn't, Paul. She was asking about the mon—" He stopped, realizing his mistake. Guarding his words carefully, he continued, "Um, it was what Paul said. She just wanted to know how to get a hold of our parents. She wanted to hire them or something."

He turned around to face the windshield and glanced sideways at his brother who was watching him with narrowed eyes. Paul started the car but held his brother's gaze.

"She was hot?" Tanner laughed. "Figures that's what you would notice, JJ."

Tanner placed his earbuds in his ears and buckled his seat belt, readying himself for the twenty-minute ride home. Taylor, however, wouldn't let it go.

"You're telling me a woman named Sierra Skinner came to school and pulled you guys outta class to ask you about doing business with your parents? I'm sorry, but I don't buy it."

There was no reply from the front seat. From the angle he was sitting, he could see the looks exchanged between the pair, but they were done talking.

Taylor leaned back and fastened his seat belt. He couldn't let that stand. Waiting five minutes, he changed his approach.

"Hey, guys, I'm hungry, let's stop for a burger on the way home— I'll buy."

Paul and JJ seemed to relax a bit. It took Paul a moment to work something out in his head.

"Sounds good, Taylor, but you have to let me buy. I got paid yesterday, and I need to break a hundred. Smaller bills are easier to use, less worry about counterfeits or something."

JJ just watched his elder brother as he spoke. What was he doing? Didn't they just decide not to spend any more hundreds?

Paul pulled into Garbo's Grill, a local favorite. Tanner exited first. Taylor jumped out and left the brothers in the front seat. He eyed them carefully, watching the pair quietly argue over something. Paul abruptly ended the conversation and exited the car. Stepping up to the counter, he ordered his burger and fries then handed Taylor the hundred and headed to the restroom. JJ was next, followed by Tanner. The two of them wandered off to explore a tourist stand. Taylor finalized the order and handed over the bill for payment.

Paul returned, and Taylor handed him his change. They secured a table for four as Taylor returned the subject to their earlier conversation.

"Paul, you know, I'm pretty good at telling when someone's lying. So spill it. What did this Sierra Skinner woman really want?" Paul smiled and shook his head. Taylor had a way of seeing right through him.

"We really didn't lie to you. She did ask about our parents and why they were out of town."

"So you gave us partial truths. If it was all so innocent, why did you get so mad and stop JJ from telling us? Are your parents okay?"

"Well, to be honest, I don't know if our parents are okay. If you ask my aunt, she says they call her all the time, but I haven't heard from them in over two months."

"Wow! Two months! That's a long time." He paused. "Did this Sierra have any news for you about them?"

"No, she was from the bank or something and wanted to know about some money JJ and I spent the other day. It's nothing."

"Money? What money? From your marina job?"

"Yaw. I guess after that money fraud in Key Largo last year, they're watching deposits like a hawk. JJ and I just bought some new wet suits and spent a few hundred dollars. With all the attention, you would've thought we robbed a bank."

Taylor forced a laugh to keep the air light, but something was off. Was this woman connected in some way to their missing parents?

"Taylor." His name was being called to pick up their burger order.

"It looks like our burgers are ready, and here comes JJ & Tanner." Paul grabbed his arm.

"Taylor, do me a favor and don't let JJ know that I told you, especially after I got mad at him in the car."

"I got your back. Don't worry." Taylor and Paul did a fist bump and headed to the counter to get their order.

It was after four o'clock when they arrived at Palm Shores Subdivision. Dropping Taylor and Tanner was their first stop and then off to the marina. Jack was in his office working, and Paul walked right in and sat down. JJ followed, timidly hiding in his big brother's shadow, trying desperately not to draw attention to himself, his last encounter with their neighbor fresh in his mind. Jack looked up, studying the uncertainty on the two boys' faces. He countered with a smile.

"What can I do for the Choate boys?" Neither seemed to want to start the conversation.

Jack sat back in his chair and gave the brothers his complete attention. After a pregnant pause, he broke the ice.

"Paul, if you're here to see what I found out, I'm afraid I don't have any new information. However, my friend Agent Medina is checking his sources."

JJ seemed confused and looked at his elder brother. Paul just waved him down.

"Thanks for that, Jack. That was fast. But actually, we are here to ask you for a job."

"A job, huh? Huh, normally this time of year, I would turn you away, but right now, with the dock repairs, I could use extra hands to handle the Jet Ski rentals and any boat cleanings that our guests request. Some of these boats are in pretty bad shape. I could give you about ten hours a week, give or take, but you will need to be patient with me. Some weeks I will need you more and some less."

"Both of us, ten hours a week?" JJ was excited.

"Maybe ten hours a week, but like I said, you will need to be flexible. Some weeks there will be ten, and some only a few."

"Sounds good to me," Paul piped in. This was great, not too many hours yet enough to make his cover story legit.

"Well, before we make this final and I send you home with an employment packet, I have to know that I can trust you both to follow instructions. I won't have the time to double-check your activities, and you will be representing the Palm Shores marina. Do you understand?"

The boys stood, and Paul moved toward Jack with his hand outstretched. "You won't be disappointed."

Jack shook his hand, and JJ timidly added his to the fray. Jack gave their hands one last shake and motioned toward the outer office.

"Follow me, boys." He walked them to the secretary's desk and handed each of them their employment packet.

"I have a check list inside. All you have to do is fill out what it says and then bring it to me. If I get it back tomorrow, you can start the day after." Paul thanked Jack and JJ nodded as the boys left the marina office.

JJ was excited as he jumped into the car and slammed the door. "We need to get these filled out and back to Jack without anyone knowing. How are we going to do that?"

"Well, it's Monday night. All we have to do is hide them in my backpack and wait until Aunt Cindy heads to the club tonight."

"That'll work."

JJ scanned the club parking lot as they drove past.

"I don't see her car, so I'm guessing she's home." Paul nodded. "But before we get there, I want to know what you were thinking spending the last hundred we had in our wallets for burgers. I thought we agreed not to spend any more hundreds."

"I started thinking about that Sierra woman and how she singled us out, and then Taylor mentioned getting burgers. I figured if I handed the bill to Taylor and he gets questioned, then we'll know there was no mix-up and the money we have is either stolen or counterfeit. I want to know for sure. Plus, by not having one of us pay and spending it in Marathon, it may confuse things a bit."

"So you want Taylor to get in trouble too?"

"No, he will just tell them the money came from me, so I will be the one getting into trouble." JJ seemed to be in deep thought. "Putting that aside for a minute, the way that Sierra woman was questioning us, I'm not sure if she was more interested in the money or who we knew. What was that about some guys named Julio and Max? And it seemed our parents' whereabouts was even an afterthought when she asked if they knew a guy named Juan Perrone. Like I said, was she really there about the money, or was it a rouse to question us? All in all, the whole thing was odd. Times like these, I really wish I could talk to Mom and Dad."

"If you're right, we should call them. We can use the phone numbers they left for emergencies. I'm pretty sure this qualifies."

Paul thought about how to answer his younger brother. Could he handle the truth after the day they'd just had? He pulled the car into the driveway, turned off the engine, and began speaking before JJ got out.

"I did. I tried the phone numbers and couldn't get through, so I asked Jack for help. That's what he was talking about when we walked in."

JJ looked shocked. "Jack? The same man that yelled at us in our tree house?"

"Yes, and the same guy that just gave us jobs." JJ's posture seemed to deflate. "Listen, I talked to him the other night after I spent some time calling Mom and Dad's emergency numbers. Jack understands about loss. It wasn't that long ago that he lost both his parents and his wife. He agrees that not hearing from our parents is suspicious. I'm just hoping he can find us some answers." He thought he saw a pair of eyes looking through the drapes. "Well, we better get inside. She knows we're home."

25

Behind the Gate – Palm Shores

Sierra pulled up to the Palm Shores Subdivision security gate a little early for her appointment. She explained her business and handed the attendant her ID. Checking for her name on the guest list, he gave her a map and waved her through. She was ready to move in, and with her need for urgency, her realtor Carol had her complete everything online. All she needed was to sign the rental agreement and get her keys to her condo. She made sure there wouldn't be a problem.

Finding the directions to the condo quite simple, she took her time driving through the housing area, studying its layout. What caught her eye was the time of day and the number of expensive cars parked at the clubhouse. This scene set the demographics of the development, clearly indicating many retired members. She made a note to swing by tomorrow and make introductions, hoping to overhear some community gossip in the process.

She wondered about the Choate boys and why their parents chose to live in this community. She thought back to her conversation with them at the high school. They had dismissed their principal, deciding to handle things on their own. They seemed grown-up for their age, but often maturity was masked in deception.

Paul had taken on the role of protector. He guarded his answers well. JJ, on the other hand, used humor. In fact, it took every trick she had to get them to admit their parents were even out of the country on business, leaving them in the care of an aunt. Asking about the money was even more difficult, but finally, they admitted, probably because she showed them the money, that they did, indeed, spend eight $100 bills at the dive and sub shops on Friday. Of course, she had to confess that Portia was her witness and convince them that none of them would be arrested.

It was hard to believe they got that money from working odd jobs at the marina, but in this neighborhood, with all those nice cars parked around the clubhouse, perhaps they were telling the truth. It was definitely worth checking into.

She drove past the marina entrance and looked at her watch. She didn't have time to peruse the docks for the missing yacht, but she would definitely head back tonight as soon as she could get rid of her realtor. So far, her inquiries had been a bust. None of the marinas she'd checked had inconsistencies in their inventory. Her only lead was the money. So that's what she'd follow.

Carol was parked in front of the four-plex as Sierra pulled her car into the driveway. It didn't take long for introductions and a quick walk-through of the furnished unit, but the paperwork was another matter. Though her background report came through with no problems, she was astounded with the amount of triplicate forms she had to sign. It took upward of an hour for Carol to read and explain each form as Sierra, as patiently as possible, initialed every sheet and signed and dated the final page of each of the three sets.

Finally, she was handed an envelope with two sets of keys, a club ID card, a security gate sticker, and a garage remote. Carol said her goodbyes and backed her car out of the driveway.

After organizing the paperwork and her belongings, Sierra did a quick assessment of needs and headed for the marina, hoping she wasn't too late. She pulled into the lot and parked next to two other cars. It was a vast space laid out to accommodate boat trailers with a drive leading down to a series of docks. Next to the docks, there was a boat crane poised, ready for its next retrieval. The damage from the latest storm was obvious. There was much work to be done.

Sierra headed toward the building marked office and noted the office hours were listed as 10:00 a.m.-5:00 p.m. Looking at her watch, she realized it was after six. She pushed the door, and it released without complaint. In front of her lay a reception desk and an open door that led to a back room. She walked over and peered inside, finding a quaint office space. It was small with a desk positioned in the middle of the room. She strolled over and picked up a name plate that read "Jack Winters, Manager."

A noise brought her attention to another small room off to her right. Glancing over, she saw a man holding a steaming cup turning toward her. She smiled at him.

Her appearance startled Jack as both hands shot up to steady his shaking cup. Her beauty did not escape his notice as he moved toward his desk.

"May I help you?" He smiled to hide his nervousness.

Sierra reached out her hand to him. "Hi, my name is Sierra Skinner. Are you Jack Winters, the manager?"

"I am, but I'm afraid we are closed."

She couldn't let that stand. "I'm sorry to bother you, but I'm kind of in a time crunch. You see, I just recently moved into the housing area, and I need to make arrangements to have my boat shipped here. I know it's after hours, but could you possibly show me around so I can be prepared when my attorney calls for my boat's transfer information tomorrow?" Jack was ready to turn her away, but she continued before he could say anything. "You see, my husband just recently passed." Her mind flashed back to Agent Kirtland's death, and her bottled-up emotions flowed freely. She blinked to clear her vision.

"I'm no good at handling all our affairs. All I know is that I need to move our boat by the end of next week. My attorney is looking into it, but he told me to find a place to dock it this week so he can arrange the transfer. I have been looking for a housing area I can afford with a marina, and today my realtor found me a condo here at Palm Shores. He's calling tomorrow to see if I've found a place." She wiped her tears away and looked up into Jack's eyes. "Could you just walk me around the marina and let me know what it takes to dock a boat here? I promise I won't take much of your time."

Jack walked past her and laid his coffee on his desk. "Well, I guess I can spare a few minutes. Follow me." He put his arm out for her to take, and the two of them strolled out the front door.

At first, they walked in silence, and then Jack said, "I'm sorry for your loss. I lost my wife a couple of years back. I wish I could tell you things will get better, but I have to admit I miss my Maria every day. Staying busy helps dull the pain most days, but what actually gets me through is knowing she is with me, watching over me."

Sierra squeezed his arm. She felt bad for lying to this nice man who was truly mourning his wife's death, even though made-up personas were part of her job. "Thank you, Jack. I am sorry we have such a sad thing in common." Sierra turned their attention to the boats docked in front of them. "Is all this damage from the storm?"

"Yes, when those winds come, they can really leave a mess. If you move your boat here, you will need good insurance, and it won't be cheap."

"Did you lose any boats or have any drift in from the ocean?"

"All our boats are strictly inventoried and accounted for. This marina is positioned in a way that boats don't just float in, no matter the wind, unless, of course, a small one gets picked up by a tornado and dropped here, but as long as I can remember, that's never happened. Each of these boats has an owner who is a resident of Palm Shores. Making sure of that is my job."

"So no missing boats and no new ones?"

"Nope, just damaged boats, which will be fixed, removed, or replaced. Actually, this storm damaged our docks, so we'll be moving all the boats out for repairs. I'm afraid if you ship your boat here, it will need to be after the first or on a trailer. The repairs will take a couple of weeks. Thank goodness, it's fall. There's not as much boating activity after the kids start school, so that minimizes the boat traffic."

"Are all these boats damaged?"

"They all have some damage—some more, some less. The ones on the far end are in pretty good shape, but they will still need some repair. Those will be the last ones we remove and the first ones back in the water."

Sierra was eyeing each boat carefully. Besides the damage, nothing looked out of place.

Jack continued, "If you choose to bring your boat here, your application will need to be approved through our homeowners association board. They meet tomorrow night and every other Tuesday after that. Once approved, you can bring your boat in on a trailer, and then I will assign you a slip. You can either back it down the ramp or schedule a date for placement with our crane."

"Thank you, Jack, this has been very helpful. Do you have a price sheet for docking fees?"

"I have one for you at the office. Our fees are pretty standard in the area, but we offer the added privacy and security of a gated community."

They had reached the farthest dock. Sierra looked around. Her hopes of finding Perrone's yacht here were dashed.

"This is the end of our tour. Is there anything else you would like to know?"

"Just one more question, how many people work at the marina?"

"Well, this time of year, it's just me and a couple of part-time teenagers who take care of odd jobs and the Jet Ski rentals. The association also employs a grounds crew that cares for the yards throughout the subdivision, including the clubhouse property. I use them for extra muscle and odd jobs during storm cleanups and repairs. This year we will need to replace a couple of docks, so we will have a contract company here for that. We have a small operation here. If you are looking for more service, the Key Largo marina offers full service and 24/7 dock hands."

Sierra knew she couldn't ask him about the Choate boys by name, but Jack had confirmed he hired teenagers. Perhaps the boys innocently got mixed up in this mess after all.

They were turning back toward the office as the reds and yellows of the sunset painted the sky.

She gasped, taking in nature's beauty. "What a beautiful sunset."

"That's Southern Florida. We have the best sunrises and sunsets."

"I think that alone will make this move worth it." She smiled up at him. He nodded in silence.

Jack had enjoyed his stroll and wasn't sure he wanted it to end. "If you don't mind me asking, where are you from?"

"Well, my family is from Nebraska, but I guess you could say I've lived all over."

"Sounds intriguing. Perhaps next time we meet, you can tell me more about your travels." She smiled as he handed her a "slip hold" card.

"That sounds like a date." Sierra filled out the card and handed it back.

Jack was silent. He wasn't sure how he felt about the word "date." He certainly wasn't interested in dating anyone. He forced a smile and handed her a packet of information and a price sheet.

"Just fill this out and take it to the HOA board meeting tomorrow at 7:00 p.m. across the street at the club."

Sierra sensed the coolness wedged between them. She thanked him for his help, said goodbye, and left. Jack was left struggling over the unsettled emotions stirring inside him. He walked over to the window and watched as her car exited the parking lot.

Rosa walked in. "Who was that?"

"Just a new resident wanting to dock her boat at the marina. I was showing her around."

"Where is she from?"

"I think she said Nebraska."

Rosa sighed. With Julio's situation, new people made her nervous. They had waited until the voices receded back to the office before she showed Julio to the Cutler's boat and got him settled. She then headed up to the office, just minutes behind Jack and his guest. She watched the woman leave. She wasn't sure how long she could keep Julio hidden from Jack. She knew she would need to tell him eventually, but right now, the less he knew the better.

"What brings you back here?" Jack was watching Rosa's face. She seemed worried about something.

"I was on my way home and decided to see if you needed anything." Though this seemed odd to Jack, he just shrugged it off.

"Actually, I'm locking up and going home. Nothing I'm doing can't wait until tomorrow."

He walked around locking doors and turning off lights. He put his arm out for Rosa and walked her out to the parking lot. Jack did his visual sweep and thought he saw a light in the Cutler's boat on the end but decided it was a reflection. He opened Rosa's car door and placed his hand on the hood. The car seemed cool to the touch, but he didn't pay it much notice. He shut her door, and she backed her car out of her stall and headed home. Jack followed.

26

Juan's Gang – Key Largo

It was early evening when the plane touched down at Miami International Airport. Perrone and his two sidekicks, Carlos and Mondo, grabbed their carry-ons and headed to passenger pick-up. A black SUV pulled up and honked. Oswaldo, the driver, got out and opened the door for his guests. After settling into their seats, Oswaldo handed Juan a personal attaché case filled with weapons and money. Juan opened his bounty and handed his cronies each a weapon and pocket money. He then went over his expectations and plans. This was a search-and-recovery mission. The money was the objective, but Juan also wanted to find Julio and Max. He needed answers from his captain before he planned to dispose of the troublesome pair for good. Silence followed his instructions, and Juan settled back for the long drive.

Oswaldo drove expertly through Miami's stop-and-go rush-hour traffic and the congestion on the eighteen-mile stretch entering the Florida Keys. Though he came highly recommended by Victor Ramos, he was still an unknown to Perrone, and this fact made him nervous. Here he was, trying to track down two traitors, and his crew consisted of one of his own warehouse men and two Ramos's hires.

He would have to say, on the surface, he trusted Victor Ramos and his tactics, but in the last few months, there had been too many changes—some were with his permission, but some were without.

Ramos had helped clear out the riffraff from his organization, and though that should have made him feel safe and secure, something still smelled fishy. He wasn't one to let slivers of doubt creep in, but lately, he felt he was losing control. New additions made him nervous. Even though two of these men came with him, he did not trust one. He would not turn his back on either of the three.

Arriving at the Key Largo Hilton, they handed their keys to the valet and their luggage to the steward and checked in. Making their way to the dining room for some nourishment, they were seated at a table with a view of the water. The room was sparsely populated, which was perfect for their plans. After some flirtation with the waitress, the men placed their order and were left alone.

Turning to business, Juan laid out his strategy for the next morning. Oswaldo handed each person a packet filled with a burn phone, credit card, and fake IDs. Carlos and Mondo were assigned to find the missing yacht. They were to contact the concierge in the morning about a rental car and use the supplied map to check out the marinas in the area. Juan and Oswaldo would take their forged credentials and follow the money starting with the bank.

"What do you want us to do if we find Max or Julio?" Mondo asked.

All eyes turned to Perrone, seeking the answer for the question on everyone's mind.

"Let me just make this clear up front—Julio is expendable. If you find him, make it quiet and deep. Max, on the other hand, needs to have a word with his boss. Bring him to me!" The irritation was evident in Juan's face. He excused himself and headed to the restroom.

Mondo waited until Juan was visually out of sight before allowing himself to comment. "So we're supposed to kill Julio?" He was keeping his eyes peeled in his boss's direction as he vocalized his concern for an old friend.

Carlos seemed uncomfortable. Oswaldo was playing with his phone, outwardly ignoring both of them.

"Listen, Mondo." It was Carlos. "I know you and Julio were friends, but you have to look at the facts. He crossed the line when he stole from the boss. I think we all know where that leads."

Mondo kept his eyes focused on Perrone's return, but his words were for his companion. "The problem is, Carlos, you are new to Juan's crew. You never got to know Julio. He was a good man. Many times he would go right up to the boss and launch an appeal for others on the crew, often succeeding in his efforts. Are you sure he wasn't set up?"

"No one knows what really happened with Julio, but even if he was set up, where is he? Why hasn't he contacted the boss? That alone makes him guilty in my eyes." Mondo thought about that and only had time to nod before Perrone was back within earshot.

Their food arrived, hushing any further conversation. Juan looked around at his motley crew, wondering if these three would be up to this mission. He had Mondo. Victor suggested him for this job, and even though he could be a benefit in determining Julio's thought processes, their closeness could be a stumbling block. Carlos, on the other hand, was new, untested. He was hired by Ramos during the mole cleansing. Though Victor said he was one of the best, his loyalty to Juan was unproven. He could be a great asset or a wild card.

Then there was Oswaldo, he also came highly recommended from Victor Ramos, but to Juan, he was a mystery. He would have to be watched carefully. This small crew had one thing in common, his second-in-command, and it was his trust he was relying on for success.

He didn't like the limited amount of information they had to work with, but he was all in. He was giving himself two days to wrap this up and head back. Though that was aggressive, he needed to get back. Victor Ramos may be a good second-in-command, but his backers were nervous when it came to change.

There rooms had been booked next to each other, and they parted company in the hall. Juan had his own room and disappeared behind his locked door. He had to check in with Ramos and make sure his instructions were being followed to the letter. Mondo and Carlos were sharing a room, and they ordered a movie on TV. Oswaldo also had his own room—per his request.

27

The Money Trail – Key Largo

It was agonizing for Paul and JJ as they sat in the living room watching the clock, waiting for Aunt Cindy to declare that she was leaving for the club. She was becoming more and more hesitant with her departures. Most days they hardly cared about her comings and goings, but tonight they had plans to make and forms to fill out, and they needed her gone.

In the eyes of two teenage boys, Aunt Cindy was the perfect guardian. She was carefree and lighthearted. No rules, no fuss. Most times it fell on Paul to play the adult role, making sure he and JJ made it to school and other functions. Cindy's life, however, reflected that of an out-of-control adolescent, spending her nights at the club trolling for rich companions and her days sleeping. Many mornings she was returning as the boys were readying themselves for school. She was not one to instill a curfew on her or the boys, but recently, things had changed, and their carefree keeper was becoming obsessed with their every move.

"She's finally gone." JJ was the self-proclaimed lookout, announcing her departure from the driveway.

Paul grabbed his backpack, and the pair rendezvoused at the dining room table. He pulled out the envelopes they got from Jack and slid one across JJ. They opened them, and their concentration began.

Both applications had their own set of forms, two each, one for their personal information and background history and one for a list of references. Paul finished the first page quite quickly, skipping over the work-experience section. This would be his first job, another sign of his maturing age that he wasn't quite sure he was ready for. He was finishing up writing his two references, that of Tanner's mom and his friend Taylor, hoping that Taylor, being older, qualified him as a reference, when JJ pulled his thoughts in another direction.

"Paul, do you know my Social Security Number? I'm not sure where Mom and Dad put my card."

"Here, I got both of ours out of Mom's jewelry box. She told me where they were in case we needed them."

"That was nice. Why didn't she tell me?"

Paul looked up and watched his brother concentrate on printing his number. He wished he could let him keep his childish innocence, but ignorance wasn't always bliss. He wanted JJ to trust him, but he would be mad if he kept something this important from him.

"JJ, while you're filling that out, I want to talk to you about something. I touched on it in the car." He paused trying to figure out how to begin. "I think something may have happened to Mom and Dad since we haven't heard from them for over two months."

"Why would you think that? Aunt Cindy says they call her every week." JJ's eyes barely left his form.

"Maybe, but you know how Mom is when she calls, she insists on talking to each of us. I haven't talked to her. Have you?" JJ shook his head. "She has our cell numbers, so why would she only be calling Aunt Cindy? Plus, they were coming home, remember? What happened with that?" JJ looked up at his brother, and back to his form.

"Something must've come up. I'm sure it's nothing."

Paul shook his head. "I disagree. I think Aunt Cindy is lying to us."

"Why would she do that?"

"Perhaps she's trying to protect us or something. All I know is she's different. I'm not sure you've noticed, but about the time we quit hearing from Mom and Dad, Aunt Cindy was home more, poking her nose into everything. She interrogates our friends when they're here, asking them about their parents and if they've ever traveled overseas."

"I just assumed she was looking for a single dad. Wouldn't that be cool to have our aunt as one of our friends' moms?"

Paul returned JJ's smile. "That may've been part of it, but look at her nights. She is home by midnight every night. Before, we were lucky if we saw her in the morning when we left. That also changed about the time the calls stopped."

"She has been acting odd for Aunt Cindy."

"I also called Mom and Dad's emergency phone numbers, both of them. All I get is ringing and a recording saying the phone is not in service. At first, I figured it was because of overseas reception, but I have been calling every day, and the recording is the same." This brought JJ to his feet.

"That can't be right. Do you think they're hurt? They're in Africa, right? Isn't that close to where the pirates steal boats and kidnap people for ransom?"

"I think that if our parents were being held for ransom, we would have been contacted in some way by now? I haven't seen anything on the news lately about pirate activity, but I'll have Jack check on that also."

"So that's why you asked Jack for help. Do you think he can find out something?" JJ looked hard at his brother. "What are we going to do if Mom and Dad don't come back?"

"First of all, let's slow down here. Jack's friend is FBI. If anyone can find out anything, I'm sure he can. Second, I asked Jack the same question. He told me not to give up hope. I think that's good advice. In the meantime, we wait. Also, we need to keep this between you, me, and Jack. There's no reason to let Aunt Cindy know we're questioning things. I'm sure she has her reasons why she feels she needs to lie to us." Paul turned his head to briefly hide his angered face.

"Do you think that Sierra woman knows anything about what happened to Mom and Dad?" JJ asked.

"Maybe? But she seemed more focused on the money than on our parents. I think the hundreds we spent are being singled out at the bank.

We need to be careful where we spend them." Paul was visualizing a plan.

"Are you saying it's okay to spend more?" JJ was hopeful.

"I've been thinking about it. You know Aunt Cindy took one of them, I'm thinking she'll use it at the club. It'll be interesting to see if the bank turns its focus there. Maybe spreading a few more around wouldn't hurt, perhaps down the Keys, a bit. But we'll still need to keep it on the down low. Our jobs at the marina will help, but mum is still the word."

"Sounds good. Do you think Aunt Cindy stole from us because Mom and Dad stopped paying her?"

Paul laid down his pencil and picked up his laptop. That hadn't even occurred to him. He opened his parents' online banking page and put in a username and password. It worked.

"You know their username and password?" JJ was stunned.

"I watched Mom a few times. I guess she didn't change it."

The account balance was quite healthy, showing a considerable amount of money. They looked at the activity and saw that only money for the house payment, utilities, and car payments were being deducted. As for deposits, there was an identical one every two weeks. Opening the "bill pay" section, they could see assorted payments that had been sent to a Cindy Parrish, their aunt Cindy. The last payment was sent just over two months ago. That was odd.

"So Aunt Cindy hasn't been paid for the last two months. That says something, but I'm not sure what." Paul shut his computer and gathered up his application. "Hey, grab your application. I want to show this to Jack."

JJ grabbed his papers and hurried to catch up with his brother as they ran out the back door, heading for their neighbor's house.

***

Jack parked his truck and walked toward his back door. Ahead were two shadows carrying something in their hands, running straight at him. He opened the door and switched on the porch light illuminating the path. The two figures slowed their approach, and one started to speak.

"Jack. We have something you need to see. It might be a clue about our parents. Can you take a look?"

"Sure, come on in." He held the door for the two boys. Paul sat at the kitchen table and opened his laptop. JJ sat next to him and continued with his application.

"Can you put in your wi-fi password? I need to get online. It's about our parents' bank account. Something is definitely wrong."

Jack leaned down and typed in his password. Paul once again opened the bank's web page and typed in the username and password.

"Your parents gave you the username and password of their bank account. They must really trust you." Jack looked at Paul.

"Actually, I got it from watching my mom, but to be honest, I haven't used it until now, and I think them being out of reach for two months gives me permission to snoop."

"You're right, it's none of my business. But it does make me wonder who may be watching my innocent keystrokes. What did you want to show me?" Jack looked worried.

"Right here, you can see that our aunt Cindy was last paid almost three months ago, but it seems that the house payment, car payment, and the utilities are still being paid each month."

"Those could be set up on auto-pay. That's how I do mine," Jack interjected.

"That explains the bills, but what about this regular deposit every two weeks, with no money being taken out. How can they live without using any money? The last withdrawal was just over two months ago - $500. From there, it looks like everything stopped about the same time as the phone calls. There has to be something wrong."

Jack pulled a chair up next to Paul on one side, and JJ moved in closer on the other.

Rosa had wandered in and was watching the three of them from the doorway. She was curious as to what the fuss was all about. Everything unusual made her worry about Julio being found. When she realized the group was talking about Charles and Sara Choate, she quietly slipped away to her room.

Jack looked through all the Choate's accounts, not trying to be nosy, but searching for clues. Sure enough, he could see that the $500 ATM transaction was at a bank in Djibouti, Africa; that being the last sign that the couple was alive. After he thoroughly searched through the account, he stood up and walked across the room.

"Paul, I will relay this information to Agent Medina. Can I let him know you are available if he needs more information?"

Paul looked at the sadness in Jack's eyes but hung onto the optimism in his words. "I'll do whatever it takes to get my parents back. There has to be an explanation."

Jack watched the two boys process what they found. Paul was finding his courage, and JJ was fighting tears. "I'm sure they're okay. We just need answers." Paul did his best to comfort his younger brother.

It was time to change the subject.

"So I see you brought your job applications. If you want to leave them with me, that will be fine. Then you can meet me at the marina after school tomorrow."

The boys signed their applications and left them on the table. Paul closed his computer, and the pair walked to the door.

"I know you don't have to help us, and we haven't been very good neighbors, but I just wanted to say thank you." JJ stepped forward and hugged him. That opened the flood gates. Now they were all fighting back tears.

"I'll let you know as soon as I get any news, I promise." And with that, the boys left.

On their way past the tree house, Paul stopped, which caused JJ to stumble.

"We're here, let's take another thousand and perhaps leave a few out for Aunt Cindy to find."

"I don't know . . ."

"It's not fair for her to take care of us and not get paid."

"Okay. What about the rest?"

"I think we can spend it here and there, if we're careful. I'll be right back."

Paul took his backpack and climbed the tree. JJ waited at the bottom of the ladder. Standing in the dark, JJ felt more and more uneasy with each minute his brother was gone. Within a few minutes, Paul was finished, and he locked the small door and climbed down.

Once inside the house, they each took $500, agreeing to each leave a hundred on their dressers for Aunt Cindy to take at her leisure. They still weren't sure what to believe about their caregiver, but things were starting to make more sense.

28

The Club – Palm Shores

It was still early as Sierra arrived back at the condo. She couldn't sit still. She felt unsettled. Pacing, she mentally replayed her visit to the marina. It was a quaint out-of-the-way place that would have been perfect for hiding a boat, but according to Jack, all was accounted for.

She smiled thinking about his face. If only she had time for a real relationship, she could see herself with someone like Jack. He was a perfect gentleman, and she liked how comfortable he made her feel. *Wait a minute!* After what she had been through, her emotional feelings screamed caution. Anyone who made her lower her defenses, she needed to investigate further. Was he trying to use his charms to throw her off the marina's scent? Could Jack be that man? Was he purposely deceiving her? She needed more information about Jack Winters.

Sierra walked into the kitchen and opened the refrigerator. Her stomach growled. Her grocery excursion had been forgotten after the marina tour, and she wasn't in the mood to drive to Key Largo for food. Looking around, she spotted the envelope that Carol had handed her as she left. Glancing inside, she pulled out a club card with her name and account number and a flyer that looked like a restaurant menu. The hours were generously displayed on the flyer, along with the list of daily dinner specials. She looked at her watch. She had an hour. She would have to change, but if she hurried, she could make it. She grabbed her suitcase and headed to the master suite.

The restaurant was buzzing as Sierra walked into the club. The hostess met her at the door and seated her by the window. It wasn't long until an older woman stepped up and took Sierra's food order—the daily special. After she left, Sierra looked around at the dimly lit room. She was impressed. It was quite nice. She turned back to the window and the lit grounds below. She was beginning to relax when a younger woman about her own age walked up and introduced herself.

"Hi, I'm Cindy, can I get you anything from the bar?"

She glanced up into her face and smiled. "I'm not much of a drinker. Alcohol messes with my thought process, and I like to stay alert."

"I know what you mean. I have recently changed my limit as well. However, we have a full-service bar, we can do any drink nonalcoholic. You look like you could use a treat, perhaps, a virgin daiquiri?"

"That actually sounds nice. Can you bring me a virgin piña colada?"

"Sure." As Cindy was writing down Sierra's virgin piña colada, she asked, "Are you new to Palm Shores? I don't remember seeing you here before."

"Actually, yes. I moved in today, and I'm already enjoying the beauty here." Sierra turned back to the view before her.

"I know what you mean. In my opinion, this is the best table in the club."

Sierra turned and looked at her waitress once again. "Since I'm new here, what do you suggest for fun?"

Cindy smiled. "Well, the club always has something happening into the night, and there's the marina, if you like boats or Jet Skis. My neighbor, Jack Winters, is the manager. He can be opinionated and somewhat strict, but most of the people here trust him with their boats. Other than that, this is the Florida Keys—your options are unlimited. Well, I better get your order in."

"Thanks, Cindy."

As Sierra watched her leave, she questioned Cindy's description of her neighbor. Something must have happened between her and gentleman Jack to cause such strong feelings. Jack seemed nice, and

Cindy seemed pleasant, but neighbor relationships could be tricky. Sierra had known neighbors who had sued each other over animals, trees, or even not returning something that was borrowed. This could have been one of those things.

Cindy—she had heard that name earlier today. The Choate boys were in the care of an aunt Cindy. Could she be one and the same? Could Jack Winters and the Choate boys live next door to each other? That was an interesting twist. Jack was becoming more and more relevant to her case. She would need to get to know them better.

Her salad arrived, and that brought her attention back to her stomach. Soon after, Cindy arrived with her drink. She seemed to linger, so Sierra asked, "Do you have a minute? Perhaps you can sit down and tell me more about Palm Shores."

"Well, it's almost time for my break. I'll be right back."

As she walked off, Sierra's food arrived. She had eaten all she wanted and had asked for a to-go box before Cindy returned and sat down across her.

"Are you done already?"

"Done eating but not done talking. I know your name is Cindy, let me introduce myself. I'm Sierra Skinner." Her hand only floated briefly before Cindy put forth hers.

"Nice to meet you, Sierra Skinner. I'm Cindy Parrish. What brings you this far South?" Both women were fishing, though they each sought different prey.

Another cocktail waitress stepped up and asked Sierra if she wanted another virgin piña colada. She nodded. She turned to Cindy, and you could tell there was tension between the two. She asked for one of the same, and the waitress moved on.

"To answer your question, I am a young widow, and I needed a sanctuary for a while, so I rented a condo down here. What about you? How long have you lived here?" Sierra waited for Cindy to answer. She seemed to be struggling with her thoughts.

"Well, I'm a divorcée who is down here taking care of my nephews while their parents are overseas on business." She went with the truth, interesting. "I've been here longer than I expected. It's a nice place, but the quiet can get to you sometimes."

Their drinks arrived. Sierra thanked her waitress and turned back to Cindy.

"Wow, babysitting and waiting tables, you're a super sister! How old are the boys?"

Cindy blushed a little at the compliment. "To be honest, they don't take much. They're teenagers, practically adults, and my job here is just for spending money and a way of getting out of the house. Sometimes I just need a break. Do you have children?"

Sierra didn't know if she would consider Paul and JJ Choate as practically adults, but she smiled. "No, my husband died before we could conceive. We planned for children up until he was diagnosed with cancer. Less than nine months later, I was alone." She lowered her head to show grief.

"I'm sorry for your loss. Sometimes I think the good ones die young. My husband was horrible to me almost from day one. I put up with it for a couple of years. Then decided I was done. Coming here actually helped me make that decision. I've had my fun here, dating most of the eligible bachelors, but that got old after a while." Cindy looked stressed.

"I think we need a happier subject. Have you been out on the water? I watched the sunset tonight, and it was just beautiful."

"No. I pretty much stay away from the marina. My neighbor Jack runs it, and he hates me."

"Wow. How'd that happen?"

"When I got here, I was quite the wild one. Let's just say he didn't approve and felt the need to tell me so."

"That sounds like it was ugly."

"To be honest, he was right, but I'm not ready to grovel over to his house and tell him so. I think I like our paths divided just the way they are. He stays out of my business, and I stay out of his."

"Probably a lot more peaceful that way." Sierra smiled at her.

"My sister says Jack lost his wife a couple of years back, and he really struggles with it."

"I know how that feels." Sierra thought of Jason's death, and a tear came to her eye, and she brushed it away.

"I guess I better get back to work before they fire me. I can't afford to lose this job."

Sierra thought her comment was odd. Wasn't her sister paying for her help? "Will your sister be back soon, or are you here for a while? I could use a friend around here."

Cindy answered before she thought it through. "I'm not sure, they're lost." She realized what she said and tried to fix it. "I mean, they tend to lose track of time when they're away."

Sierra caught the odd answer but let it slide. "Sounds like me when I travel. I get caught up in the adventure and want to stay as long as I can." She gave Cindy a smile. "Before you abandon me, can you tell me how this club works? What does this number on my card mean?"

"That number is you. Have you gone online and hooked it to a form of payment?"

"No. How do I do that?"

Cindy pulled a small form out of her apron and handed it to Sierra. Written on the paper was a web address and instructions. "Go here and use your account number and attach it to a credit card or bank account. Then whenever you eat at the club, you just show your ID card and sign your receipt, and they will automatically charge your method of payment."

"What about tonight? What do I do about tonight?"

"I'll tell you what, tonight's on me. Next time, it's on you. I'll be right back." She pulled out a hundred-dollar bill, took the check, and disappeared before Sierra could stop her.

Sierra did what she was told and sat at her table looking out across the well-manicured lawns lit up by the moonlight. Cindy had surprised her with her offer, and it bothered her. From what she was saying, how could she afford such a kind deed? Still, it was seeing that hundred-dollar bill in the hands of the Choate boys' aunt that made her question. Could that be one of Julio's hundreds? Was this playing out right in front of her? The bank was supposed to call her personally if any more arrived, but did this club use that bank? She didn't know if she wanted that bill to be one of the marked bills or not, especially after what she was hearing about the boys' parents. Were they really lost? How did Julio, Max, Juan, Jack, Cindy, and the Choate boys figure into this whole thing?

Cindy returned to the table with her apron off and her purse draped over her shoulder. She handed Sierra a folded piece of paper. Sierra started to open it, thinking Cindy was going to ask for payment for the check after all.

"What's this?"

"It's my phone number and address. How about you meet me at my house for breakfast after the boys leave for school, around nine? I haven't had a friend around here for a while, and I'd like to get to know you better."

"Sounds like fun. Are you done for the evening?"

"Well, with my job, but now the fun begins. They have some nice dance clubs here that go till midnight. Girls gotta blow off steam. Do you want to join me?"

Sierra smiled. "I'm not ready for that kind of fun yet, perhaps another time."

"Okay, but I'm holding you to that." Cindy returned the smile.

Sierra stood up and walked with Cindy to the hallway. Saying goodbye, they each went their separate ways.

It was after 10:00 p.m. as Sierra settled down for the night. She pulled out her computer and connected to the wi-fi for her condo. The day's events were swirling in her head. It was the comment Cindy made about Paul and JJ's parents that she couldn't shake. What did she mean by "lost"? Were they missing?

Signing into her FBI account, she did a background search on Paul Choate, Key Largo, Florida. He came back as a seventeen-year-old Paul Winston Choate, grandson of Paul Winston Choate, son of John Charles and Sara Larsen Choate, and brother to John Charles Choate Jr., age fifteen.

She plugged John Charles Choate in and found that his file was blocked. She tried Sara Larsen Choate, and her file was also blocked.

She knew what that meant: She would receive a call from Homeland Security soon. Her phone rang.

"Special Agent Cortez." She answered on the first ring.

"Special Agent Cortez, Agent Suarez here. What's your interest in Charles and Sara Choate?" She knew he was looking her up as he spoke.

"First of all, their names have crossed my case, and second, what's their connection with Homeland Security?"

"I suppose you aren't at liberty to disclose your case, but I see you have logged in from Key Largo, Florida, the Choate's home location, which tells me you know they've been away for a while."

"I can tell you their boys are connected on the fringes of my case, and I need to know if their parents are involved in some way."

"When did your case begin?"

"I've been embedded for over three months, but the connection to Key Largo started just this last week."

"The Choate parents have been gone for over six months. They work for Homeland Security, undercover, as shipping agents in Djibouti, Africa. They disappeared a couple of months back. We are zeroing in, but it's unlikely they're mixed up in your case in the States."

"Who's watching out for their boys and their aunt?"

"We've had an agent embedded with the family in Florida since their parents left. They're well protected."

She thought he was finished and expected him to hang up, but he came back with his own question.

"Special Agent Cortez, are you working with a Special Agent Medina? He has also inquired into Charles and Sara Choate."

That surprised her. "Agent Medina from Miami?"

"Yes."

"I know him, but he isn't part of my case. When did he inquire?"

"This morning."

"Did he say why?"

"He said he was checking for a friend of the family. I had to shut him down. If there's nothing further, good night, Special Agent Cortez."

"Good night, Agent Suarez." Sierra was confused.

Sierra hung up the phone and shut down her computer. Her thoughts were trying to put together all the pieces she had learned since coming to Florida. She had two teenagers on a spending spree of FBI-marked $100 bills, an aunt who was worried that their parents were missing, and Agent Medina in Miami snooping into this whole thing. She had more questions than answers. Her mind was restless as she lay down for the night.

29

On the Hunt – Key Largo

Juan was up early. He couldn't sleep. It was his conversation with his protégé that left his night in a fit of restlessness. Victor Ramos was capable enough, but he was dismissive, curt, and downright rude. He knew the job had its challenges, but Ramos had only been doing it one day. Something wasn't right. He needed to get this business with Max and Julio settled quickly and get back. He was giving himself two days. His shower, shave, and clean suit swayed his anxiety some. He was dressed to kill, and it was time to get started.

His room was a suite, well laid out, with a large workspace. Sitting at the desk, he went over his plan for the day. He pulled out his phone and sent a text to Oswaldo; they would meet out front at 9:45 a.m. to arrive at the bank before 10:00 a.m. He opened his briefcase and removed the money from the envelope he'd received at dinner, placing a thousand in his wallet and the rest in his briefcase's lining. Sorting through his forged identities, he placed the FBI credentials in his suit pocket. Next, he picked up the map and marked the marinas he wanted searched. Lifting the desk phone, he first called the concierge and verified that a rental car was scheduled for Carlos and Mondo, and then he called their room. Carlos answered.

Mondo was restless. He was dreaming. The kitchen was beautiful but unfamiliar. Where was he? He saw a flash and heard a scream.

Stepping forward, he was engulfed in pain. He hit his knees on the floor. He hit hard. His head lay on the concrete surface—not concrete but ceramic tile. It was red, or was that blood? Someone else was there, lying next to him. It was Julio—no, Carlos. He didn't know. He couldn't tell. A woman leaned over him. She looked familiar, but he could only see her eyes.

She spoke. "He's dead. What about the other one?"

A man's voice with a Spanish accent replied, "He's dead too."

He was surrounded by people, so many people, all strangers to him, except for the woman. Her touch was tender. She was shutting his eyelids. He tried to scream, but no sound emerged. The woman stood. She was talking to a second woman. She was leaving—leaving him to die.

His eyes opened. Panic gripped his heart. There was a light, so it was true. He was saved. He blinked, and his eyes reawakened to darkness. He blinked again, and his eyes adjusted to the hue. He turned his head seeing Carlos standing in front of the window. He let out the breath he didn't remember holding and slapped himself in the face to verify life. His ears were ringing. No, it was the phone. Carlos reached over and picked it up, cupping the receiver to shield his words. He didn't care. He wasn't in the mood for games. He felt the tightness in his chest lighten. It wasn't real. He was fine. Taking a deep breath, he grabbed his clothes and headed for the shower.

Carlos waited until he heard the shower start before he walked to the adjoining room door and unlocked his side. He knocked. Juan opened his door, and the two exchanged maps and conversed briefly. There was no reason for an explanation of expectations; he understood his job and the consequences. He just wished he could get rid of the deadwood he was tasked with. Mondo was a nice-enough guy, but he had been Julio's friend. That made him untrustworthy as far as he was concerned. The meeting ended, and the doors were locked back in place. Pulling out his personal cell, Carlos walked across the room and looked out the window. He scrolled through his contacts and found "Ramos, Victor" and pushed send.

He was finishing up his call when Mondo stepped out of the bathroom fully dressed.

"I gotta go." He quickly hung up and headed for the door.

"Juan handed me a marked map, so if you're finally ready, let's go." Mondo followed Carlos to the concierge desk.

Oswaldo was sitting in the black SUV watching as Juan Perrone exited the lobby and headed in his direction. He couldn't figure this guy out. Why was he here? Who were these two men, Max and Julio? Why were they so important that their boss was willing to drop everything and find them himself? Part of him respected the man for being willing to get his hands dirty, but he knew where his loyalties lay.

Perrone climbed in and buckled his seat belt. He typed the address into his phone, and ten minutes later, they were parked across the street, waiting for the bank to open. The clock ticked by in silence. At exactly nine fifty-eight, Oswaldo started the engine and drove up to the door and parked.

Standing outside the bank doors, a figure of a woman appeared through the glass. She sent a smile their way and clicked the lock open. Stepping aside, she allowed them to pass. Upon entering, they noticed a man sitting behind a desk in a glassed-in office. The door was labeled "Jose Santana, Bank Manager." Ignoring the customer service steward who stepped forward to help them, Juan and Oswaldo made their way through the manager's door, taking him off guard.

"May I help you?" Jose closed a file folder sitting on his desk and gave his guests his full attention.

"I'm Supervisory Agent Sanchez, and this is Agent Perez." He flashed his ID. "We are here to follow up on the flagged bills you called in."

"The ones Special Agent Cortez picked up yesterday?"

This took Perrone off guard. He was shocked the FBI had already sent someone in to retrieve the bills.

"Yes. That's why we're here. We do a random follow up to keep our agents honest, if you know what I mean." He forced a smile. Jose gave a wry smile in return.

"Can you verify that Agent Cortez picked up and replaced eight $100 bills yesterday?"

The manager reached into his file drawer and pulled out a red file. Opening it, he read aloud, "On Friday night, 9/16, The Dive Shop." He added, "A local business, for clarity. "Deposited seven $100 bills, and on the same day, The Sub Shop, another local favorite, deposited one $100 bill. They all had serial numbers flagged in the system. A Special Agent Cortez arrived Monday morning and picked up and replaced the bills. I spoke to her personally."

Perrone wasn't expecting Agent Cortez to be a woman. He hesitated for a minute but soon recovered. "Was she professional?"

"She was a little casual, but this is South Florida, we are more laid back here."

"Did she replace the bills she took with her?"

"Yes. She handed me eight $100 bills, and I gave her the FBI-flagged ones. I have the serial numbers here, if that will help."

Perrone took it all in. Special Agent Cortez had the money. He could get nothing more here. "No. That's fine. I have what I need." Perrone and Oswaldo stood up and left Santana's office.

As they exited the bank, a clerk stepped into the Santana's office and handed him another red file folder with two more flagged bills attached. He quickly dismissed her. Glancing at the closing front door, he shook his head. He wasn't sure what was going on, but there was something about his recent guests that he didn't trust. He picked up the phone and called Special Agent Cortez.

Juan and Oswaldo pulled up to The Dive Shop just a few minutes after they left the bank. The sign on the door read "OPEN." Looking around, Juan noted The Sub Shop across the street. They were definitely in the right place. Oswaldo turned off the engine and reached for the door. Juan caught his arm to halt his exit.

"Oswaldo, we are going in there to get information, and we aren't leaving until we get some. Do you understand?"

"Got it. I'll follow your lead."

Oswaldo brought up the rear as the pair made their way into the dive shop. Juan headed for the checkout counter, while Oswaldo locked the front door and turned the open sign to closed. Spying a camera by the door, Oswaldo redirected it toward the wall. Looking around the room, he couldn't see any other cameras. He joined his boss. Juan had waited at the counter for Oswaldo to finish securing the premises before he rang the bell for service. A middle-aged man exited the back room with a smile on his face.

"Hi, I'm Nick, may I help you?"

"I'm sure you can. Last Friday, you sent seven $100 bills in with your night deposit. What I need to know is where they came from?"

He looked over the two men. "Who are you?" he asked.

"Well, let's see . . . If you cooperate, you can look at us as simple satisfied customers. But if you choose to make this difficult, you won't be alive to care. So I'll ask you one more time, who came into your store last Friday and spent seven $100 bills."

Nick held his ground. "I'm afraid, without proper identification, I can't release that information."

Juan looked long and hard at the stalwart man. He seemed unmoved by the odds against him. It was a battle of wills that Perrone had no interest in playing. He turned to his lackey. "Oswaldo, take care of him."

Oswaldo stepped toward him with the force of a linebacker. Nick shied away but not far enough for escape. It all happened in a blur as the back of a monstrous hand smashed across his face, leaving knuckle imprints on his cheek. His body followed his neck unwillingly. He hit the floor, pulling a rack of dive suits down on top of him. A hand reached through the debris and pulled him back to his feet. He was unsteady, cradled in his captor's grasp.

Juan tried again. "Right now, I own you. If you give me what I want, I will have my friend here let you go, but if you keep trying to be a hero, you can kiss your family and this establishment goodbye." He paused briefly, taking a deep breath to still his anger. He would have preferred to wring the man's neck and be done with him, but he needed a name. He searched for a calmer voice. "Listen, we are not unreasonable people. All you have to do is tell me what I want to know, and we'll let you and your business live on."

Nick was bleeding. A gouge above his right eye was impeding his vision. He blinked, causing the blood to smear. It didn't help. In all his years as a shop owner, he had never experienced such violence. He was visibly scared and with good reason. His life was in danger, but what frightened him more than his own safety was the nearing hour. With his good eye, he glanced at the hands on the clock across the room and quietly prayed that today, of all days, his niece would be late for her shift. If not, she would be walking through the back door in the next few minutes.

His hesitation cost him. Before he could agree with his attacker and halt the assault, Oswaldo's other hand, balled in a fist, made contact with his stomach. His body crumbled, and he would have met the floor, once again, if his abuser wasn't holding him with his other hand. He turned his face upward, toward the man calling the shots.

Gasping for air, he mouthed the word "okay" and nodded his agreement. A name wasn't worth his life or his niece's.

He pointed to the register and was escorted behind the counter with his feet swaying from the brute's grip. He reached into his pocket and pulled out a key. Turning the lock, he opened a drawer and removed a file. Still trying to clear his vision, he drew out the deposit form dated Friday, 9/16. Attached to the back was a handful of receipts marked cash sales. As he began to separate them, he was pushed out of the way, barely steadying himself with the counter's edge. He was where he wanted to be. He only had to move his finger an inch. Slowly, he inched his hand toward the button. He felt it give way under his pressure—the alarm had been tripped. He could only hope that they would arrive before his niece Portia.

It was Oswaldo rifling through the handful of receipts, then Juan was there pulling them from him. There was definitely a territory issue between these two men. It was no wonder they missed Nick's call for help. Then everything changed. The back door opened, and in walked a teenage girl.

She was humming as she stepped from the backroom into the shop. Her uncle, desperately trying to secure her attention, was waving his arms and edging in her direction. His captors were busy rifling through the receipts and wouldn't have noticed her if she hadn't yelled "hello!" with a reply wave in Nick's direction.

It took only two steps for Oswaldo to regain his hold on the shop owner. Juan, stuffing the receipts in his pocket, headed for the girl. Portia, realizing that her uncle was in trouble, turned and headed back the way she came. Running through the back room, she made it outside and across the street before her pursuer reached the exit. She was safe.

A distant siren grabbed his attention, and Juan headed back to the showroom. Their time was short. With the girl on the loose, the police wouldn't be far away. He nodded to Oswaldo to mete out another round to Nick, for his trouble, and they left the store with a crumpled shop owner gasping for breath. They were long gone before the police arrived.

Portia was on the phone with 911 as the police pulled up in front of her uncle's shop. She heard the sirens. Handing off the phone, she ran outside. Two officers directed her behind their cruisers as they questioned her and cleared the scene. The ambulance pulled up, and her Uncle Nick was wheeled out before she was allowed to move from her position. She ran to him and crawled in the ambulance behind the paramedics, calling her aunt Arlene to meet them at the hospital. His appearance and the oxygen mask on his face frightened her, and she began to break down. She grabbed her phone and texted Paul. She just hoped he would check it between classes. She needed him.

Oswaldo and Juan drove away from the strip mall as calmly and quietly as they arrived. They had the receipts, and with the shape of the shop owner, they were pretty sure he wouldn't survive to be a problem. As for the girl, they expected to be long gone before she could finger them. Juan reached into his pocket and pulled out a fistful of receipts. Shuffling through them, he found a sale for a Paul Choate for $700 with a Key Largo address. He punched it into the GPS, and they headed toward the morning sun.

30

Breakfast at Cindy's – Palm Shores

Sierra arrived at the Choate's home at exactly 9:00 a.m. She was interested in finding out more about this family. It baffled her how Cindy and her charges were freely spending hundred-dollar bills all over Key Largo, yet Cindy needed to work as a waitress for money. If their situation was so dire, why spend so recklessly? Perhaps they were being paid to spend those hundreds. Was Max using this family to gage the FBI's interest? Or was Julio trying to send a message to his handler? Did he even know Jason was dead? By default, Sierra was his handler now, and she needed to find him and protect him. If the money was his plea for help, she was listening. Answers—that's what she needed, and she hoped Cindy would oblige.

Sierra knocked on the door and waited. A sleepy-eyed mussed woman dressed in PJs answered.

"Am I early?" Sierra was puzzled.

"No, I'm just late. Come on in."

She walked into a beautiful upscale home adorned in posh furnishings and famed artwork. There was money here. It had to be flowing through from somewhere. Just inside the door and to the left was a baby grand piano centered in a formal space. Next to the shimmering beauty sat a pair of white wingback chairs, complementing the ebony structure. To the right was a home office handsomely laid out and observably locked—a clear sign that any secrets left by the Choates were secured in place. She made a mental note of the lock. It was a step above standard, but she felt she could pick it if the need were to arise. As they continued forward, she observed a formal dining room almost sterile in nature and a family room where the family actually lived. There were video game controllers and empty drink bottles lying on the coffee table, as if the boys had just stepped away.

Cindy didn't slow her pace until they reached the kitchen, where she proceeded to pull out a package of French toast from the freezer and handed it to her. "Can you take care of this? I'll be right back."

Sierra wasn't sure how to respond. Instead, she just watched Cindy's back as she disappeared down the hallway. Realizing her opinion really didn't matter, she turned the bag over and read the heating instructions. Laying the package on the counter, she made a visual sweep of the kitchen and noted its striking layout. It was square-shaped with a breakfast bar along one side. The granite countertops, stainless steel appliances, and floor-to-ceiling cherry wood cabinets were beautifully designed in the space. Her attention was drawn to the two unwashed cereal bowls in the sink. The Choate boys took care of themselves. This was a home with missing parents, a thought that left her saddened but she couldn't allow herself to get drawn in. She had her own mystery to solve.

Her eyes caught the back patio. There were two sets of sliding glass doors—one off the side of the kitchen and one off the breakfast nook. The view across the back lawn would be perfect on a postcard. There was a decaying tree house lodged in an old oak tree whose branches reached into the sky and flowed over to the water's edge. It was breathtaking.

She turned her attention back to the task at hand. Deciding where to start, she began looking through the cupboards for plates. Putting them on the counter, she placed three pieces of toast on each. Waiting, to allow her hostess more time to change, she walked over to the office door. The door was definitely locked. She looked through the glass, noting a large model of a Spanish galleon ship lying on the desk. Behind the desk was a shelf filled with nautical books, from sailing to exporting.

This family was definitely familiar with boats. She was intrigued. Could this room hold any answers to the missing Choates? She moved around, looking at different angles. What struck her as odd was the amount of dust she could see lying across the woodwork, very different from the piano in the front room, which was immaculately cared for and dusted. The office must have been locked up before the parents left with strict rules of access. That boundary had been honored.

Sierra looked at her watch and headed back to the kitchen. She didn't know how long Cindy would take to dress, but she didn't want to be caught snooping. She preceded to follow the printed instructions on the bag. It was when she pulled the second plate from the microwave and placed it in the oven to keep it warm that a fully dressed and primped Cindy emerged from the hallway. Cindy quickly filled two glasses with orange juice and carried them to the kitchen nook. She then went back to the refrigerator and brought back butter, fruit, and syrup. Sierra, pulling the plates from the warming oven, followed in kind. They sat opposite each other. Sierra broke the silence. "You clean up well." She smiled as Cindy looked up.

"I'm sorry about that, but I am a total bear in the morning. I probably did you a favor staying clear. I appreciate you taking care of things."

"No problem. Let's eat."

Between bites, Sierra let loose a string of compliments about the house and the backyard. She had just finished her first piece of toast when Cindy changed the subject and got to the meat of her invitation to breakfast.

"If you don't mind me being blunt, what are you really doing here in Palm Shores?"

Sierra was taken off guard. She didn't expect to be interrogated, though her companion's odd behavior should've given her notice. Placing her fork on the edge of her plate and pushing it aside, she looked at her inquisitor. "Cindy, what's wrong? You look like you're carrying the weight of the world."

Cindy burst into tears. She was ready to be tough and defend her question, but she wasn't prepared for tenderness. "I-I can't tell you. They told me I can't tell anyone."

Her answer piqued Sierra's interest. Who was threatening this woman? Perrone? Max? Julio? Would Julio do such a thing. "Who's threatening you?"

"No. No. No one is threatening me."

"Then what's wrong? Why can't you tell me?"

"It's my sister." Cindy was struggling to speak through her sobs. "Someone took them, and-and the government can't find them, and they won't let me tell the boys. They've been lost for over two months. What am I going to do? I'm not their parent. Besides, they don't even like me."

Sierra felt her pain. She handed her some napkins from the holder in the middle of the table. Here it was, the rest of the story, but not the one she was seeking. Yet she felt for this family, and though she knew more about the Choates' situation than Cindy, she couldn't blow her cover to help her find the peace she was looking for. All she could do was listen and let her release the pain she'd silently carried for so long.

Sierra slid her chair closer and gave her a one-armed hug. Soothingly, she whispered, "Cindy, I'm sure if the government is keeping it quiet, they have a plan. Don't give up. Good things are bound to come your way soon."

Cindy laid her head on Sierra's shoulder and let loose. The house was deathly still except an occasional sniff. Suddenly, Cindy sat up, wiped her eyes, and blew her nose. She stood up and turned to Sierra. "I think it's time for you to go."

Sierra smiled. Cindy was back. The spunky, strong-willed woman had returned. She would let her keep what pride she had left.

Sierra stood. "I would like to thank you for a lovely breakfast. We should do this again. Next time, it's on me."

Cindy accepted the compliment gracefully and walked her to the door. They parted company.

As Sierra made her way to her car, she noticed that the Choate house was secluded from the street, but the neighbor's garage was less than ten feet away. She wondered if the two properties were once one. The smaller home next door could have been the caretaker's cottage. This must be Jack's place. She could see how a wild Cindy could have easily caused an uproar creating a wedge between the neighbors.

As she was sitting there musing, she watched an elderly woman carrying a sagging grocery bag exit the smaller house. She climbed into an old car parked on the far side of the drive and backed onto the street. The bag reminded Sierra that she still needed groceries. She looked at her watch and noted it was almost eleven. She did a GPS search for grocery stores, finding a Winn-Dixie in Key Largo. She pressed the "Go" button and backed out of the driveway, heading for the front gate.

Her phone rang. It was the manager at the bank. She listened to the short call and reprogrammed her GPS for the First State Bank in Key Largo.

As Sierra slowed past the security gate, she observed some kind of commotion going on between the guard and two men in a black SUV. It reminded her of when she first tried to get into the neighborhood and how strict they were to outsiders, but with these men, there was yelling. She expected the police would be called to straighten it out, but a little while later, the same black SUV sped past her. She figured he must've given up, much like she did. For some reason, the whole situation bothered her. A cold chill ran down her spine. She shook it off. She was getting sidetracked again. She needed to go to the bank, get some food, and then pay Jack another visit.

The bank visit was quick, and he had some news for her: Her supervisor and another man had made a follow-up visit to check up on her. He felt she should know, though he was instructed to keep it quiet. Santana informed her that the whole thing seemed odd to him. She was rattled but smiled. She thanked him and took the names of the businesses that made the deposits. Her fear was confirmed: There was one from the club at Palm Shores. It was Cindy's hundred.

Back in her car, she phoned Director Smith's private cell number. It went to voice mail. She left him an inquiry about a supervisor following up on her at the bank. That was all she could do for now. Her stomach growled. She headed for the grocery store. It didn't take her long to gather a few easy meals and basic items. She was nearing the checkout counter when she realized she forgot breakfast cereal and milk. The cereal was easy, it was behind where she was standing, but the milk was at the far end of the store. It was this errand that changed everything.

31

Hide and Seek – Key Largo

The grocery store deli was filled with people ordering sandwiches when Carlos and Mondo arrived for lunch. They were frustrated. The marina search had turned out to be a bust. At first, it was a problem getting past the secured gates and onto the docks, but they found a way. It was a simple matter of overloading themselves and pretending to struggle with the lock, bringing a Good Samaritan to the rescue. Once they got through the gate, they would choose a rundown vessel near the end as their destination. The slowness of their progress would bore any lingering observer yet allow them visual access to each boat they passed. At times they would raise their voices of curiosity and lean over the edge to get a better look. If someone was working on their vessel, Mondo would chum them up and ask for a tour. These methods gained them access to more than half of their targets. The rest, they looked for signs of life or daily use. In their search, they had seen everything, from dinghies to massive-size boats, but none of them matched Juan's description. They had a picture. It was a beautiful medium-size yacht, about seventy foot in length, with the name *Macon It Easy* printed on the stern. Though this should be making it easy, so far, their efforts had fallen short.

Mondo needed food. They had skipped breakfast, hoping to wind things up by noon, but here they were with nothing to report. If Julio or the yacht were in Key Largo, he wasn't hanging out at the marinas, at least not the ones they had inspected. They were hoping for more luck after lunch. His stomach growled from the smells around him. Carlos stepped up and pulled a number. There were ten people ahead of them. Glancing at each other, they walked away from the deli counter to explore the grocery shelves, seeking a quick alternative. That's when it happened. Coming around the corner of the cereal aisle, a shocked Mondo stopped in his tracks. This caused a collision of their two bodies as Carlos, following too close, crashed into him.

"What are you doin—"

Mondo, with his finger to his lips, had grabbed him and turned him around. "Shhh," he hissed.

"What is it?" Carlos's whisper was barely audible. "Is it Juan? I'm sure he can't fault us for stopping for lunch. We haven't been here that long."

Mondo shook his head and whispered as he quickly glanced back over his shoulder, "No. It's someone else, and you won't believe me if I tell you. I'll have to show you. Follow me."

Carlos gave him an odd look. Who would they know here? But curiosity had a seductive taunt. Quietly, he followed Mondo, watching closely as he surveyed each aisle before heading to the next. They were at the last one, which was lined with glass-door coolers, when Mondo quickly pulled back. Grabbing Carlos, he traded him places and pointed for him to look. He timidly peeked around the corner and saw a short woman with long dark hair. He was puzzled at first, but then she turned her face toward him. He jumped back, nearly knocking Mondo over.

"It's that babe from the bar. Wait." He looked again, trying to fit this narrative into his reality. He jumped back.

"It's her, all right. What's she doing here?" Mondo also looked puzzled, trying to fill in the pieces. It was all coming together, but before he could speak, they heard footsteps. Almost running, they moved over two aisles, keeping their voices at a whisper and their eyes peeled.

Mondo stopped. Turning, he grabbed Carlos's shoulder. "I think she's here to meet Julio."

"She knows Julio?" Carlos was confused.

"It was before your time. She and Julio were kind of a thing."

Carlos just smiled. "You should have told me. I could have had some real fun with her."

"Well, she's all the proof we need. He's here. And she'll lead us right to him."

"Do you think she saw us?"

"I don't know. Let's split up. We need to find her."

She was paying for her groceries the next time Mondo saw her. Grabbing some chips, crackers, and soda, he slipped into an empty cash lane and paid for his items. As he finished, he noticed the woman exiting the store. Taking his bag and casually walking out after her, he followed her to her car. She was moving quickly. He stopped at a small black sports car a few stalls away and pretended to dig for his keys while noting the make, model, and license plate number on hers. Then she was gone.

He headed for their rental on the opposite side of the parking lot and waited for Carlos. It was ten minutes before he appeared, and by that time, Mondo had already eaten through one of the boxes of crackers and started in on the next. He was glad he thought to pick up something to eat.

It was too late to follow her by the time Carlos arrived, and it was decided that their stomach discomfort outweighed driving around blindly. They went back inside to order their sandwiches. By then, the line had fizzled out, and they quickly placed their order. They grabbed an empty table by the window.

"How are we going to explain this to Juan? He will be furious that we let her get away." Mondo looked as worried as he sounded.

"Personally, I think, until we can produce her, we should keep this to ourselves." Mondo was a little shocked by Carlos's answer. It seemed out of character. The real question was, could he trust him?

However, trust was a two-way street. Relying on Carlos to honor his word was not a feeling with which Mondo was comfortable. Then again, he was also holding back. He thought about the rest of the information he had gleaned from her car. Telling Carlos the color was all he was willing to disclose. It was Carlos's comments and treatment of women, especially this one, that bothered Mondo. He would play it by ear and see what information was needed when. He didn't have to decide right now.

"So we're in agreement—before we talk to Juan about Sierra, we both need to agree. Right?"

"Sounds good to me. What Juan don't know doesn't hurt us." Their eyes met, and they nodded.

***

Sierra was frightened. The face she had seen at the grocery store was that letch Carlos, one of Juan's men. He was here. The men at the bank that morning and the scuffle at the security gate had to be him and one of his cronies. Were they following her? It looked like Carlos definitely was. She looked in her rearview mirror—no one was behind her. She calmed her nerves and entered Palm Shores and headed for her condo. Her time schedule had just shortened. She unloaded her groceries and headed for the marina. It was time to have another talk with Manager Jack.

Her phone rang. It was Director Smith.

"Hello, Director," she answered.

"Sierra, what's this about an audit at the bank?"

"Director, the bank president said there were two men, one claiming to be my supervisor, following up on my visit on Monday to pick up the marked bills."

"So our mole strikes again. Listen, Sierra, you be careful. It sounds like Juan and his men have arrived and are fast on your heels. You should contact Miami and get some back up to help you finish this."

"Sir, I am so close, I can feel it. Give me till the end of the day and let me see what I can find out. Tomorrow I will reassess things and look into getting help, okay?"

"Okay, but be careful! And if Miami hasn't called me for operational approval by end of day tomorrow, I will call them in myself. Understand?"

"Yes, sir."

Sierra hung up as she pulled into the marina. There was a heavy stillness in the air.

32

Rosa's Secret – Palm Shores

Jack laid down the last page of his daily report. It was still early, but he was ready to walk the docks, close up shop, and go home. Construction at the marina had ground to an abrupt halt shortly after noon, leaving him frustrated. The first boat should have been loaded on the trailer that morning, but it had been postponed till the following day. That left him with workers standing around, being paid to do nothing. He had insurance companies, boat owners, and crane operators lined up in a domino effect, waiting for their cue, each vying for work order priority. His job was to maintain order and keep things steady. He hated waste, especially his own time. Giving up on productivity shortly after lunch, he acquiesced and sent his workforce home.

Leaning back in his office chair, he blinked at the sunlight streaming in through the window. It beckoned him to the sea. He closed his eyes, basking in the heat of its rays as he envisioned a wave-touched sunset. If he hurried, he could witness it anew. He was done with his paperwork, and all that was left was to walk the property and head home to ready his boat. Perhaps he could salvage the rest of his day, after all. As he was preparing for a quick exit, his cell phone buzzed. Glancing at his caller ID, he answered, "Louis, it's good to hear from you. Does this mean you have news?"

"I do, but I would like to discuss it in person. Can you meet me at the Fish Shack on Route 1 in Florida City at five this evening?"

"That shouldn't be a problem."

"Great. See you soon."

Jack pocketed his phone, grabbed his keys, and headed for the door. His final security check wouldn't take long, which would allow him ample time for a shower and shave before heading north. Reaching for the front door, it opened to his touch. Then a familiar face stepped in.

"Welcome back. It's Sierra, right?" Closing the door, he offered her a chair.

"That's right. Are you always that good with names?"

"It comes and goes." He smiled. "What brings you by? Did you have more questions?"

"Well, I wanted another look around, if that's okay? Before they load my yacht, I thought I would take one more tour."

"I was just getting ready to do my afternoon check. You are welcome to join me."

"Sounds like an adventure." Standing, she took his offered arm.

It was near the end of their stroll when Sierra thought she saw movement in the boat at the end. She halted her steps, which pulled him up short.

"What's wrong?"

"I thought I saw someone."

"Where?"

"That boat down on the end."

"Well, let's take a look." He smiled at her and led the way.

Jack didn't expect to find anyone on the boat, since the owners were traveling, but he was happy to make this an adventure for his guest. He led her toward the farthest dock, leaving her on the pier as he stepped on the bow. Casually, he walked around the vessel, performing a serious security search for his audience. As he approached the stairs, a familiar face stepped into his view.

"Rosa? I didn't know you were here."

"I was just running an errand for a friend. I was going to stop up at the office before I left. Is there something wrong?"

"No. Not really. We thought we saw someone, so I was just checking it out. Have you been here for a while?"

"Not long . . . Who is 'we'?"

Jack was still trying to figure out what Rosa was doing on one of his owner's private yachts when her words pulled him back. He turned and acknowledged his companion. Rosa stepped up to his level and followed him onto the pier.

"Rosa, this is Sierra, one of our new residents here at Palm Shores."

"Sierra, this is my friend and housekeeper, Rosa." The women stepped toward each other and performed a traditional Latin greeting, a double-cheek kiss, which seemed comfortable to both women.

While they were so engaged, Jack looked down the steps at the closed door. It bothered him that Rosa didn't mention her visit or her friendship with the owner. He decided her curious behavior was worth noting. Rosa sensed his uneasiness with her presence. She quickly changed the subject.

"Well, I'm done. How about I walk back to the office with you two? I would like to get to know Sierra better. It seems her ancestry is Cuban, like mine."

Jack stepped over to the dock and held an arm out for each woman, and off they went. He would have to question Rosa later. He was sure she was purposefully leaving something out. Any place else, he wouldn't care, but the marina was his responsibility, and if anything was going on, he needed to know.

It wasn't long until the women were deep in family history. Jack just enjoyed listening to their accents, allowing the memory of his Maria to settle in his thoughts.

At the office, Rosa motioned to leave, and Jack excused himself from Sierra and walked her to her car.

"Is everything okay?" he asked her.

"Everything is fine, Jack." But her eyes drifted toward the boat on the end.

He left the silence between them linger, hoping she would confess her secret, but she just smiled and seated herself as he opened her door.

"Well, I guess I should tell you that I won't be home for dinner tonight." He ended the tension before she drove away.

"No problem." He heard her call through the open window as she drove off.

He turned toward the office and found Sierra walking toward him. She thanked him for the tour and left as quickly as she had come. Back up at the office, he paused in the doorway and sought out the Cutler's boat that had caused so much interest. He watched for a few minutes, then locked up, and set out to find answers to Rosa's mystery.

By the time Jack arrived, he had nearly changed his mind. It was Maria that pushed him on. Her voice was in his head, urging him to see this through. He would still give Rosa her chance to explain, but he couldn't let his suspicions go unresolved. He carefully boarded the boat, feeling the movement with each step. He descended the stairs and knocked on the door below. To his surprise, it opened.

He didn't expect to see Roberto, the young man he rescued from the ocean, standing there, yet it made sense. Rosa had formed a bond with this young man. Still, their secrecy puzzled him. Rosa should've taken him to the authorities to start his paperwork. Something wasn't right.

Realizing he was staring, he forced himself to speak. "Roberto, what are you doing here?"

He stepped aside, motioning for Jack to enter. Roberto shut the door behind him and joined his guest. He was several words in before Jack realized his question was not only being answered, but also the young man before him was speaking English.

"Jack, I will answer your questions, but I need you to promise me that this conversation won't go any further. Rosa said I can trust you." Jack nodded, still stunned. "My name is Julio Roberto Torres." Jack stuck out his hand for a formal greeting, and they shook. "First of all, I want to thank you for saving my life. When the boat went down, I had given up on expecting any kind of rescue." He paused, remembering. Shuddering, he continued, "I was making peace with my ancestors, believing it ironic that I would perish so close to their homeland." Reaching up, he wiped away the moisture forming on his cheeks. Jack stayed silent, letting this young man tell his story in his own way. He could see that he was working up the courage to share a part of his life that had caused him deep pain. "You see, I killed my mother."

"What? Why? How?"

"Rosa just showed me her obituary. She was killed the day I left. I might as well have pulled the trigger myself. It's my fault she's dead. I should've known he'd shoot her when he didn't find the money." He brushed another line of tears away with his hand.

"Okay, slow down. Start over, from the beginning."

Julio wondered where he should start. When he first met Juan? Last week? He decided to start with the boat and fill in what he needed to as he went.

"About a week ago, I was arrested by the FBI. I still don't know how or why, but I woke up in a cell. There was this Special Agent Jason Kirtland. He made me a deal I couldn't refuse . . .," he grimaced. "If I would help him, they, the FBI, would drop the charges against me. You see, they had bigger fish to fry than little ole me. They wanted my boss." He took a deep breath and sighed. "All I had to do is replace some bills in a money shipment, thereby exposing my boss's contact in the Caribbean. Agent Kirtland said if I cooperated, I would be protected, and my boss would go to jail. But I failed, and my mom was killed for my failure." He paused and bowed his head in his hands.

"It sounds like it was a pretty big order. Did you have access to the money?" Jack's thoughts were on his find, hidden at Cay Sal. Was his treasure FBI-marked money?

Julio looked up. "I'd seen money come and go, but that had nothing to do with me. My job was warehouse security, not inventory. But I was stuck. If I didn't help the FBI, they would make it look like I did, and my boss would kill me. If I said yes, I at least had a chance to save my own skin. I didn't know the game was rigged. I wasn't out more than a few hours when everything changed. Somehow he had found out, and the next thing I knew I was on a boat headed for Saint Maartens with a captain who had orders to kill me. At least I'm pretty sure he was going to kill me, he threatened me enough." He looked off in the distance and shook his head. "Anyway, let's just say the boat didn't make it. You saw the last of it floating with me. I would've been a goner, if it wasn't for your help." He smiled at Jack.

"So you were a prisoner on that boat."

"Yes and no. I was there against my will, but Captain Max trained me to drive while he slept. At the end, I learned that I was not needed. He could have programmed the autopilot while he slept. He put me on three-hour driving shifts, which left me sleep-deprived, all the while feeding me the guise that my clothes and passport would be shipped and waiting for me when we arrived. I tried to get away when we pulled into Miami for fuel, but there were cops everywhere, and I wasn't sure who to trust. My boss, Juan Perrone, has eyes and ears everywhere, and if he finds out I'm alive, I won't be for long. Then there's the FBI. I disappeared with $15,000 of their money. They probably have a warrant out for my arrest."

"What were the cops doing at the Miami fuel dock?"

"There was some dead woman in a small boat docked at the pier. I don't know what happened, but the fuel attendant seemed awful nervous."

"Okay, let me get this straight, you were put on a boat to the Caribbean with just the clothes on your back. Where was this boat coming from? And what does this have to do with your mother?

"We left from Washington DC. As we were leaving the pier, my car was being searched by Perrone's lackeys. Somehow they had heard about the FBI money and were looking for it. What they didn't know is that it was strapped to my leg. I'm guessing when they couldn't find the money in my car or my apartment, they went after my mom, searching her place and killing her." He paused to wipe his eyes once more. "It had to be Vic, Perrone's new second-in-command, that killed her. He hated me." He looked up at Jack. "The saddest part is my mom didn't know anything about the money."

"I'm sorry you had to find out about your mom from an obituary."

"I actually knew before. The police told me when I called her house from the boat."

"I'm sorry for your loss." Jack truly was. He knew what it was like.

"It was my fault. I should never have gone to work for someone like Perrone. I should have gone to college like she wanted."

Jack waited a couple of minutes for Julio to process his remorse. He decided to change the subject. "You know, Julio, we all have decisions that when we look back. We think, if only, I woulda, I coulda, I shoulda. It sounds like you didn't have much choice in the matter." He nodded. "So let me get this straight. You left DC with $15,000 strapped to your leg? Did you lose it in the ocean?"

"Well, that part has its own twists and turns. It was strapped to my leg when Juan ordered me to go with the boat, but I took it off to take a shower, and I think Captain Max found it."

"So where is this Captain Max?"

"That's another story. I'll try to explain. I realized just before we fueled up in Miami that Max and Perrone had their own plans to kill me on this trip. When I realized that Max was going to do it before we reached Saint Maartens, I decided my only hope was to attack him first. With little or no sleep and fearing for my life, I readied myself to strike. I lunged toward him, but I clumsily tripped on the door frame, pushing Captain Max just right to send him over the boat's railing. The last I saw of him was his body sinking on the downside of a wave . . . I guess he had my money pack with him because I couldn't find it anywhere on the boat. I tore that place apart, but neither Juan's money nor the FBI money could be found."

"Juan's money?"

"Oh, I left that part out. Juan Perrone was shipping the boat along with a million dollars in cash to a supplier in Saint Maartens." His furrowed brow deepened as he stared across the room. "What you see before you is a walking dead man. At this point, I believe I'm wanted by Perrone, the FBI, and probably the local police."

Jack lowered his head, shaking it. This was a lot to take in. His windfall now had an origin—cartel money. He would keep it hidden for all their sakes. He wasn't sure how else to help this young man. He was associated with the wrong people, dangerous people. He thought about Rosa. She wanted to help, and so did he. His Cuban refugee group in

Miami may be able to help Julio secure papers and a new identity, but they would have to work fast. It could already be too late.

"Listen, Julio, I have a contact in Miami, and I will work with them to get you a new identity, but in the meantime, you will have to stay hidden. Rosa did well placing you here. I'll keep you concealed. However, as the work rolls forward on the marina repair project, I may have to move you from boat to boat. Trust me, no one else will know you're here."

Julio smiled. "I'm getting pretty used to boat living. My first few days, I was perpetually sick, but I think it's growing on me. Thank you, Jack. I appreciate all you and Rosa have done for me. Because of you two, I may actually live through this."

"We'll do our best. For now, I need to run and meet a friend of mine. Just stay here and keep a low profile. Is there anything I can get you while I'm out?"

"Junk food and soda? Rosa's food is excellent, but I have missed good old chips, cookies, and soda."

Jack laughed. He knew exactly what Julio meant. Rosa was an excellent cook, but she was no-nonsense when it came to sweets.

"Coke, okay?"

"Sounds great."

"I'm not sure how late I'll be, but I'll knock twice, then twice again. Don't open to anyone you aren't expecting. There is a camera on this boat for security. Jack opened a cupboard and turned it on. This will help you see who's coming and going. This"—he showed him a security key—"is to turn on the alarm. Only do that if you are settling in for the night. It is kind of an infrared motion detector. You will set it off if you move around after it is activated. So on at night, off in the morning. On board, there are books to read and a TV and radio combination that will give you the local stations. Just use the headset. What will give you away is noise and visible lights after dark. If someone boards the boat, hide in one of these storage compartments. They are your best bet. I need to get going, but I should be back before nine."

"Thanks, Jack, I appreciate this." They shook hands.

He was much more cautious as he left and walked back up to the office. Now he was worried about leaving his post early and driving so far from his ward. Sitting in his car, his phone beeped a message from Louis. He was heading out and would be there in about thirty-five minutes. Jack returned the text with the same travel time. As he was backing out, a convertible pulled into the parking lot. It was the Choate boys, arriving for their first day of work. Putting his car in park, he jumped out and met them before they opened their doors.

"Sorry, boys, I have an appointment in Florida City. I'll leave it up to you, you can either go clean all the Jet Skis while I'm gone or you can call it a day and start tomorrow." The boys looked at each other, and Jack could see they didn't want to look bad, but the thought of skipping work appealed to them.

"If you don't mind, I think we'll feel more comfortable starting tomorrow with you around." It was Paul who formed his words carefully, trying to be more mature than his age.

"That's fine. Enjoy your day off." Jack was walking back to his car when he heard Paul answer his phone.

"Calm down. We'll be right there . . ." was all he heard before the convertible sped out of the parking lot.

Jack exited the housing area by the back gate. He had his contact for the Cuban refugee project on the line as he headed north. He hoped the eighteen-mile road between Key Largo and Florida City would be the road less traveled tonight. That stretch was often congested and full of tourists. It required patience and time that he didn't have.

***

Jack arrived ten minutes late. He walked in and was escorted to the back patio where Agent Medina was waiting. Louis stood up, and they shook hands. It had been too long since he had seen his friend. They started out with small talk as Jack perused the menu, finally deciding to order a blackened mahi-mahi sandwich. After the waitress left, Louis got right down to the brass tacks of their meeting.

"Jack, anything I tell you tonight is between two friends. This is top secret—at the highest level. I want your word you will keep this private—need to know only—and my name must never come up. Understand?"

"No problem, Louis. I get it. So what have you found out?"

"I just got word from my contact at the CIA that Charles and Sara Choate were kidnapped about three months ago. They were working undercover and were snagged. But my understanding is that they have been found, and there is a recovery team assigned to bring them home. They may already be rescued. That might be why my contact was forthcoming with the information now. I have to tell you, though, I don't know what shape they are in or when they will be back in the States, but I wanted you to know that there will be a resolution soon."

Jack thought back to the phone call Paul got as they were leaving the marina. Could that have been about his parents' return? Louis had used the words "a resolution soon." That didn't seem immediate or necessarily positive. At least he had answers. Now he knew why his neighbors weren't home with their boys.

Life was so unpredictable. Here, he had lost his sweet Maria and their child along with his parents, and then there was young Julio losing his mom. Would the Choate boys fall into the same curse? Oh, how he hoped not.

Louis was saying something else. "Now I have a question for you. You know people in Key Largo, right?"

Jack shook his head, not knowing where this was going. "Some."

"I am looking for a woman who was seeking my help on a personal matter. Her name is Sierra." Jack glanced up at Louis. "So you know this woman, do you?"

"Maybe, I know of a Sierra who just moved into my housing area. Is she wanted by the FBI?"

Louis looked perplexed about Jack's information. So she hadn't introduced herself as an agent. She was still undercover. "No, no. I just did a background check on a woman of that name living in Key Largo and wondered if you knew her."

"A background check? For what?"

"Oh, it was nothing. A member of her family was applying for a security check, and we have to check all who have lived in the same house. It's a small-enough world. I just wondered if you knew her."

Their food arrived, and that gave Jack some time to ponder Louis's words. Sierra hadn't mentioned any other family but her husband, and he was deceased. What Louis was telling him may have had some truth, but the rest was highly suspect. He put condiments on his sandwich as his mind raced on. Louis knew Sierra but most likely couldn't tell him more. His mind was bouncing around with thoughts waiting for them to form into something cohesive. Who was Sierra? Could she be FBI? He looked across the table and watched Louis struggling with his own thoughts. Now he was curious. Would Louis ask another question about Sierra? And why was he asking?

They were halfway into their meals when the silence was broken.

"Jack, I was out of line asking you about Sierra." Louis had realized what he had done, and it was time to waylay any curiosity that Jack may have. "The truth is that I met her in the airport, and she said she was moving to Key Largo, and I wanted to ask if you knew who she was so I can figure out how to get in touch with her. She's a beauty. The background check was a lie. Sometimes my FBI status gets me information where other avenues fail. I should have known better than to use it on you. You looked downright irritated at my inquiry."

Jack still didn't know whether to trust him or not. It was all too easy to shift the truth. What was the truth? Was he interested in her personally or professionally? Maybe before the boys' drama and Julio's appearance, he wouldn't have questioned his friend, but now everyone was suspect, and until proven innocent, they all looked guilty. How was he going to end this with Louis? He wasn't there to lose a friend or a resource. He finished his dinner in two bites. Pushing his plate away, he addressed his companion.

"I'm not sure which of those yarns you spun for me is true, but let me tell you the Sierra I know. This woman is a widow who recently lost her husband and moved to Florida. She is, indeed, a beauty, as you said. I don't know any more about her than that. I have only seen her a couple of times, and both of those were in reference to a boat she is having shipped to the marina I manage. If this sounds like your Sierra, I guess you will just have to come visit me some time, and perhaps we'll run into her at the club or something. If she has additional family, I do not know. Is that what you wanted to know?"

"Sorry, man." He looked around them for anyone who might hear their conversation. He seemed satisfied. He leaned in, and Jack did the same. "I can get fired if you breathe a word of this, but the Sierra I met here in Miami last weekend was an agent for the FBI."

Jack was more shocked that his friend divulged the information than the fact that she was who he said she was. It was time to end this visit.

"I wish you wouldn't have told me that. I'm not sure what that means. Do you think she is there to watch over the Choate boys?"

"No, Homeland takes care of that."

33

Home Security – Palm Shores

As they neared the gate to Palm Shores Subdivision, Oswaldo knew they couldn't survive another confrontation with the security guard, especially after what had just happened at the dive shop. Key Largo was a tropical tourist town, and word of their attack would spread quickly, causing all strangers to look suspect. They needed someplace to lie low. This was not the time for rash decisions; this was the time for strategy. Slowing their SUV, he pulled off the main road and parked partially hidden among a row of conifers. The sudden outburst of his companion put him on guard.

"What are you doing?" The derision was heavy in Juan's voice.

"We need to think about our next play . . . unless you already have a plan? This road is taking us right back to the same security guard that threatened to call the police at our last visit. Barring ramming the gate, which will also bring cops, we have no way of getting into the housing area. What we need is a less-hectic access point." He pulled out the map and located the back entrance into the housing area.

They were back on the road. Juan took a deep breath and pondered on his companion's words. There was stillness in the air, only interrupted briefly by a bright red Mustang zooming past. He looked over at Oswaldo and noticed how he was intently pacing the convertible. They stayed at a prudent following distance, coming up the road toward the

subdivision's back entrance, dropping back as the panel gate inched
forward, allowing the four teenagers entry. They watched as the wall
before them reversed and started to advance. But before it finished, a
white Jaguar jetted around them, breaching the threshold, reversing
the gate's motion, and allowing the car admittance. Inching their SUV
forward, Oswaldo followed in kind and passed through without so
much as a hiccup. It was all too easy. They were inside Palm Shores
Subdivision.

The GPS continued its directions, and they were soon passing by a
row of condos, where they saw the red Mustang sitting in the drive. A
park in the center of a big open field butted up to the condo lots, and
then the houses started. They were modest homes, at first, but the closer
they got to the water, the homes were grander. Some had their own
built-in docks and boat houses. They would need further investigation.
As they neared the marina, Juan urged Oswaldo to do a circle of the
parking lot. It was a quiet place with no noticeable activity. There were
two cars parked next to a one-level brick building that was in need of
a coat of paint. The docks looked neglected or damaged. There was a
crane positioned but no operator in sight. They parked, and Perrone,
using the crane as cover, walked to the dock. He perused the boats, each
showed signs of damage, perhaps from a recent storm. He heard a noise.
Hiding, he watched an elderly Spanish woman walk toward the boat on
the end, carrying a large purse. She was on her cell phone.

"I'll check, but I don't think he'll get to it till next week. I appreciate
your help." She disappeared below.

Juan had seen enough. This was Florida, where there were many
people who lived aboard boats; activity of this kind was far from
unusual. He would have to be careful. Many eyes could be on him. It
was time to leave and find Paul Choate.

A couple of blocks later, they were on a street with houses set back
behind a hedge row. The first two homes looked to be connected, with
the smaller one being the caretaker's cottage and the larger one, the
estate home. It was the garage's foundations, built less than ten feet
a part, that painted the picture. The lesser of the two was quaint and
could be seen from the road. Set back just off the water's edge was the

majestic estate home with its long-angled drive. Though it was mostly blocked by frontal foliage, the address was well displayed. They had found the Choate address.

Juan Perrone assessed the property and its sheltered setting. Neither home had any cars or activity visible from the front. He noted how the seclusion of the home would work in their favor. Security would be a different story. It was hard to tell if the home was wired or who was actually living there. He needed recon, and that was a job for his two lackeys, Carlos and Mondo. They moved on. Their browsing had caused a line of cars behind them. To avoid unwanted attention, Oswaldo pulled into the parking lot of the club. Their target had been acquired, and he needed to know Juan's next step in his plan.

Perrone took out his phone and called Carlos. "Progress report."

"We have searched the entire list of public marinas in Key Largo, and we haven't found any boat fitting the description of your yacht. We have been told that there are private marinas in gated communities that require membership to access."

"That won't be a problem. We figured out a way to follow on the bumper of another car, but we may need a quicker solution. Head to the Palm Shores Subdivision and follow an exiting car. When they have parked, take their gate clicker. We need our own access. We are closing in on the money, but in the meantime, we'll secure a base here. Get here as quick as you can and bring pizza. I'll text you the address." Juan ended the call.

"Let's go find a home, Oz."

Oswaldo was annoyed by the nickname. It irritated him. *Two days*, he thought. He shifted into gear and pulled out of the parking lot. "Which way?"

"Let's drive farther into the subdivision. We are looking for a foreclosure notice or a for-sale sign where the property has been neglected—as secluded as possible. I'm sure we'll know the place when we see it."

34

Night Games – Palm Shores

Carlos backed into his concealed parking stall for the fourth time and leaned back in his seat. It wasn't that they didn't have cars to follow, but their efforts had been in vain. Each prospect was a mystery that only revealed itself after a long game of cat and mouse, and thrice now, they had returned empty-handed. If it was the matter of simply getting through the gate, their task could have been completed long before, but Juan wanted a gate remote. That meant they were on people-watch, singling out the right target. The first two cars they followed headed straight for the eighteen-mile stretch toward Florida City, and the third continued to the southern part of the Keys, along A1A. Each had pulled them away temporarily, only to once again return and start all over again.

Frustration hung between them as they each tried to get comfortable in their cramped space. They weren't friends, just associates. It was evident with these two that small talk wasn't comfortable. Carlos was napping, jerking himself awake every few seconds. It had been a long day of searching for yachts, chasing a bar waitress through the grocery store, and now awaiting the opening of the gate ahead. Waiting was the worst part. It gave a man too much time to think, and Mondo wanted his mind busy. It was the only way to keep the images out. Seeing yourself dead was an unsettling feeling, and the stillness allowed access, peeking in and out like a slide projector.

He thought about fate. Was there a possibility he could change his? The image was there, and he pushed it away. Was he going to die? Leaning back, he wiped his face with his hands. A thought formed. Could his dream have been an omen and not his doom? Could there be a chance? Taking a deep breath, he freely opened his mind and allowed the vision. He was lying on the floor with his eyes open. He flinched but stayed in the moment. The room didn't seem familiar. Searching his limited angles, he surmised he was in a square space with large red tiles—no, wait, not red tiles. It was blood that covered the tiles. Feeling nauseous, he forced himself to look past the blood. He could see something white. It was a small square, compared with the overall space. Squinting, he saw what looked like tan streaks. The longer he stared, the clearer it became. It started to glow, emitting a reflection from the light. It was mesmerizing. He had to force himself to look away. Redirecting his vision, he looked to the right, searching for more clues. There was a bright silver strip of metal just raised from the floor. Was it on legs? He couldn't be sure. His brain surmised it was the base of a stainless-steel refrigerator. Was he in someone's kitchen? Moving his eyes to the left, he was blinded by a pure white light. Was he to follow the light? Was this his exit? He blinked his heavy eyelids. Looking again, he could see dark fuzzy rectangles surrounding the blurring light.

His mind was muddled, and he was so tired. It was time to sleep. He was fading, dying. Someone knelt beside him. It was the woman. She leaned over him, her voice floating across the room to someone else. What was she saying? He couldn't tell. Concentrating, he focused on her face. His vision was fading. He found her eyes. Was that pain? For him? He couldn't tell, but he would remember those haunting eyes.

He heard the familiar sound of the gate's creak. Carlos had heard it too. In unison, they sat forward, waiting anxiously for the emergence of their next target. Exiting the subdivision, they watched a white 911 Porsche convertible pull slowly through the back gate, gunning its engine and heading west toward town. The gentleman driver had to be in his seventies, tall and lean with ample forehead and streaming a snow-white ponytail. Barking his tires, he shifted through the gears. It wasn't long till all that remained was a white blur and Bon Jovi floating over the sound waves. Glancing toward each other, they laughed. Carlos hit the gas. Not only did this prospect amuse them, but also the convertible would allow them unfettered access to the subdivision's gate clicker.

They had topped out the speedometer on their rental and were giving up the chase when they saw a dust flume ahead. Arriving on the scene, they found the little sports car parked comfortably in front of Hole in the Wall bar and grill. It seemed the car's owner had chosen to mark his destination with a power slide—the smooth curves across the gravel told the story.

"Well, it looks like he left his mark for us." Mondo smirked.

"Looks like, and that's good for us. Look at his visor. He left us a gift."

They parked next to the Porsche, blocking the view of the main entrance to the bar. Mondo opened his door and purposefully bumped his neighbor's car. He took his time exiting the car, waiting for any possible hidden alarm response. Nothing happened. Reaching across the open car, he pulled not one, but two remotes from the visors. Slipping back into his seat, they sped off. It was so easy.

Arriving back at the gate, they tried each clicker, but neither moved the iron structure. It took numerous tries, including a battery assessment, before the two men gave up with a realization that they had stolen the wrong remotes. They headed back to the bar, hoping their prey would still be inside.

Carlos chose silence, rather than let his anger toward Mondo openly flow. However, his body language expressed his inward frustration. With the gas pedal floored and his blood vessels bulging, it was easy to see that their setback was stirring his mind. Mondo had missed something. There was no other explanation, and now they had to go back and risk being seen or, worse, caught. *Such incompetence! What an idiot! I'll have to do this myself.* He parked in their previous spot. He got out. Using every ounce of self-control not to slam his door, he walked around the Porsche. Checking each angle, he saw nothing. He opened the glove box and pulled everything out, still nothing. He opened the passenger side door and felt under both seats. His anger toward his companion, who was being his lookout, was deflating, yet still, he was confused. Shutting the convertible's door, he pushed the lock button on the rental car remote, it clicked.

"So what now?" Mondo questioned.

"I think I need to have a chat with our seventies friend." Carlos turned and headed toward the entrance.

Watching him disappear into a black hole, Mondo turned toward the little white car parked so innocently next to them. He walked over and opened the driver's door and sat down. He glanced at the mess Carlos had left. Quickly cleaning it up, he ran his fingers along the dash and checked every indentation and compartment to no avail. He sat back against the head rest and closed his eyes.

He wasn't sure how long he had napped, minutes or perhaps half an hour? Upon opening his eyes, he saw a magnetic decal stuck to the windshield next to the side-view mirror—the sun illuminating the wire through the plastic case. He had seen cars with electronic passes for tolls, but those were attached next to the rearview mirror. Looking around for stray eyes, he carefully peeled the strip from the windshield. It was then that he realized that Carlos had locked him out of their car, and he could not simply move the sticker over. This created a problem since most decals could be quite sensitive. By simply removing them from the windshield, the conductor could be damage, and the sticker would be worthless. However, there was no way to know until it was tested. For now, he had to find a safe place to lay it while he got the keys from Carlos. He reached into his wallet and found a laminated card. He attached the decal to try and preserve the adhesive. Now where to store it? Putting it back in his wallet could cause undue stress on the wire, so he devised a plan to hide the card between the lower windshield and the car's hood. Placing it out of the way of the windshield wipers, he headed toward the bar.

Blinking several times to adjust his eyes to the dim lighting, he quickly found Carlos sitting at the bar, talking to the white-haired man. As not to interrupt, he walked over to an old juke box and selected a song on the seventies list labeled "American Pie" by Don McLean.

When it started, both men at the bar turned toward him, their laughter changed to the solemn drunken melody.

"A long, long time ago
I can still remember how that music used to make me smile
And I knew if I had my chance
That I could make these people dance
And maybe they'd be happy for a while…"

Words failed them as their emotions took over. Slithering back into their drinks, the two friends commiserating over old times, as the song continuing in the background.

Mondo was shocked at the emotions emanating from the two men. He was hoping the 'Bye, Bye Miss American Pie' would be a hint to Carlos that it was time to leave, but as it turned out, he was crying with a stranger. He walked over to the bar and ordered a beer and sat down two seats over and waited for a lull in their conversation.

"Excuse me." He steered his comments to his partner in crime. "Could you pass me the peanuts?"

Carlos slid the bowl across the counter toward him, turning in the process.

He took that opportunity to mouth "I found it."

At first, he seemed a little confused, blinking and squinting, but then he nodded. Mondo took a handful of peanuts, a sip of his drink, and headed toward the bathroom. When he returned, Carlos had already exited the bar. He met him at the car and retrieved his card from the windshield. Carlos put himself in the passenger seat and handed the keys over. Sitting in the driver's seat, he attached the sticker to the windshield and headed for Palm Shore Subdivision. Carlos, on the other hand, was three sheets to the wind and snoring away.

Worried that the pony-tailed man would report his loss, he was anxious as they approached the iron bars, but the gate swung open without complaint. He didn't know how long the pass would work, most likely only a matter of hours. After testing it a few times, they headed back to pick up food.

Once again, Mondo was alone with his thoughts, and he didn't like the feeling. All his mind would conjure up was his nightmare. Was this job going to be his last? Should he be worried? He pushed aside his fear and focused on his task. It fell to him to fill Juan's food order. He had seen this before. Carlos would often crawl home from the bar loaded and unrecognizable until morning. At least he was a happy drunk, though unhelpful for the moment.

Parking at the grocery store, he called the pizza place next door and placed an order. He then went shopping. With muffins, bagels, and coffee piled into his cart, he added rolls, deli meats, and condiments. Picking up a case of Coke, he paid and loaded them into the car, then went for the pizzas. Now they would find out if the owner of the Porsche had noticed their theft.

The ride back left Mondo with more thinking time. His vision always ended with the eyes of the woman. It was beginning to haunt him. Who was she?

He was happy to hear the buzzing of Carlos's cell phone. They were already inside the gate and driving past the townhouses when the vibration awakened the snoring lump. Mondo let him take his time to adjust to his surroundings and answer the buzz. It was Juan with a pin-drop. Carlos touched the screen, and soon his phone's computer voice began to spill out directions.

They would soon be back in Juan's presence. Mondo slowed the car to observe the scenery. They passed the entrance to the marina on the left and the club surrounded by classy cars on the right. He summed up the neighborhood as being upper-middle class. They drove on, passing many estates that backed up to the water, long driveways obscuring their entrances. Slowing down even further attracted the attention of his buzzed companion.

"What are you doing? The boss is waiting for us?"

"Can't you feel it—the peace?"

"Peace? Stop all this sappy crap. Just take us to Juan."

Mondo ignored his companion and moseyed on down the road, enjoying the calm and serene feeling this place was giving him. With what awaited him in the next few days, he wasn't in any rush to hurry it along. So if he couldn't stop it, he could certainly make the most of the time he had remaining.

They pulled up to a small cul-de-sac at the back of the housing area. Mondo surveyed the properties around the circle. The one on the right was partially constructed and looked abandoned with the materials lying weathered across the makeshift driveway. Straight ahead was an empty lot with a "For Sale by Owner" sign stuck in the ground. The third home was Perrone's pick. It looked to be one of the original homes of the subdivision. He had chosen well. They would not be bothered here. It was an old one-level ranch that showed the neglect of years. Mondo wondered what history was hidden in this forgotten structure. He could see the potential. It just needed some care. He would start with yard work to clear the two feet high weeds and grass, followed by some much-needed scraping, painting, and sealing of the aging wood. Then he would focus on the vast number of bushes that were overpowering the wooden fences, which edged the property. He would take great pride in that, learning at a young age how to sculpt shrubbery. The driveway wrapped around the side of the house and allowed only visual of the front porch. The privacy was perfect for their base of operations. Pulling up to the garage door, it opened to them. They followed Oswald's beckoning and parked the car inside. Once inside, he hit the button again, closing the large quiet door behind them.

Emerging from the car, Mondo opened the trunk and handed Carlos a bag of groceries and Oswaldo the pizzas, following to the rear with the sodas. Upon entering the home, he was shocked at the beauty that met them. This home had not only been updated, but also completely refurbished, making it quite a contrast to its dilapidated exterior. They would be comfortable here.

"Wow," he couldn't stop himself from saying. "Who'd you have to kill to get this place?" His three companions looked at him. Juan laughed. Carlos had a blank expression, and Oswaldo just smiled.

"Didn't have to. It was empty." Oswaldo shrugged and walked over to the kitchen counter and lay the pizza boxes down. Pulling a plate from the cupboard, he filled it and sat down with his bounty.

Carlos and Mondo followed with their bags and emptied them into the refrigerator then grabbed a plate and did the same. Juan watched the three, and though he was anxious to get started, he too was hungry. They were each on their fourth slice of pizza when Juan broke the silence. "I hope you two enjoyed your dinner, but now you need to earn it." They slowed their chewing and gave him their full attention. "I need you both to do some reconnaissance tonight. We got an address of two teenage boys who have been spending Julio's FBI money. I want to know who else is living in their house, and if they are hiding Max or Julio."

Mondo and Carlos glanced at each other. Juan had found a clue, but they had shown up with nothing. They both knew this was more than a mere spying assignment. They would need something concrete, or they could not return until they did.

"If they have the FBI money," Perrone continued, "they most likely will have mine. We are close. I can feel it." He paused, looking across the room, thinking about how he needed to get back to DC before Victor Ramos ruined his business. He regained his focus. "At this point, we are staying under the radar until we have more information, but once we know what we are walking into, it's go time. No mistakes!"

He looked across the table at his two lackeys. He made eye contact one at a time, just long enough to accentuate his message. They were completely engaged, and he was pleased. He finished, softening his voice, though the intensity of his words were not diminished.

"Tonight's job is to monitor and report. We need to know what threats exist and our best access point. Do you understand?"

Both men nodded. Questioning their boss was never an option. You either did what you were told, or you didn't work anymore—for anyone.

They headed out. Carlos, loaded up on coffee, was losing his buzz. He pulled out his phone and searched Perrone's pin-drop. Looking up the address, he found that the house backed up to the water and had another smaller home only a few feet away from the garage. They would need stealth. Mondo was driving, slowly as before, but this time there was no complaint. They both knew what this assignment meant to their lives, and they didn't know what sort of night games they were walking into.

They parked at the club and set out on foot using Juan's pin-drop as their guide. Neither spoke as they casually traversed the two blocks to the teenager's home. The sun was far spent and preparing for its final curtain call as streams of cars filled with families returning from their daily routines filed past. The weather was warm and sticky, humidity hung low in the air. Their decision to walk was being questioned with every sweat drop.

"Your destination is on your left." Their phone had alerted them to their arrival.

Slowing their pace, they continued forward, assessing their target. Mondo recognized the place from their first pass-through the neighborhood.

Mondo pulled up short, and Carlos followed in kind. He had been silent since they left, and Mondo wasn't sure if he was completely aware or still in la-la land. He turned to him. "I saw this home when we entered the neighborhood. It is almost completely hidden from the street. The smaller home may be connected or separately owned, so we'll have to be careful. Are you ready?" Carlos just nodded.

Looking closely at the green shrubbery, Mondo noticed an opening, and they slipped through, emerging into the front corner of the property. Hiding in the shadows, they made their way to the edge of the big home on the opposite end of the garage. Moving toward the backyard, they heard a noise and froze. Silence filled the air for a full two minutes. They relaxed. By then, the sun had set, leaving only the light of a quarter moon. They were camouflaged in the darkness with their dark pants and black sweatshirts. Peeking around the corner, all Mondo could see was more of the same. The house seemed dark and empty of life. He picked up a stick and threw it across the back patio.

"What did you do that for? Are you trying to get us caught?" He put his finger to his lips and motioned for Carlos to hush.

After a few minutes without sound or change, he surmised that the family was void of dog and motion-detection lights or alarms. Moving forward in a crouched position, they made their way to the patio's edge. Exiting off the kitchen, uncovered sliding glass doors faced them. Mondo peeked inside. The room was dark, except a low light emanating from the microwave. Smiling, he mused over the familiarity of his own family's routine, of leaving a small light burning so the family wouldn't return to a dark home. He moved on, creeping across the door to the other side. Carlos kept pace behind him.

His view of the kitchen changed with his angle. It triggered his vision. Fear shot through his limbs, causing him to jump back and knocking his companion to the ground.

"What is it? What did you see? Is there someone in the house?" They were mouth to ear hidden behind a tall bush at the edge of the cement slab.

Mondo didn't hear all that his partner said because he was hyperventilating.

"Breathe. Breathe. Breathe." Carlos was trying to calm him down. "Talk to me. What's wrong?"

"That's the pla . . . ce."

"The place? For what?"

"I-I." He looked at his companion and realized there was no way to explain. He would think he was crazy. He took another deep breath, trying to remember something pleasant—his home, the girl with the eyes. He would focus on her, not his death or the blood. He sat down and put his head between his knees, taking a long deep breath to release the tension trapping the air from reaching his lungs. Carlos was watching him and shaking his head.

"You need to pull it together, man. You're going to get us killed!"

That didn't help. He took another cleansing breath. He forced himself to get to his feet, inching his way toward the barely illuminated kitchen. Yup, the tiles, the stainless-steel fridge, the shape of the ceiling light he had seen reflected in the window—this was the place. He had to do something. He turned back to Carlos.

In his shortness of breath vocabulary, he managed, "No one is home. Let's look around and get the layout and report back." Though he tried to sound strong, his voice was barely more than a whisper.

Carlos nodded as Mondo set off across the lawn, surveying the layout of the backyard. He couldn't figure out what had happened. It was true that he wasn't back to his full alert self, but he didn't see or hear anything that could have set him off. It was a full-on anxiety attack, totally out of character from what he'd seen of the man up till this point. He crept to the sliding glass doors and looked inside. It was a basic, nice kitchen, square in nature with a small eating area to one side. He shrugged and set off after Mondo. He would have to watch him closely. That kind of behavior could get them both killed.

He found him at the base of a large oak tree, looking up.

"Is there someone there?" he whispered.

"No, but there is a small tree house. I've been standing here listening but haven't heard any movement. One of us should climb up and take a look.

Carlos took one look at his pale-faced friend and started climbing. He reached the door and noticed a padlock and climbed back down.

"It's locked, so if anyone is in there, they're trapped. There is a window on the side, but it's not big enough to climb through. It looks abandoned."

They heard a noise from the house next door. Hiding behind the tree's trunk, they watched as an elderly Latin woman stepped out, pulled some sheets from the line, and went back inside. It still wasn't clear whether the homes were one property or two. They looked as if they had been divided by a shrubbery fence running most of the property's length. However, there was a small area around the tree house that still connected the two yards. Looking between the two, he noticed blocks of stone that formed a visible pathway from back door to back door. It was hard to know how old the path was, but it was clearly a defined route. At one time, these homes were connected. They would have to monitor both.

A light flashed across the yard. Startled, they dropped to their stomachs at the base of the tree. A car was in the drive of the big house. The garage door sounded, and all went black. Watching, they saw the big home awake from its dark slumber. The pathway of the occupants was well defined by the lights illuminating through the back windows.

The kitchen came alive as they watched two boys open the freezer, pull dishes from the cupboard, and start the microwave. This new development renewed their interest. There were only the two teenagers, no adults. That was curious. Their animated selves showed signs of distress and anger. One kept wiping his face as if he were crying.

They had seen enough. There were no signs of Julio or Max at this home. They turned their attention to the smaller house. The elderly woman piqued their curiosity. Who was she, and was she connected to their aloof targets? Turning, they saw a boat docked behind the small home. Pointing to the vessel, Mondo moved in its direction. The tree's shadow could only give him cover for part of the distance. The owner had installed an overhead fluorescent light, most likely to ward off possible thieves. The only way to get to the boat was to expose himself to anyone paying attention. It was too early in the evening. They would have to wait until all parties were asleep. He crept back to the tree trunk, sitting in its shadow.

"Too much light. We'll have to wait them out." Carlos nodded his agreement as he adjusted his posture, placed his folded arms across his knees, and leaned back against the tree trunk. He lowered his forehead onto his arms. It wasn't long until he was out. Mondo just watched and shook his head. He must have hit some hard stuff at that bar. Of course, that meant Carlos would be napping, and he would have to be on guard.

Observing the back of both properties and keeping to the shadows, he quietly made his way to the small home. He had noticed that there were big picture windows that faced the tree house. He got close enough to see in. The elderly woman sat in a rocking chair watching TV. No one else was visible. Perhaps this woman lived here alone. If one house had teenagers and this house had an elderly woman, where could Max and Julio be? He moved back to the tree and sat down next to Carlos. He was doing those mini snores that, at first, irritated him, but now he appreciated. It was nice knowing Carlos was out of his thoughts. It gave him time to think and figure things out.

He had messed up. Carlos had seen his anxiety attack, and that would cost him. Even if Carlos would keep his secret from Juan, he wouldn't trust him the same. He had to come up with an explanation, and it had to be good. Still, he felt cold. That kitchen—his death bed—had been real, and he was right here within its grip. He watched as the bright light diminished, leaving only the small glow of the microwave. The other lights dissipated one at a time as the two small side window lights glowed. The boys must have gone to their rooms.

A light flashed through the small space between the properties. He wasn't sure how long he had been sitting there going over his dream again and again. Looking up, he heard a man whistling a tune as he appeared around the back of the small home and went inside. The porch light highlighted his frame. From what he could tell, the man was not Julio or Max. He was too tall to be Julio and too young to be Max. He watched the light in the kitchen turn on then off again fifteen minutes later. The TV glow from the living room diminished. Mondo crept closer. He could see the two adults say good night and go in two different directions—perhaps a mother and son.

He looked once again at the still small house and rechecked the bigger home. Deciding that the coast was as clear as he was going to get, he roused Carlos and told him to keep watch. Making his way to the dock, he put together a plan to minimize his time under the light. Keeping to the shadows till the edge, he hurriedly crossed the dock to the boat. Once inside, he made his silhouette as small as possible. Stepping carefully not to rock the boat too much, he pulled out his gun. Reaching for the doors handle, he took a deep breath. There was no one on the vessel. He put his weapon away, pulled out his phone for a flashlight, and proceeded to search. Opening one of the compartments, he pulled out a life raft. He took a picture of the insignia and tried to stuff it back in its place. Perusing the rest of the boat, he found bags of handheld GPS units. He stuck one in his pocket. He also noticed smears of red paint, or possibly blood, on the table and floor. He took pictures and climbed back out.

Carlos was waiting. "Did you find anything?" He sounded so hopeful.

"I'm not sure but probably not." He sighed.

"You do realize, if we come back with nothing, Juan may just kill us?"

"Well, we don't have 'nothing.' We know there are only two people living in the little house, one male and one female, and in the big house, the boys are on their own. Maybe their parents are out of town. Wait—" Something was bothering him. It was the microwave light. He was always taught that the light in the kitchen was to be turned off by the last one coming home at night. He looked over at the sliding glass doors. "Someone hasn't come home yet."

"What?"

"The microwave light is still on in the kitchen. The rule is the last one home shuts it off."

"So you're saying we better get comfortable."

"Pretty much."

It didn't take Carlos long to be back asleep, sending out his little snoring sounds. Mondo was going over their information for Juan. First of all, they knew how to sneak onto the property without detection. But they had no proof that the yacht, Max, or Julio were connected with these homes. Two teenage boys did live in the big house, but their adult supervision was still unknown. The small home housed two adults, but they didn't see any interaction between the two households this evening. However, they were or had been connected at one time. There was definitely a nice path between the two. There is a boat parked at a dock behind the two homes, closer to the small one. The boat does not have an occupant, but there was a life raft, handheld GPS devices, and some smears that looked like blood.

Mondo was doing his best to keep his mind occupied. Sleep was pushing at his thoughts and images. He gave in. Another light flash interrupted his troubled dreams, and he pulled himself out. The garage door was sounding at the big house. He looked at his watch. It was 12:30 a.m. He moved forward, adjusting his view. Sure enough, a woman entered the kitchen. She seemed too young to have teenage boys but too old to be one herself. He watched her every move. She got a drink and sat at the little table. Tiredness showed as she rubbed her face. He recognized the strain. He felt drawn to her. She finished her beverage and put her glass in the sink. From there, she checked the sliding glass door for security and turned off the kitchen lights, including the microwave's small glow. His eyes followed her exit through the house, leaving only darkness in her wake. The last glow emanated from a window behind the garage. All was dark. It was time to go, yet this home seemed to seduce him. Was it normal for someone to feel drawn to their death?

35

The Break-In – Palm Shores

Jack was awake, lying in the black stillness of his bedroom. He glanced at the clock. It was 5:30 a.m. He lay there comforted by the silence. If only he could freeze time. Somehow the darkness gave him comfort and protected him from the reality waiting outside. He had a young man wanted by a crime boss and a possible undercover FBI agent hot on his trail. Boy, did he miss his Maria, his calming balm. She would've known what to say and perhaps lull him back to sleep. "Don't worry," she would say. "Things will all work out. This boy was sent to you for a reason. It will all be clear soon." Then she would snuggle up to him, calming his breathing until he blissfully fell back to sleep.

Without her, he was left in the dark turmoil of his mind. He crawled out of bed and stumbled over his sagging clothes balanced half on and half off his desk chair. His mind sensed the danger, and though his body was slow to respond, he caught himself before he hit the floor.

Turning on the light, he removed his pajamas and headed for the shower. As the water washed over him, he mulled over the conversation from the evening before. Louis had mentioned Sierra, an FBI agent, working undercover on a case in his backyard. She had to be the one looking for Julio, but was she friend or foe? Julio had absconded with $15,000 of FBI money. Was that what she was looking for? Would she accept his story of the lost money at sea? Just how long could Julio hide

243

before someone found him? Then there was this cartel in the picture. Could they already be close?

This development changed everything. Jack had to figure out how to protect Julio without exposing himself and Rosa. Prison was not in his life plan. Jack quieted his mind and tried to relax. Perhaps Louis's Sierra was a different Sierra and not even connected to Julio. Doubtful. Her timely appearance was not by chance. She was here on a case, and her target was at the marina. How could she have known? The money! The FBI money must've turned up here in Key Largo. He would have to feel her out and decide if he could trust her. Jack needed Sierra on his side. Her help may be their only way out of this mess and maybe Julio's only hope.

Jack dressed in his work clothes and headed out to the back patio with his morning coffee. Rosa brought him his breakfast, leaving him alone in this thoughts. The daily sunrise was invigorating to his soul, something he looked forward to each morning.

Pulling out his phone, he checked for messages. He had missed a security breach text from his boat's sensor from the night before. How had that happened? He checked his sound, and it had been turned off. He remembered silencing his phone before he met with his friend Louis.

Jumping up, he headed for the dock. Cautiously, he boarded his boat and checked below. The life raft he found in the ocean had been roughly stuffed in its storage compartment, but he couldn't see any other disturbance. He chastised himself for leaving the raft and the GPS units on the boat. Someone knew. He looked through the pictures his security system sent him and found a face. It was unknown to him. He grabbed the life raft and the bagged GPS units and headed for his garage. He knew just the right place to stash them. Then he needed to get to the marina. A break-in with nothing being stolen was suspicious. This changed everything. Julio could be in danger. He had to know if he was all right.

Jack stowed his secrets and stepped back into the house to warn Rosa. She was sitting at the table, expecting to talk to him about Julio. He sat down and held up his hands to stop her from explaining. "Rosa, I know about Julio." She looked shocked at his news. She started to respond, and he cut her off a second time. "Listen, I don't have much time. I need to warn you that my boat was broken into last night. I don't know if this is related to Julio, but it's too close of a coincidence to dismiss. Be extra cautious today, and don't come to the marina to see him. The less notice we bring to him, the better. I will make sure he has food. Now, for you, I want you to stay here and keep the doors and windows closed and locked. If you see anything suspicious, call the police."

She got up and handed him a bag from the refrigerator. "Can you give this to him?"

"I will, first thing this morning. And I want you to know I have my Maria's Cuban refugee organization working on papers for him. I will keep him hidden at the marina as long as I can."

She was crying. Rosa hugged him as he hurried out the door, locking it behind him.

36

Ambush – Palm Shores

A knock on the door signaled that his presence was requested for their breakfast meeting. They had arrived back at the house after 2:00 a.m., and Oswaldo was waiting. He let them in and ushered them to their rooms, explaining that they would rally for breakfast around 8:00 a.m. to go over their findings and plan their next move. Mondo had locked himself in. It was the first time, since this assignment began, that he had his own space and time to himself. He was exhausted. He rested peacefully.

Climbing out of bed, Mondo was surprised at how invigorated he actually felt, though he didn't know why. This meeting would not be pleasant. Juan wanted information on Julio and Max, and they simply had nothing. He wasn't sure how to respond. This breakfast could literally be his last.

He quickly showered and dressed. Grabbing his phone, he met the other three at the kitchen table. Carlos was being grilled, and since he spent much of last evening sleeping off his buzz, he wasn't sure what he would say. He himself didn't have much more, a person count and a few pictures that were probably nothing. Sitting down, he reached for a bagel. Juan's question back to Carlos made him freeze.

"So, for sure, you saw Julio in the house?"

He looked at Carlos. What was he doing? And why was he lying?

"We were sitting under the tree in the backyard, and the lights came on in the house. That's when I saw him. He was standing in the kitchen. The dark night and the bright light around him made it so clear. I could see his face as if he were standing right here in front of me."

"What about you, Mondo? Did you see him too?"

Mondo was bent over his bagel, spreading it with cream cheese, trying to figure out what was the prudent thing to say. If he said yes and Carlos was setting him up, he would be in danger. If he said no, then how could he explain Carlos's sighting?

"No! Mondo didn't see him," Carlos interjected. "He was checking out a boat next door to see if anyone was hiding in there. By the time he came back to the tree, Julio had left the kitchen and turned off the light."

When Mondo looked up, Carlos smiled like there was more to the story, but he couldn't share.

"He's right, I checked out the boat, but no one had been living there. We also know that the two teenage boys and a young woman are living in the house. The boys got home about nine and the woman just after midnight."

Juan was silent as the other three ate their breakfast. It was obvious that hearing Julio's name made him angry. He stood up and went to his room, leaving the others alone with their thoughts. Carlos and Oswaldo seemed to be eyeing each other nervously. Mondo finished his third bagel and headed to the bathroom. He halted and watched the table from the hall, making sure to listen for Juan. As soon as he disappeared, Oswaldo leaned toward Carlos, and they began to talk. He only caught a few words.

"You have orders, so do I." These words left unanswered questions. Why did they wait till he left? And what orders did they have that didn't include him?

There was movement down the hall. He stepped into the bathroom, flushed the toilet, and was wiping his hands when his boss passed. He quickly followed him back to the table. There was an uneasy undercurrent between Carlos and Oswaldo. Juan didn't seem to notice.

"Okay. It's time to move forward. This ends today. Carlos and Mondo, you take over the boy's home. Search it from top to bottom. Find Julio, then call me."

"What about the woman and the boys?" Mondo asked, worried about the answer.

"Whatever it takes. Get what you can, then dispose of them. No witnesses, understand?" They both nodded. Juan made sure to look deep into both sets of eyes, cementing his orders with intimidation.

Perrone continued, "Oswaldo and I have some business to take care of. We won't be far behind." They pushed away from the table. Oswaldo followed, closing the garage door as they pulled away.

Returning to the table, he asked, "Now what?"

"Now you're going to tell me who you're working for?"

"What do you mean? I work for you."

"Then why are you calling Victor Ramos and reporting to him?"

"I'm not. The last time I spoke to him was when he set up our meeting. Besides, doesn't he work for you?"

"Presumably, yes. However, he's been blocking my calls, and trust me, he will pay for that. Then today he answered. Oddly, though, he knew more about our operation than I've shared. Someone has been feeding him information."

"Have you asked Carlos or Mondo? They worked with Ramos in DC."

"They didn't know what happened at the dive shop, you did, and for some reason, Victor does." Oswaldo stayed stoned-faced silent. Juan took a deep breath to calm his anger. Having Oswaldo on his team was an asset. Could he get him to switch loyalties? He would try. "I don't know your connection with Victor Ramos, but I need someone I can trust protecting my interests. I've seen you work, and I could use a man with your skills. Work for me and this little incident will be like it never happened."

Oswaldo sat thinking for a minute, then stood and walked to the refrigerator, opening it and stowing the cream cheese. Pulling out his gun, he turned toward Juan. "Let me just say that this has been one of the more entertaining jobs I've had recently. Yet even with that, I don't like you, and I would never work for you over Victor. He saved my sister's life, and I will always be indebted to him. I am only here as a favor to him. My job was to eliminate you and leave your body to rot. Ramos hasn't been answering your phone calls because he has been busy setting the stage for your suicide. By now, your suppliers all think you're mad, and your crew has all been replaced."

Perrone kept eye contact and let him talk. He wanted to know just how far his protégé had gone. Shifting his weight, he laid his hand on his concealed carry.

Oswaldo was on a roll, and he wasn't done. "I don't understand your personal connection with this boat and its occupants. You probably make a million dollars before breakfast. What kind of boss leaves his business in the hands of someone he barely knows to chase a boy and a boat across the country? How could you be so gullible? He played you. All he wanted was your contacts and your position, and you just handed them right over. What you're doing here makes no sense unless this boy is blood. Or the million was actually a billion. If that's the case, I get it."

Juan shifted again. The gun was in his hand, and the bullets rang out. Who shot first was unclear. There were three shots, and then one more.

37

Lies and Surprise – Palm Shore

Sierra sensed something was wrong. She was waiting for Jack when he entered his office. He was different. He looked at her suspiciously. Something had changed since yesterday. He seemed dismissive, distant, and stressed. His day looked hectic with all the workers standing around outside. He had a crane operator awaiting his cue and other men in hard hats asking for directions. She said her goodbyes and let him be. He looked relieved.

Sierra headed for the club for breakfast. Cindy was working, and she didn't look happy. Sierra knew her new friend's night life wasn't conducive to an early morning shift. Still, she greeted her warmly. She asked for a table by the window and was accommodated. This allowed her a daylight view of the club's well-manicured lawns. It was all very peaceful, and she was enjoying breakfast when her tired-eyed friend joined her.

"Are you okay?" she asked.

"Not really, I got called in this morning at six, which is ridiculous. Anyone who knows me can attest to the fact that I don't even get out of bed until ten unless I have to."

Sierra smiled. She had experienced firsthand what Cindy was like in the morning. "So what's your schedule today?"

"Well, I'm on break right now. I work till two, and then I'm off for the rest of the day. My only plan is a long afternoon nap. I just hope the boys will keep the noise down, or I won't be any fun this evening for dancing." Sierra just shook her head. Cindy looked at her. "Are you okay? You look like you lost your best friend." Sierra just shrugged and looked outside. She continued, "One of those days, huh? I have an idea—why don't you join me tonight? It can be a girls' night out."

Sierra was about to turn her down when she had a thought. The teens were her only lead to the money, and Cindy was her access. This invitation would give her a chance to personally question Cindy and perhaps get back into their home. She needed information, and right now, she would take anything.

"I think . . . yes, I could use some me time. Do you want me to pick you up?"

"How about we meet here, in the foyer, around five thirty? We'll have dinner and then go to the club down the hall. And if you don't mind, could you call me around four to make sure I'm awake? That way, I won't be late."

"Sounds like a plan."

They parted ways; Cindy back to work and Sierra paid her bill and left.

After a few hours, Sierra returned to the marina. She sat in the parking lot, watching as a big crane lifted a boat out of the water and placed it on a waiting trailer. She was fascinated by the process but wasn't sure why she felt drawn here. Her eyes followed the crane's arm as it disembarked from one vessel and swung over to the next. It stopped. Jack stepped up to converse with the crane operator. His presence energized her. There was something about him. Was he the reason why she was sitting here watching? He stepped down, backing away from the machine. The process resumed as the second boat was lifted and relocated next to the first.

Turning her eyes to the docks, she noticed that the boat on the far end had someone sitting on the deck, watching the men work. At first, her brain dismissed him as one of the workers, then something hit her. He was the only one not wearing a hard hat. Pulling out her phone, she took a picture. It wouldn't be clear from that distance, but it didn't hurt to try. She needed to get closer. Grabbing her purse, she reached for the door handle; it moved. Jack stepped into the gap between the door and the frame. She glanced at him and back at the boat. The figure had disappeared. She focused her mind on Jack's voice, though her thoughts were processing her sighting.

"Hello. What brings you back?"

Sierra turned, giving him her best smile. "Oh, just curious. This morning, when I was here, I saw the cranes and decided to come back and observe. It's amazing watching those big boats floating in the air like that."

He smiled. Jack squatted down next to her seat. He had seen her looking in Julio's direction. It was all starting to become clear: Julio, the FBI, and Sierra—she was here for him. Her eyes looked busy, processing her vision. She would want more information. A stroll around the marina would be her next play. He needed to redirect her focus.

"Well, we're all stopping for lunch. Would you do me the honor of joining me?"

She was taken off guard. His plan was working. "I don't know. Do you mean sandwiches in your office or at the club?"

He shook his head. "Don't tell me you're not the sandwich-and-thermos type?"

"Actually, I am. Any egg salad?"

He smiled. She swung her feet to the side, waiting for him to back up so she could exit her car. "Actually, I have an errand to run in town, and I thought we could grab a sandwich there."

"I'm game. Your car or mine?" She lowered her head so he wouldn't see her disappointment, but something occurred to her. Searching the marina was her preferred quest but waiting till the men were back and otherwise engaged would offer her cover to sneak around unnoticed. Her mood changed.

"How about mine?" He extended his arm, and she smiled and permitted his escort.

The workers were leaving the parking lot, and all was quiet. She glanced over to the last boat and saw the remnants of a shadow recede.

Whether it was a tree limb or a man, it was unclear. She turned to look at her lunch date. Had she really just seen her target? If so, what was Jack's role? Or was he oblivious to the danger? She needed to find out. His help could put him in the line of fire. She would need to keep a close eye on him—an assignment she would definitely enjoy.

"Are you up for seafood?"

"Sure."

"Sundowners, it is. They have great food with an ocean view."

"Sounds wonderful. I haven't seen much of Key Largo yet. Who knew moving would be so much work?" He gave her a smile.

They had just exited the housing area, and their chitchat had reached a lull. Jack decided to press his guest. "So, Sierra, I heard a rumor about you. Perhaps you can put it to rest."

"Okay, really? A rumor, huh? What have I done that's so salacious?"

"Well, not so much a rumor, I guess, but more like information from one friend to another."

"I'm intrigued?"

He glanced at her, trying to decide whether to call her out with Louis's information. "I was informed that you are an FBI agent. Is that correct?"

She was floored. It took all the muscles in her face to hold her smile, but she was sure part of it was drooping. "Where in the world did you hear that?"

"I have my sources." She thought of Julio. Had he recognized her and outed her? Did he have a message? If it was Medina or Macdonald, she would make them pay. Or was Jack just messing with her? She had to save this somehow. She fabricated a laugh. Not one of those cute styles that makes someone fall for you, but one of those full-blown fake laughs. She had to admit, though, it was a work in progress.

"Jack, Jack. You are so funny. How long have you been working on that one? Do you pull that on all your dates? You almost made me pee my pants. Me, an FBI agent? Really?"

He had his answer. She was. He knew she would guard her identity as long as she could, but he knew. Now he needed to find out if he could trust her. He started to laugh with her.

"You got me. If you could've seen your face."

On and off, they laughed. Neither wanted to expose what they knew.

They arrived at Sundowners, and Jack came around and held her door. She took his arm, and he escorted her inside.

Their lunch was full of small talk about the marina and her fictional boat. They ordered key lime pie, a tradition in the Keys, and as the waitress left, Jack decided to tell Sierra about the break-in on his boat and gage her reaction.

"Sierra, I wish you were FBI. You could help me with a problem."

"Well, you're stuck with just me, but perhaps I can help."

"Last night my boat was broken into."

"At the marina?" Her thought went to the man who could be Julio.

"No, behind my house."

"Did you call the police?"

"No, nothing was stolen." He watched her struggle. She seemed to bite her words off before she spoke, monitoring each carefully.

"How did you know someone broke in if nothing was stolen? Was the door lock broken or anything disturbed?"

He knew she would have a hard time controlling her knowledge of a criminal act. "I have a security system on my phone. It texts me when someone breaks in and sends me pictures. I would have caught him in the act if I hadn't turned off my ringer last night at dinner."

"You have pictures? Can I see them?"

He smiled, logging into his phone. He handed it to her. "These were taken around midnight."

Watching her reaction, he didn't expect to see her flinch. Her fingers seemed to hover close to the surface of the phone. Her cell beeped. He wasn't sure, but it looked like she AirDropped the pictures to herself. That made Jack nervous. It meant his boat's break-in was somehow connected to Sierra and Julio. He needed to get back to the marina.

Their pie arrived. They both refused coffee, and Jack asked for the check. In three bites, his pie was gone. Looking over, Sierra was only one bite behind. He paid the bill, and they left; both hurrying without trying to seem anxious toward the other. They stopped at the local hardware store. As Sierra waited in the car, Jack quickly ran in and was back in five minutes. His part must have been waiting for him at the register. Fifteen minutes later, they pulled into the marina parking lot. The conversation on the way back revolved around the break-in on Jack's boat. He answered every question she put forth, and she didn't hold back.

As they said their goodbyes, Jack was backing toward his office. He would wait for her to leave before he checked on Julio. She scared him with her guarded reaction to the face on his camera. She knew him. It proved her connection. Julio's capture was close. Could she help him, or was she the catalyst that would bring them trouble? Whoever was after Julio knew where he lived, and it wasn't a big leap to connect him with the marina. Was there any place safe for Julio in Palm Shores?

As soon as the coast was clear, Jack hurried down to the Cutler's boat. The boat was eerily quiet, except for the groan of the mooring lines. Stepping down to the cabin, he knocked his code. There was no response. He tried again. Still, silence filled the air. He reached for the door, and it opened to his grasp. The room had been neatly tidied. On the counter laid a note scribbled in a mixture of print and cursive. It read,

Jack,

Thank you for your help, but I must go. Please say goodbye to Rosa for me and be careful who you trust.

Roberto

***

Sierra left the marina's parking lot and headed for her townhouse. She had to tell Director Smith that Mondo, one of Juan's henchmen, had broken into a boat next door to the Choate home last night. Those teenage boys were in danger. She had to act, or there would be dead bodies.

Sierra was in a waiting pattern. Calling the director's cell gave her access to him, but he had more important matters to handle before hers. He would call her back. Turning the TV on, she laid the phone on the counter while she showered and dressed for her night out. She had to look the part if she was going to absentmindedly drop in on Cindy and her brood, though showing up two hours early would be a hard sell. Forty-five minutes later, finishing up her hair, the phone rang. It was Director Smith.

"Sierra, this is Director Smith. Sorry about your wait. What's going on?"

"Director, thanks for returning my call. I found out some information that pushes my timeline forward. I have conformation that Juan's men are not only in the subdivision, but also have been seen behind the teenager's home."

"You are sure about the sighting?"

"Yes, Director. The neighbor has a picture of one of them on his boat last night."

"On his boat? Is there any evidence that this neighbor has anything to do with Julio? Was he hiding him there?"

"That information is unknown at this time, but I would guess that if he was, there would have been a bigger stink raised. This was all done quietly, and the neighbor didn't even report it to the police. He said nothing was taken."

"You saw the picture then?"

"He showed it to me. It's a long story. He thinks I'm FBI."

"You are FBI. How did he get that information?"

"He said a friend told him. That part bothers me, but it's not my current concern."

"True. But this could be the work of our mole. Are you sure this neighbor is not connected with Juan's organization?"

"Pretty sure. He seemed genuinely worried about the break-in on his boat. He seemed to not recognize the perpetrator."

"So what are your plans?"

"I have a night out with the boy's aunt. I hope to get another look inside their home and get her to tell me about where they got the hundreds. I think that will lead me to Julio, though I may have another lead on his whereabouts."

"It sounds like you are making real progress, but I can't hold off any longer getting you backup. You have proven that Juan has men in the area. Your safety needs to be factored in." Sierra barely heard her boss.

The TV was updating a story on the condition of the dive shop owner. She turned it up. She hadn't heard about the incident. They showed an image from the security camera. It was jiggled and blurry, but she recognized Perrone. He was here, and he had already put a man in the hospital.

"Sierra. Sierra, are you okay?" The director was trying to get her attention.

"Sorry, Director, I just watched some news footage. The dive shop, where one of the marked bills turned up, was broken into Tuesday, and the owner is in the hospital, in a coma. They showed an image from the video surveillance. It's Perrone. He's here." She used her most calm voice, but she wasn't able to block out all her anxiety.

"Okay, Perrone is there. I will call Miami and get you backup. I want you to go to the teenagers' home and keep an eye on them until help arrives. It will most likely be Supervisory Special Agent Macdonald and Special Agent Medina. In the meantime, if you see anything nefarious, call 911. I'll also call the local PD to explain the situation and give them a heads up so they won't be walking in blind. Can you handle that?"

"Yes, sir. Have Miami meet me at the boys' home—97 Ocean Ridge Boulevard, Palm Shores Subdivision. I'll wait an hour for them, but then I'm going in around 4:00 p.m. Oh, and let them know I'll be wearing a white dress."

"Stay safe, Sierra," was his last words as he hung up.

Sierra stood in front of the TV and paused then replayed the picture of Juan Perrone. It gave her chills. He was here, and he meant business. She looked up Cindy's number on her phone and pushed send. There was no answer, only voice mail. Sierra tried again, this time leaving a message. "Cindy, this is Sierra with your wake-up call, like we talked about. I forgot the meeting time. I'll just meet you at your house at four. I hope you get this in time. See yaw soon."

***

The clock struck 2:00 p.m. as Cindy punched her time card and headed home. She was tired and ready for her afternoon nap—it had been a busy shift. The club had been overrun with guests and participants for their annual charity golf tournament, and though the tips had been good, Cindy was fed up with the "hey, babe" comments. At first, she liked the attention, but there was a limit to her patience with alcohol and handsy men.

The garage door was a welcome sight, and it opened to her remote without complaint. Entering, she left her purse and shoes in the laundry room. Zombified, she headed for her bedroom.

"Going somewhere?" She was halfway down the hall when he stepped up behind her.

"Taking a nap, boys." She stopped. Swinging around, she realized that the low voice didn't belong to Paul or JJ.

Ducking under her attacker's outstretched arm, she was inches from the laundry room door when another presence grabbed her from behind. Wrapping his arms around her squirming body, he escorted her to the family room. Turning her face toward his, he froze, relaxing his grip. Twisting and writhing, she broke free and ran for the kitchen door. The first man, calculating her moves, was only a step behind. He reached out and grabbed her hair with one hand and a kitchen chair with the other. Pulling her backward, he sat her down hard, back handing her across the face for her act. Proceeding to pull zip ties from his pocket, he secured her to the chair.

She was thrown back in time—a time of pain and fear, when violence had been her daily desserts. Her ex-husband had been convicted and her threat removed, but the memories were ingrained. Her scars ran deep—a constant reminder that life was not worth living in suffering. She lived because she fought back. She would watch and listen, divide and conquer. She would need an escape plan.

The first man was yelling at the second, "You idiot! What was that about? You let her go? Are you mad?"

The second man hadn't moved. He was staring at her like he'd seen a ghost. He turned toward the bedrooms. "I'll get the rest of those shoe boxes from the closet." He disappeared down the hall.

Cindy was frightened by the attention. Did he know her? Was he hired by her ex? If he was, she would be leaving in a body bag. That thought left her terrified. She needed an escape. The first man watched his partner retreat. Turning toward his captive, he pressed her cheeks with his hand and turned her face up to his.

"I don't know what you said to him, but if you try that again, I'll shoot you and those two kids you live with."

She cringed. They knew about the boys. This was no ordinary break-in. They had been targeted.

Purposely not looking in her direction, the second man returned from the hallway. In his arms were four shoe boxes, which drew the attention of her attacker. Their actions confused her. If these two were sent by her husband, she would be their target. What were they looking for?

Cindy took in her surroundings. She hadn't noticed it before, but the house had been ransacked. The den doors were broken, leaving glass shards across the floor. Wall hangings and books were strewn around the room, blocking any discernable path to the front door. She wanted to scream but knew better. Focusing on her captors, she memorized their faces; every detail burned into her brain. They were huddled across the room, tearing through shoe boxes, dumping and destroying their contents. They were looking for something. Could the boys have enemies? Or was this related to their parents' disappearance? Just who were these men?

Hundred-dollar bills were being laid out in two piles on the dining room table. Counting, she totaled five bills in one pile and four in another. She recognized the boxes. Paul kept them on the top shelf of his closet. The money, however, was a mystery to her. So the boys were hiding money. That explained the hundreds in their wallets. Was there more? Where could they have gotten so much money? She wanted answers, but that would have to wait. There would be a reckoning once this was over. For now, that wasn't important.

Cindy looked around, spotting the wall clock precariously leaning against the hutch. She was running out of time. Within the hour, two teenage boys would be walking through the garage door. There had to be a way to stop this before they arrived. Surveying the room, Cindy looked at her escape possibilities. She wasn't far from the kitchen's patio door, but she was tied up. Wiggling her hands, she worked on the plastic straps binding her, but all she managed to do was move her chair and cut her skin. Looking up to see if her slide gained her any attention, she was relieved to see both men focusing on their find. Moving the chair an inch at a time put her close to the glass door. She could touch it. Now to get free.

The silence in the room was interrupted by the second man. Cindy froze. "Less than a thousand dollars! Where's the rest? Honestly, this looks like a teenager's stash. If Julio was here, where's the money? Are we in the wrong place?" The first man just shrugged. The second man looked around and continued, "Where are Juan and Oswaldo? They should have been here by now?" He was mad.

Cindy felt even more anxious at their words. They were expecting someone else, and the odds were already stacked against her. She scooted again, pulling hard on her bindings, but her effort wasn't enough.

The first man glanced at his watch. He seemed even more annoyed. "We've been through the house and the garage. It's time to get some answers from our new friend."

Cindy gulped. They were coming after her. Cindy was stuck. She was close to the sliding glass door in the kitchen, but her bindings restricted her ability to fight back or save herself. She had nothing, and they had guns. Her leg buzzed. Her cell phone was still on vibrate from work. Though it was out of her reach, it gave her hope that someone was trying to reach her. Perhaps it was the boys telling her they would be late. She held on to that hope until she heard the garage door open. Her two captors heard it too, and they headed for the laundry room.

Cindy yelled with all her might as the laundry room door squeaked open, but her warning caused the opposite effect. They had run toward her, not away. It was too late. Each boy had a gun pointed at his head and an arm around his neck. The zip cuffs came out, and soon the teens were tied to two chairs facing their aunt. The first man backhanded each boy with his gun. Their wounds bleeding down their faces and onto the tile at their feet left quite the mark. The stakes had changed; their innocence had been breached. What they needed now was a miracle.

38

The Red Tile – The Choate House

The house seemed still and quiet as Sierra stepped into the evening shadows. She wasn't dressed for surveillance, but she needed to know if Cindy and the boys were safe. After seeing the pictures of Mondo on Jack's boat, she knew her time was running out. If there was any chance in finding Julio or ending this case without more bloodshed, she had to act and act now.

Sneaking along the row of bushes between the two properties, she crossed a small open area and hid behind a big oak tree. The back windows of the Choate home lay before her, but the sun's reflection was disfiguring her view. She had to get closer. Making her way back to the hedge row, she hid behind the bushes until she felt safe hugging the home's exterior.

Carefully making her way along the siding, she arrived at the first window. Though there were mini blinds and curtains that blocked part of her vision, she could tell by the memorabilia on the walls that it was a boy's room. Moving to the other side of the opening to get a different angle, she noticed that the room was in disarray. It was unclear, at first, if this was normal teenage behavior or if the room had been searched, but the knee-high pile of clothes and shoes were suspicious.

Silently, she moved farther along the wall until she reached the next window opening. She slowly raised her head to peer inside. It was also a boy's room with rock-and-roll posters adorning the walls. This one had been ransacked more thoroughly with model cars lying broken on the floor and the contents of the closet tossed around the room. She heard muffled voices and ducked.

With her back snug against the siding, Sierra put her ear close to the window pain. She listened. There were two distinct male voices. They were low and deep, unlike the two teenage ones she interviewed on Monday. However, their sound was growing distant. She waited until she could no longer hear them and moved to peek in once more. Things were definitely searched, the drawers were on the bed, and the clothes that had been tossed were still attached to their hangers. They had to be looking for the money. The boys were in danger. Hearing the voices returning, she flattened herself against the wall and tried to overhear. This time they were closer to the window.

"I've been through every box, drawer, and under the bed. There isn't any more money."

"There has to be. Juan said the boys have it."

Sierra barely heard this voice.

"Where are Juan and Oswaldo? They should have been here hours ago."

"I'm sure they'll come when their business is finished!"

That time, the second voice was loud and clear. She recognized it—Carlos, the letch from the bar. The other one had to be Mondo.

She could hear items being thrown about, slamming against the walls. Suddenly, there was silence. She held her breath, hoping they didn't suspect her presence.

All of a sudden, Carlos's voice broke the stillness. "We are wasting our time. Let's go beat it out of those kids."

Sierra was shaking. Juan and another man were expected at any time, and they had the boys and probably Cindy too. Their lives were in immediate danger. She glanced at her watch. It was only four o'clock. Her backup wouldn't be there for another half hour, and that was only if the director had connected with the Miami bureau right away. Moving away from the house, she hid in the bushes and called 911. She needed help now.

Her phone call was short and to the point. "This is Special Agent Cortez from the Washington DC FBI field office. I'm in the Palm Shores Subdivision, 97 Ocean Ridge Boulevard. I'm undercover, and I have a hostage situation with three possible hostages and multiple armed felons. I am armed, on scene, and wearing a white dress. I need strategic backup. I have also notified the Miami FBI field office, and they are en route, ETA 4:30 p.m."

Sierra ended her call and made her way along the back wall to the patio doors. She hid behind the tall shrub. Inching toward the glass doors, she tried to see inside, but there was too much glare from the sunlight. As she was defining her possibilities, she heard a muffled scream. It was a woman. It had to be Cindy.

"Stop! Stop! You're hurting him. He's already said he doesn't know anything."

"Shut up!" It was Carlos. Mondo had his back to Cindy. He refused to look at her. She turned her comments to him.

"Can't you see what he's doing to these innocent young boys? You showed me kindness, can't you do the same for them? We don't know you or have what you're looking for. Please just let us go, and we'll keep our mouths shut."

The blow was hard, knocking her unconscious. Her chin came to rest on her chest. Carlos was not in the sympathy mood. Fear was evident in JJ's eyes, and he was crying, sobbing. Though he had withstood his captors beating thus far, Paul knew he had to do something, or they would all end up dead.

"I have the money. I can take you to it, if you let my brother go."

Carlos grabbed Paul and cut him away from the chair. "You are going to show me where it is, and your brother is going to stay right here with my friend. Do you understand?"

Paul reluctantly nodded. "It's in the backyard. I'll take you there." His voice was quivering.

"Let's go, but if you try anything foolish, these two are dead, understand?"

Paul nodded again.

Carlos unlocked the glass door. As it opened, Sierra secured her hiding place behind the tall bush once again. Paul led his captor across the backyard to the tree house, and they climbed the ladder. Paul searched his pocket for his key.

Sierra was trapped and couldn't move, or she would be exposed. She watched as the two went inside the little structure, and the door closed behind them. This was her break. She crept along the house and back to the bush line, keeping one eye on the tree house and one on the sliding glass door. Retracing her steps to the edge of her concealment, she was stuck. If she crossed over to the base of the tree, her movements would be exposed long enough for either party to see her. She wouldn't be able to take Carlos out at the tree, but perhaps she could sneak up behind him on his way back to the house. Of course, that would put JJ in danger.

***

JACK'S HOUSE

Rosa had seen the woman in the white dress before. Jack had introduced them at the marina. But what was she doing skulking along the bush row between the two houses? Jack had warned her about strangers on the property, which was making her attentively check the windows each time she passed by. She never expected to see Sierra hiding in the bushes or witness an older man emerge from the tree house with a gun pointed at one of the boys next door. She quickly surmised that the boys were in trouble and the woman in white was trying to help. Rosa slowly backed away from the window and called 911. Then she called Jack.

***

THE CHOATE HOUSE

Sierra didn't have time to formulate a plan before Carlos and Paul reemerged from the tree house. Paul was shoved into the lead with zip ties securing his arms behind his back, followed by an armed Carlos with one hand on his gun and the other carrying a small black bag. They crossed the backyard and went back inside.

Sierra followed their movements from the shadows. As they reentered the house, she took up her place behind the bush and listened. The men's voices were slowly fading away. Chancing a look through the glass, she shaded her eyes enough to see Cindy's back, her head slumped forward, and the two boys, which were facing her, were shrouded in fear; all three tied to their chairs. She watched them only a few seconds then pulled back. She needed to wait for backup.

Most of her operations, she could separate herself from the action, but this time she knew all the players—it was personal. It was up to her to protect this family, and she had failed. Every inch of her wanted to break the door down and take Juan's men out in body bags, but she couldn't think that way with innocent lives in the balance. This was the time for strategy.

She heard something. Turning her head, she saw someone making their way to her position. It was too early for her backup to have arrived. She braced herself for action. Sliding deeper behind the shrub, she watched as a sole figure cautiously made his way to her side. He raised his hands to her and whispered his introduction, "I don't believe we've met, but you must be Special Agent Cortez. I'm Agent Taylor from Homeland Security. I understand you require some assistance and backup." He carefully pulled out his ID.

"So you're the undercover agent watching over the boys while their parents have been missing?" she whispered back, lowering her gun.

He nodded. "If all goes well, they should be home soon."

"Good to hear, but I'm not sure what they will come home to."

"So what's the situation here?"

"The boys and their aunt are tied up, and there are two hired killers from DC in there, searching for some money from a shipment that went off the rails. They are expecting their boss and, I believe, one other. I have FBI backup from Miami on the way, but they won't be here until around four thirty, if traffic cooperates. The local strategic backup team has been called, and I expect them within the next five to ten minutes.

However, I'm not sure how much longer Cindy and the boys are going to last once their captors realize the boys don't have the money they're looking for."

"How about I go and meet the backup and send someone to you."

She nodded, and he was gone.

It didn't take long before another figure crept up beside her.

"Are you Special Agent Cortez?" She nodded and offered her hand. "I'm Detective Rios. Can you fill me in?" he whispered.

She motioned for him to squat down beside her. Whispering, she explained, "There are three captives—one woman and two teenage boys—tied to chairs on the other side of this sliding glass door. There are two perpetrators, with two more on the way. They are drug dealers and murderers from DC, and they will not hesitate to kill."

"What do you suggest?"

"If you can get a sniper in that tree house and another along that tree line"—she pointed to the big oak and the line of trees along the shoreline—"the sunlight will be masked soon, and the light in the kitchen will illuminate the figures inside. They should have a pretty clear shot in about ten to fifteen minutes. I just hope our hostages can hold out that long."

"We'll just have to make sure they do."

They finalized their plans, and he left to set up his men.

Sierra could hear the voices rising inside.

"Where's the rest of the money?"

"We don't have anymore." It was Paul. "That's all we found."

"Where? Where'd you find it?"

"Behind our house, by the dock. It was in that bag I gave you— $15,000. We spent some, but that's the rest."

She could hear the tears Paul was choking back as he spoke. She knew he was being honest, but honesty wouldn't save them from these men. They only cared about results.

"Stop lying! Does Julio have it? Are you hiding him somewhere? He's not worth it! Trust me, if he gets the chance, he'll stab you in the back!" He paused and softened the tone of his voice. "I'll tell you what, if you tell us where he is, I'll make your deaths less painful. Otherwise, we got all night to make you talk. Spare yourselves the pain and tell us where he is."

Cindy's voice was back and growing louder as their volume increased. "We don't know any Julio. Please, we don't know anything."

"I'm not talking to you—"

Then from out of nowhere, the doorbell rang. Everything went silent, except the sobbing. Sierra knew it came from Cindy. Sierra didn't dare move. The doorbell had been her signal that the snipers were set, and the plan was in motion. She glanced up at the sky. The sun was slipping behind the tall branches reaching toward the heavens, and the evening shadow was growing across the lawn. It wouldn't be long now.

"Paul and JJ, stop being jerks, and let me in!" Sierra recognized Taylor's voice as the yelling, ringing, and banging on the front door continued. Then it stopped.

Sierra moved toward the window and peeked in. She could see Mondo waving his gun at the three captives. He looked scared, shaking and pacing. Carlos's voice was coming closer. He had Taylor in tow. It didn't take long for him to be tied up next to the brothers. As Carlos backed up, he swiped his gun across the young man's face. Taylor spit out the blood that formed in his mouth.

"What are you doing?" Mondo asked. "Who is this?"

"Some nosy kid who couldn't mind his own business."

"Now what? We don't have the money. We don't have Julio. And where are Oswaldo and Juan?"

"Well, I guess we work with what we've got. There are other ways to get information. I think we'll start with the young one."

Sierra pulled back, watching the backyard shadow climb up the sliding glass door, the glare was lifting. The scream came before she heard the glass break. It was Cindy. Sierra braced herself as she felt her phone vibrate with the words "It's finished." Gun drawn, she stepped through the shattered glass and assessed the scene. Taylor had cut himself free with a blade he had hidden in his belt. He was now releasing his friends who were in a state of shock. Blood was splattered everywhere—a mixture of torture and death. Securing the guns and Carlos's knife, she stepped across the red tile.

There was a commotion coming from the front. The tactical team and the FBI were streaming onto the scene. She checked Carlos for any signs of life. His pulse was still. "This one's gone."

Mondo's breathing was ragged. He would be dead soon. Cindy was in pain, bleeding from her face and arms. She had been hit and cut numerous times. Sierra went to her and cut her free. Reaching for a kitchen towel, she handed it to her bloody friend. Cindy dropped to her knees next to Mondo and cradled his hand in hers. "Thank you," she said.

He looked up at her, his eyes dimming with each passing moment. "I knew it would be you. Be careful, he . . . won't . . . quit . . . until . . . he . . . gets . . . Julio . . . and . . . the . . . money."

"Who? Perrone?" It was Sierra, dropping to her knees beside Cindy, but Mondo had said his last word. He was gone.

It was the EMTs who unclenched Cindy's fingers from her captor and helped her onto a gurney. "Who is Julio?" she asked. No one responded. She was wheeled away with the boys who were also being treated and carted away. It wasn't long until multiple sirens were wailing toward the hospital.

Sierra looked around at the once beautiful kitchen floor, now tainted with the blood of monsters. In her mind, she was back at the mall in Nebraska watching the horror on the faces of the innocent teenagers. She had seen those same looks on Paul and JJ; their lives had been touched by violence and would ever more be changed. She wanted to cry, but this was not the place. An FBI agent had to hold such emotions for private reflections. It was time to focus on the scene. She needed to know who else was with Perrone and what happened to them.

Turning, she saw Supervisory Special Agent Macdonald and Special Agent Medina approaching. She wondered if one of these two sold her out to Jack or was somehow connected to the mole in the agency. However, that would have to be a conversation for another time. Looking through the shattered glass, she saw a familiar face. Jack Winters was staring in at her. His questions had been answered. Though her identity had been exposed, Sierra forced a smile. He met her smile with an expression of concern. As she watched, Jack's gaze moved from her to someone behind her. He waved. Looking back, she saw Special Agent Medina acknowledge Jack's greeting. Now she knew who couldn't be trusted. But was he the mole?

Sierra turned back to the task at hand. The scene had to be contained. There were police and agents everywhere. She would have to explain what happened, but what bothered her was what she couldn't explain. Where was Juan Perrone and his third lackey? They didn't show, and with this police presence, they wouldn't chance an appearance now. She knew they were there, in Key Largo, and if they weren't found soon, there would be more dead bodies. Her investigation wasn't over. Sierra had to find Juan Perrone before he found Julio. The manhunt was still on.

EPILOGUE

Palm Shores

Watching the house go up in flames made him smile. It was time to settle the score. Driving back to Washington DC would take close to seventeen hours. It was his only way out. If only his picture hadn't ended up on the television set. Oswaldo screwed that up at the dive shop. He should have destroyed the camera. Flying home was out of the question, with so much exposure. Besides, he was in no shape to fly. The scans would reveal his bullet. That would trigger the police.

Perrone was bleeding. Oswaldo's aim had been good. If only he'd seen through the treachery sooner. He would have contained it before it got out of hand. Instead, his life and his business were almost taken by Victor Ramos. It was time to fight back. He saw the police presence as he slowly drove past the Choate residence. There were no sirens or flashing lights, but the cars were lining the streets. Carlos and Mondo were in trouble, but he wouldn't be stopping. They were on their own. If Carlos and Mondo were following orders, Julio and the teenagers would already be dead. He would worry about the boat and the money another time. It wasn't worth exposing himself. For now, he was done with Key Largo. It was time to go home.

The bleeding made it difficult to stop for gas without raising suspicion. He wasn't sure how long his jacket could hide his injury, or how much blood he could lose and still make it back? Filling up a cooler with food and soda from the house would be enough to get him to DC, but he still needed to stop for gas. He had plenty of money but paying with cash exposed his face to the cameras. Using his credit cards were risky, they could be tracked, but that was the only way to stay out of sight. Driving itself would take its toll; he would have to nap at rest areas and keep going. But would he get there in time? He had to. Victor Ramos was opening a powder keg. Secrets would be revealed, families destroyed, and businesses would crumble. His death would have severe consequences. He had placed safeguards to protect himself and others. Destroying him would destroy them. If he made it in time, he might be able to stop the bloodbath before it was too late. If not, DC power players would be no more. Juan Perrone turned right out of the housing area and headed to DC.

Printed in the United States
By Bookmasters